THE JAGUAR PRINCE

THE
JAGUAR
PRINCE

KAREN KELLEY

B
BRAVA

KENSINGTON PUBLISHING CORP.
www.kensingtonbooks.com

To Megan Hope Wheeler

The first rule of life, believe in yourself.
Well, that, and shop till you drop.

BRAVA BOOKS are published by

Kensington Publishing Corp.
119 West 40th Street
New York, NY 10018

All Kensington titles, imprints, and distributed lines are available at special quantity discounts for bulk purchases for sales promotion, premiums, fund-raising, educational, or institutional use.

Special book excerpts or customized printings can also be created to fit specific needs. For details, write or phone the office of the Kensington Special Sales Manager: Attn.: Special Sales Department. Kensington Publishing Corp., 119 West 40th Street, New York, NY 10018. Phone: 1-800-221-2647.

Brava and the B logo are Reg. U.S. Pat. & TM Off.

ISBN-13: 978-0-7582-3836-8
ISBN-10: 0-7582-3836-3

First Kensington Trade Paperback Printing: April 2010

10 9 8 7 6 5 4 3 2 1

Printed in the United States of America

Chapter 1

That creepy crawly feeling was back, and goose bumps were popping up all over Callie Jordon's arms.

Damn it, Callie was certain, well, almost certain, someone lurked in the shadows. The feeling was the same as when she watched a scary movie late at night and hadn't pulled the curtains. She rubbed her arms to take away the sudden chill as her gaze scanned the park.

The last visitors in the zoo had left a couple of hours ago. There was no one in this area except herself. She was all alone.

It could be security, although Ben usually worked this side, and she knew he was still at the employee office. He wouldn't leave until he'd had at least two cups of the too strong black coffee and a couple of the jelly-filled doughnuts.

The feeling persisted, though. Not in a stalker kind of way. More as though whoever watched her was waiting to see what she would do next. The spooky sensation had been with her for a few days now so it was nothing new.

She closed her eyes and took a deep breath. *Get over it,* she told herself.

"Hey, Callie, you still here?"

Her eyes flew open and she jumped, slapping a hand to her chest. "You scared the hell out of me, Pete!" Pete worked at the park, cleaning pens and any other odd job that came along.

The money he earned helped pay his way through college. He was cute, in a nerdy kind of way.

He blushed. "Sorry."

She took a deep calming breath. "It's okay. I just thought . . ."

"That I was the bogeyman?" He grinned.

Now it was her turn to blush. "Yeah, something like that."

"You on your way to see Sheba?"

"Yes."

He shook his head. "I'll never understand your fascination with that jaguar."

She couldn't explain it, either.

"Don't stay too long," he told her. "There is life beyond the zoo."

"So they tell me. Have a good night."

They parted ways, but she still felt a little uneasy for some strange reason.

Shake it off. It had been a long day, and an even longer week. She worked around kids most of the time. No wonder she was edgy.

The petting zoo was not what she would call a fun place to work, let alone being the person in charge. She'd been pinched, prodded, and bitten—and that was just this afternoon.

Still, pride washed over her. Not once had she threatened to feed the little monsters to the lion. Well, at least she hadn't today. Monday could very well be another story. Thank God she used birth control, and thank God she was off for the weekend.

So why was she still here? Yeah, yeah, Pete was right. She'd finished all her paperwork ten minutes ago. The answer was easy. She *couldn't* resist checking on the jaguar one last time. Crazy? Probably, since she didn't work with the big cats.

She released a deep sigh of longing. One day she would. As soon as the next animal keeper job came open, it was hers. It had been a long time coming. And she damn well deserved the job, too. She'd more than paid her dues.

A soft breeze carrying a hint of jasmine and ginger caressed her face, immediately calming her. She stopped, closed her eyes, and drew in a deep breath. The scents created the illusion of the rain forest. Tropical palms and a mist so light that she barely noticed added to the atmosphere. This was her Zen, her Chi.

The very first time she'd visited this part of the zoo, Callie had known she was meant to be here. Then, when Sheba arrived, she knew it for a fact. There was something special about the jaguar.

She opened her eyes and crossed the rustic bridge, then went around to the backside that was off limits to visitors.

The cats were in cages at night for safety reasons. A long row of them with a concrete roof and solid walls held the animals. The pens were small, but they connected to separate pits, as everyone at the zoo called them. The pits gave the animals a little more room to roam, and were more like their natural habitat. There were only two other cats at the small zoo. A mother lion and her cub were caged at the end of the row.

The zoo was family owned, and would never be able to compete with the bigger Fort Worth zoo, but this one was nice. At least it was until Mr. Campbell had retired and his son took over. Now, she wasn't so sure. His son seemed more concerned with publicity and making money than the animals or people who worked at the zoo.

She slowed her approach, not wanting to startle the jaguar. Sheba was in the far corner of her cage, lying on a bed of fresh hay. "Hi, girl," Callie kept her voice soft.

The big cat looked up, purring from deep in her throat, as if to welcome Callie. Callie knew not to get too close, even though Sheba was double caged at night. As much as she loved the cat, it was still a wild animal, and she respected that. But Sheba was so beautiful, her coat a rich reddish-brown with black spots.

There was something in the cat's eyes that Callie could relate to, as though they were kindred spirits. Not that she would do more than think that thought. But Sheba didn't have anyone, and neither did Callie. Two lonely souls. They had that in common.

"I brought you something." A little extra meat. No biggie. She knew she wasn't supposed to feed Sheba. It would be grounds for dismissal, but she hadn't been able to resist. And Sheba loved the extra treats.

Sheba suddenly came to her feet, but rather than walk closer to Callie, as was her norm, she backed away. Her head swung to the left, then right, as though she sensed something wasn't right.

Callie tensed. "What's the matter, sweetie? Still upset about all the kids today?" But Callie didn't think it was that. Visitors had never bothered Sheba in the past. No, the cat was acting really strange.

The sudden roar of a cat echoed through the zoo.

Callie's blood ran icy cold as dread washed over her.

The noise hadn't come from Sheba or the lion. The sound had come from the opposite direction.

And she knew something else. This cat was close. Close as in she-didn't-stand-a-snowball's-chance-in-hell-of-not-getting-eaten-alive close.

Stay calm.

Deep breath.

Yeah right, easier said than done.

Think, she had to think.

Her gaze searched the area. Nothing moved in the shadows. She could hear the guttural purr of the unknown cat, though. The sound coming from low in its throat.

Then padded steps.

Then silence.

Callie's stomach churned as her gaze slowly moved up, inch by inch.

She spotted the cat lying on the concrete roof of the cage, staring right at her.

Lunch time!

Fear clogged her throat, making it impossible to swallow. She couldn't move, she couldn't breathe.

The cat probably weighed nearly two hundred pounds. A rare, solid black jaguar, his black on black spots barely discernible in the fading light. It wasn't one of their cats.

Tame?

Maybe?

Please.

Sheba snarled, pacing her cage as if she knew the danger Callie was in.

Callie closed her eyes and took a deep breath. *God, just let me get through this without being ripped to shreds.*

Cautiously, she took a step back, then another. The jaguar didn't move. This was a good sign, right? Five more steps and she felt a little better. A few more and she would be around the corner and she could take off running. She would survive this encounter. She would . . .

The cat came to its feet.

She froze.

How far would she get if she turned and ran right now? Two feet? Maybe farther if the cat was in the mood to do a little hunting. Jaguars liked to stalk, then ambush their prey, clamping down on the heads of their poor victims, their sharp teeth sinking into the skull.

So much for the new haircut she'd gotten yesterday. She stifled hysterical laughter. Nice, she was already losing what little mental function she had left.

The jaguar jumped to the ground in one fluid movement, barely making a sound when it landed. Any other time, she would have admired its grace and agility, but right now, she just wanted it to go away.

Was it a good sign her life wasn't flashing before her eyes? Probably not, since she really didn't have a life.

The meat! God, she'd forgotten about the meat. If she could tempt the big cat with it, she might be able to escape.

She eased her hand inside her pocket and brought out the baggie with the chunks of meat, then scooped out as much as she could hold.

"I have food," she squeaked, then tossed it toward the cat. It landed with barely a thud. Why hadn't she grabbed a big juicy hunk of meat just this once, rather than the measly one-inch chunks?

The animal ignored it. Ambled past without so much as a glance, its golden eyes never leaving her face.

Of course, why would it go for a handful of food when it could dine on her? One hundred and twenty pounds of juicy—she swallowed hard—steak.

The cat moved closer, circling her. She froze to the spot. She tried lifting one foot, but nothing moved. She figured this was what was meant by being scared stiff. Oh, hell, she was going to die.

As the cat sauntered in front of her again, a fog began to roll in. The guttural purr of the cat became louder.

"Please forgive me of my sins," she whispered. Oh, God, there weren't that many. Not nearly enough in her twenty-six years. She didn't go to bars and get totally zonkered, or have one-night stands.

She read lots of books. She lived vicariously through the heroines on the pages of a romance novel. Her life was boring. Well, except the books were really good. Still, the closest she'd ever gotten to a hot guy was drooling over the cover models, and praying that one would come into her life.

A drop of sweat slid down the side of her face. She squeezed her eyes closed. If she was going to die, then she didn't want to watch it happen.

The cat's hot breath was on her hand, moving up her bare arm. Trembles of fear swept over her. So, this was the end of her life. Would anyone even miss her? It was sad, but she couldn't think of a soul besides her friend, DeeDee. She didn't have any relatives—not one. Her landlady would miss her, but only because the rent was due tomorrow.

The jaguar's purr grew louder. She flinched. Her eyes opened. The cat walked behind her again. She trembled so hard her whole body shook like a California skyscraper during an earthquake. Not that she'd ever felt one since she'd never been out of Texas—at least, that she could remember.

She couldn't take any more suspense. "Oh, hell, just end it now," she finally whimpered.

Silence. The fog rolled in thicker, more dense.

She heard someone groan. Her? Oh, no, her mind was going fast. Her brain had already stopped functioning.

"End it now? You're ready to die?" A deep, husky male voice asked close to her ear.

She whirled around.

The jaguar was gone.

A man stood behind her.

"Did you see the jaguar?" she frantically whispered, squinting her eyes as her gaze searched the shadows. Nothing moved.

He smiled. "He left us."

"Not possible. The cat would have attacked. Why would it just leave?"

"It was time."

"I don't know what you did to make it go away, but I'll be eternally grateful." She looked at him then. Really looked. There were flecks of gold in his dark eyes. They were just as mesmerizing as the jaguar's. The man's black hair brushed his shoulders, and he wore a medallion that had a diamond in the center, encircled by jewels in different colors. The stones shimmered in the dim light.

Of course, it couldn't be real. The diamond was as big as her thumbnail. Her gaze moved lower, then jerked back to his eyes. "You're naked."

His smile was slow and lazy. "It would seem that way."

This wasn't happening. It couldn't be. Maybe she was already dead and this was heaven. Wow, it looked pretty good to her!

No, no, no. She would know if she was dead. Then again.

"Is your name Adam by any chance?"

He shook his head.

She hadn't thought so. "I'm going to close my eyes and when I open them, you won't be here." She closed her eyes. There wasn't really a hot, sexy, naked man standing in front of her.

It was a shame really. Her imagination had outdone itself this time. First a jaguar roaming loose in the zoo, then poof, it's gone, and in its place is a tanned, very sexy man with longish hair, a slight accent that she couldn't place, dark eyes with flecks of gold that made her want to melt into a puddle when he looked at her, and he was hung like . . . yeah, it had to be her imagination.

She opened her eyes.

He was still there.

What was happening? Had one of the little monsters at the petting zoo drugged her water? No, not possible.

"You're not real," she said.

"I'm real." His deep sultry words boldly rolled over her.

"I'll prove you're not real." She reached out, her hand coming in contact with his hard male chest. She could feel the strong beat of his heart, the smoothness of his skin, the sinewy muscle. She swallowed past the lump in her throat. If she moved her hand a little to the right she would just graze his nipple . . .

She jerked her hand away, but tingles of anticipation still lingered. "You are real," she choked. Unable to stop herself, her gaze moved downward . . . again. He was still naked.

"I'm as real as you. I'm Prince Rogar Valkyir from New Symtaria."

She cleared her throat and kept her gaze on his face. "Thank you very much for . . . for whatever you did to get rid of the jaguar, but you can't run around in the zoo without clothes. Public nudity is against the law, no matter where you're from. I won't say anything, but you really need to leave."

What the hell was she thinking talking to a naked man?

He could be a serial killer for all she knew, and the cat his pet. She might be in more danger now than she had been with the jaguar.

"I have to go." She turned on her heel.

Walk slowly and calmly. Don't spook the naked serial killer.

She didn't hear him following, but then, he was barefoot and she probably wouldn't hear him until he clubbed her over the head. She picked up the pace until she was running.

She was almost out of breath when the door to the employee building loomed in front of her. Every horror flick she'd ever seen flashed across her mind where the victim reaches the door only to have a knife plunged in her back. But nothing happened when she got to the door, not that she wasted any time flinging it open, and falling inside.

"You okay, Callie?"

She screamed.

"Hey, it's just me, Ben." He ran to her, putting his arm around her, and leading her to the nearest chair. If she could have picked a father, Ben would have been her first choice. Her heart slowed to a normal thud-thud.

"What got you all fired up?"

"There was a jaguar loose."

"Sheba?" He straightened, his hand moving toward the tranquilizer gun that was holstered at his side just like a real gun. "Are you hurt?"

"No, I'm fine, and it wasn't Sheba. This one was black. But then the jaguar somehow disappeared, and now there's a naked man running around inside the zoo." Her words tumbled out.

Ben laughed. "That was a good one. For a second there, I almost believed you."

She opened her mouth, then snapped it closed when she realized how ridiculous she sounded. A jaguar? Then a naked man? Maybe she was losing her mind. If word got around, she would also lose any opportunity to move up the ladder at this zoo, and probably any other zoo for that matter.

Her smile was weak at best. "Yeah, I almost got you."

Ben patted her on the shoulder. "You'll have to get up earlier in the morning to pull the wool over my eyes."

She sobered. Her story did sound as though she was pulling his leg, but she knew there had been something out there. She couldn't leave Ben with a naked man and a jaguar running loose in the zoo, except now she wondered if she had actually seen them. She wanted to warn Ben in a way that he wouldn't think she'd been doing drugs or anything.

"Seriously, I thought I did hear something, and it spooked me. You might want to be a little more cautious tonight, and tell the others, too."

"When it comes to wild animals, I don't take any chances. You don't have to worry about me or the others on duty tonight, but I'll tell them to keep an eye out for anything strange."

She knew Ben would be careful. But what had she really seen? The man had felt real. She rubbed her hand over her eyes, knowing she needed more sleep. That had to be it. At least eight hours tonight, and no more staying up late to read another romantic suspense.

After she gathered her things, Ben walked Callie to her car. She looked around, but the night was still, not even a breeze now, not even a hint of fog. "Thanks, Ben," she said as she unlocked her door and got in.

It took a few minutes for her car to start, but it finally made it past the chugga-chugga stage and the engine fired off. It was cheap, what could she say. It was also paid for, and it got good gas mileage. Of course, it leaked oil, too.

Even her rattletrap car couldn't keep her from thinking about what had happened with the jaguar and the naked man. Was she losing her mind? She didn't know if insanity ran in her family or not since there was no one to ask. Maybe that was the answer. As soon as her ancestors turned twenty-six, they all went crazy and committed suicide, and that's why she was dumped on the doorstep of an orphanage.

She pulled into her driveway and went inside the one bedroom fixer-upper that the landlady never had time to fix up. It was cheap, too. The only thing she regretted was the "no pet" rule. As soon as she had the animal keeper job, her pay would increase, and a lot of things would change, unless she *was* going crazy. That might possibly upset her plans.

Her imagination had definitely been in overdrive. Now that she was safe, she could look at it a little differently. She loved jaguars, and the black one had been beautiful. The sexy man was an added bonus. She frowned. He'd felt real enough. It would be nice if she could imagine him in her bed tonight. Not in a stalker, serial killer kind of way. More like he wanted to worship her body way.

Man, she really had to get out more.

After a quick shower, she slipped on her comfy granny nightgown. If she had a hottie in her bed, then she would wear something sultry and sexy, like a lacy red teddy. For just a moment she indulged in a fantasy of her zoo man strolling toward her, his heated gaze never leaving her body.

A dog barked, ruining the moment. Not that it made much difference. For now, she chose the old lady look. It wasn't like the guy from the zoo would show up at her door.

She snorted.

Even *her* imagination wasn't that good.

Tiredness spread throughout her body. Staying up past midnight, then getting up at five had not been one of her brightest ideas. Then add the kids, who were particularly obnoxious this afternoon. Today had literally drained her. All she wanted was a bed, and to look at the inside of her eyelids.

Her stomach growled. Food first.

Her cabinets didn't yield much. A box of cereal, a can of soup, a jar of peanut butter and a loaf of bread. Even her food supply was pathetic. Soup it was. After opening the can, she dumped it into a plastic bowl and heated it in the microwave, then took it to the living room, and clicked on the television. Rerun, rerun, rerun. She finally settled on watching the end of a movie she hadn't seen in a long time. The dog died in the end. She really hated when writers killed off an animal, especially after the animal saves the hero's life.

She sniffed. So what if the dog had been shot. Miracles happened all the time. Especially in the movies. She swiped at the tear that rolled down her face. Great, now she was about to go on a crying jag.

Before that could happen, she switched the channel to one of the reruns, and finished eating her soup. It was so past time for her to go to bed. She glanced at the clock. It was only nine? Not that she really cared. Her body was telling her it was much later.

But when sleep did come, she dreamt of the man at the zoo. He pulled her close, nuzzled her neck. She ran her hands over his body, touching, caressing. He moved closer, tugging her gown over her head, then pressed her body intimately to his. She sighed, letting sleep transport her to a series of erotic dreams where his hands explored her body.

When Callie woke the next morning, she stretched like a contented cat, and opened her eyes.

Then screamed.

The naked man from the zoo sat on the end of her bed, legs crossed as he studied her.

And he was still naked . . . and so was she.

Chapter 2

This wasn't happening. Callie closed her eyes and took a deep breath. "You're not real," she repeated over and over until she could feel herself beginning to relax.

The naked hottie was only the last fragment of a delicious dream she'd been having. Right before she went to sleep, hadn't she wished he would magically materialize in her bed?

She relaxed and smiled. It had been a great dream. The way he'd touched her, nuzzled her neck, pressed his naked body against hers. It had been one long sensuous dream. That was probably why she'd apparently gotten rid of her hot granny gown sometime during the night. Okay, now she was back to normal. No more fantasies that a hot, sexy man was in her bed. The idea was ludicrous.

Deep breath. Inhale. Exhale. She was wide awake now. She opened her eyes.

He was still there, sitting on the end of her bed, staring at her with what appeared to be . . . amusement? He laughed at her! He was in her house, her bed, and he laughed at her!

Callie sat up, the cover fell to her waist. His gaze dropped. She grabbed the sheet and pulled it against her chest. "Get out! Who are you? How did you get into my house? Where's my gown?"

One eyebrow arched. "Are you always this emotionally unstable?"

"Emotionally . . ." she sputtered.

"Unstable," he slowly and distinctly repeated.

"I am not emotionally unstable!" Oh God, she was arguing with the serial killer. She took another deep breath, then exhaled once more. She needed to stay calm. "If you don't leave right now, I'm going to call the police."

Oh, yeah, now he really looked nervous—not! He didn't even flinch. Just sat there staring at her. And why wouldn't he? He probably weighed around one-ninety. She would be no match for him.

Maybe if she kept him talking, he wouldn't kill her right away. She'd once read somewhere that if you could befriend your abductor, then he would be less likely to kill you. Not that he'd abducted her, but he had apparently broken into her home. God, she hoped this worked.

"How . . . uh . . . did you find me?" Surely someone would've noticed a naked man following her car. For the first time in her life, Callie wished her rattletrap car went faster.

She frowned. How had he followed her? Her car wasn't that slow. He probably had his own car. He'd waited for her to leave, then followed.

So, he drove around naked. And no one noticed this?

"Does it matter how I came to be here?" he asked.

"I guess not." If she knew where he came from, then maybe she could talk him into going back, though. "Where are you from?"

"New Symtaria."

"Never heard of it. Is that a suburb of Dallas?" New ones were cropping up all the time.

"It's in another galaxy."

All righty. "Another planet?"

He nodded, still looking amused about something.

"And you are?"

"Prince Rogar."

Delusional. Probably escaped from the state hospital. This was worse than she ever could have imagined. Not only was he naked, but he was a nut. Automatically, her eyes strayed downward. She swallowed, then quickly jerked her gaze to a safer place. She had to stop looking . . . looking at him . . . down there. It wasn't like she'd never seen a naked man before.

This was ridiculous. She needed help and all she could think about was staring at his . . . his nakedness. She had to call the police or something—911. Her cell phone was in her purse. From now on, she was keeping it on her bedside table. If there even was a from-now-on in her future. Okay, keep him talking.

"And why are you here?" She smiled. At least she tried to pull it off as a smile even though her stomach rumbled, and her hands were sweating, and she was probably going to throw up any second.

"To take you home."

She looked around. "I am home, so . . . bye-bye."

He grinned and she noticed his teeth were pearly white, and he had a nice smile. Ted Bundy probably had a nice smile, too.

"You're part Symtarian," he continued.

"Okayyy . . ." He thought she was from another planet, too. This was worse than she could've imagined.

"When our planet was dying, some of the people were sent to other places. An expedition went in search of a new planet to call home. Some of our people were forgotten, and became integrated with the aliens. Now we're searching for them so we can bring them home."

"And you're doing it without clothes."

"It happens when I shapeshift."

"Well, of course, I should have guessed." The guy was a raving lunatic. "And what form do you take?"

A fog began to roll across her bedroom. She glanced nervously around, then looked at her crazy guy. Her mouth dropped open as he slowly began to change.

The prince dude gritted his teeth and downed his head. His skin changed from flesh to short black hair with barely visible spots. He stretched out across her bed, his hand curling into a fist, becoming a paw.

Oh, God, she was crazy. Now she would never get her chance to work with the big cats—except in her warped mind. It wasn't fair.

The fog rolled in thicker until all Callie saw were patches of black fur, a glimpse of golden eyes boring into her. She couldn't move. She tried, but her legs wouldn't budge.

The fog slowly dissipated.

The black jaguar from last night lay across the end of her bed, panting slightly. It met her gaze, and seemed as though it was gauging her reaction.

She opened her mouth, then closed it when no words came out. The cat purred from deep in its throat. She swallowed past the lump in hers. What if the jag was real? Maybe she wasn't crazy. Oh, yeah, now she felt better. She was going to die. Then again, she might already be dead and this was hell.

Whatever it was, the jaguar was still stretched across the foot of her bed.

The room began to tilt, then grow dark, and she knew without a doubt, she was about to faint. She'd never fainted in her life.

Rogar's spirit melded with that of the jaguar Balam, his animal guide. They were one, yet separate, their thoughts intertwining.

She didn't take that very well at all. I told you it was too soon to change in front of her. She's not used to it like we are, Balam's thoughts mingled with Rogar's.

Yes, this complicates matters, but surely the woman that bore her explained her existence, Rogar told him, hating that his animal guide had been right . . . again.

From her reaction, it's doubtful. She can't return without some knowledge of her ancestors. The shock would be too much. You'll need to teach her our ways.

An irritation, but I will learn more about this planet while I'm here so all is not a waste.

Are you so sure she will leave Earth? Balam asked.

Of course she will return with me, she has no choice. This is her heritage. I shall convince her. I am a prince after all.

The fog rolled across the room, and the change began. The familiar ache in Rogar's gut, the burning sensation that he had grown used to long ago.

Rogar became a man once again. He studied the young woman. She was quite beautiful, with dark hair and deep green eyes. Odd, but beautiful. The oddness must come from her Earth heritage.

She also seemed quite disturbed about his ability to shape-shift. She apparently had no knowledge of Symtarians. Did those she was born unto explain nothing? Others before him had brought back stories. Stories that some of the non–pure bloods were unaware of their origins. He wouldn't be able to take her home until he taught her the ways of their people. Balam was correct that this complicated things.

He frowned.

She still hadn't moved.

Could she be dead? He reached forward and took her hand, then let it fall back to the bed. Limp. It was a possibility the shock had killed her. He pulled on the cover, exposing more of her. No her chest moved up and down, so she still breathed.

Her chest moved very nicely. He pulled the cover to her ankles. She had a nice form. Her breasts were full, her waist small, and she had very long legs.

He moved closer, running the palm of his hand over her body, watching the nipples tighten. Her skin was soft and smooth. She moaned when he brushed his fingers through the dark curls at the juncture of her legs.

Her eyelids fluttered, before slowly opening. "What?" She glanced around, then threw her hands across her chest and jerked her legs up.

"You looked at me!" she sputtered.

His brow wrinkled. "And that angers you?"

"Of course it angers me."

She grappled for the cover but it was just out of her reach so he handed it to her. She seemed quite upset with him.

"You took advantage of me after I fainted."

"It's wrong to look at the naked body?"

"Yes!"

"But what about when you look at mine? Is that not equally wrong?"

"I'm not looking at you." Her gaze moved downward, then shot back up.

"Aren't you?" He smiled. This part Earthling, part Symtarian, was a mass of contradictions.

She grabbed the cover and wrapped it around her, then stumbled into the other room. She came back a few minutes later with a large white cloth.

"It's a towel. Do me a favor and wrap it around your waist."

She really had a problem with his nakedness, yet he could sense a passionate nature within her.

"How did you do it?" she asked, changing the subject.

"Do what?"

"Change into a jaguar."

"I told you, I'm Symtarian. We are a race of shapeshifters."

"Or you're a damned good magician."

"Would you like me to show you again?"

"No!"

She was very fervent when she was cornered. And he could almost feel the rapid beat of her heart as it pounded inside her chest.

"The towel?" she reminded him.

He slowly came to his feet, noting the way her gaze lowered, then quickly darted elsewhere. He grinned as he knotted the towel at his waist. She looked at him, saw that he was smiling, and frowned. She was even more alluring when she frowned.

"What do they call you?" he asked.

"Callie."

"Callie," he said, testing the sound of her name on his lips. "I like it." It seemed to unnerve her when he said her name.

"Do you have someplace to go?" she asked. "Someone I can call?"

"I've finally found you, why would I leave when I just arrived?"

She closed her eyes and he wondered if she might be going through some kind of ritual. She closed her eyes quite often, losing herself in what appeared to be a trance of some kind. But then, she opened her eyes again.

"I really don't want to have to call the police to come take you away because this isn't where you belong."

"You have a mark on you. It looks like a rose." When she didn't say anything, he continued, realizing it might be harder to convince her than he'd first imagined. "On your right cheek." When her face flamed, he knew she was aware what cheek he spoke about.

She pulled the cover closer around her. "You looked at my butt!"

"No, I just know it's there."

"That doesn't prove anything." She jutted her chin forward.

Rogar had an incredible urge to cup her chin, pull her closer and taste her, inhale her scent. It hadn't been enough to hold her in his arms last night, to feel her naked body pressed close to his. But he didn't touch her. Instead, he untied the towel.

"What are you doing?" she asked, panic lacing her words.

"I have the same mark. All Symtarians have it." He turned around.

"That doesn't prove . . . uh . . ." Her words stammered to a stop. "So what if you have the same mark."

He picked up the towel, retied it around his waist, watching her facial expressions. They ranged from denial, to maybe there was truth in his words, then back to denial.

She shook her head. "This is crazy. It's absurd. You are not an alien, and you need to . . . to . . . leave. Right now."

"Did the people who raised you say nothing about your ancestors?"

She squared her shoulders. "My parents died when I was very young. I grew up in an orphanage."

Now he understood. Of course, she would deny her heritage. Earthlings weren't as advanced as other worlds.

There was a knock on her door.

She froze.

"Miss Jordon, are you awake yet?"

"Mrs. Winkle, my landlady." Her gaze flew to him. "I don't know what she'll do if she sees you. Hide!"

She seemed quite flustered by this person she called a landlady. It was interesting to watch Callie.

"I need my robe," she muttered, dropping the cover.

Very nice.

Before he could study her form, she made a little gurgling noise, then grabbed the cover, and hurried back to the other room, emerging a few moments later wearing a white robe of sorts.

"Stay here," she said, holding up one hand as if he wouldn't understand her words. Did she think he was feebleminded?

"Stay!" she said once more, this time gritting her teeth.

She would make a fierce hunter the way she bared her teeth. It didn't last long, though. Her expression quickly turned to one of pleading.

"Please?"

He nodded once in acquiescence.

"Coming," she called out as she hurried to the other room, shutting the door to this one.

He casually strolled over and reopened it. He couldn't see Callie or the landlady, but he would at least hear them talking. He was curious to listen in on their conversation.

Another door opened.

"I was sleeping in this morning," Callie breathlessly told the landlady.

"I didn't mean to wake you, but the rent is due, you know."

"Yes, it's the first of the month. I've been living here for almost a year and it's always been due the first."

Rogar heard the sarcasm in her voice. Apparently, Callie didn't like this other woman.

"And I haven't raised your rent, either. At least, not yet, even though everyone else has been raising theirs. I pride myself in taking care of my tenants. I've always been known as a fair woman."

"I've been very pleased living here, too. I'll get your money."

Rogar frowned. He could tell Callie had just lied. Why had she felt the need?

"Huh-choo! Oh, excuse me."

The woman's voice sounded closer this time. He eased the door closed a little.

"Here's the rent," Callie quickly spoke.

"Huh-choo!"

"Bless you."

"Odd, I usually don't sneeze unless I'm around cats."

There was a distinct pause.

"Do you have a cat, Miss Jordon? You do realize pets are not allowed, don't you?"

"Of course I remember the no pet rule. I don't have a cat. It's just that I was so tired last night I went straight to bed without showering. I was around the cats yesterday. I'm sure that's all it is."

"Umm, I suppose that could be it."

"It is." Callie's words were firm. "Now, if you don't mind, I have a lot to do today."

A few minutes later the front door closed and Callie returned. She planted her hands on her hips, and again, he wanted to scoop her into his arms and carry her to bed. He was pretty sure she wasn't ready for that.

"You have to leave. Right now."

He sighed. He had hoped she wouldn't be difficult. "I will leave then." He unknotted his towel, then handed it to her, before starting toward the front door.

"No, you can't leave!" she frantically whispered.

"But I was only doing what you asked."

"Not without clothes."

"Then what would you have me wear?"

She nibbled her bottom lip. He had an incredible urge to nibble it, too.

"I'm not this Symtarian you're looking for, I promise. I'll go to town and buy you some clothes, but then you really do need to leave."

"If you insist."

"I do."

"Then I will leave."

"Good." She nodded her head. "I need to get dressed." She grabbed some things out of the drawers of a chipped and scarred chest, then went into the room where she'd gotten the towel. She started to close the door, but stopped to look back at him. "Don't touch anything."

"Of course not."

She nodded again, then closed the door.

Very strange female. It must be the fact she was part Earthling. He tied the towel around his hips, glancing at a board with pictures all over it. It appeared to be modes of transportation, another dwelling, jewels, and an assortment of small animals. An odd picture to hang on one's wall.

He wandered to the other room, looking around as he went. He hadn't taken the time to inspect the dwelling last night. He'd only sensed it was a safe place. He could see that it was sparsely furnished with few personal items.

He wandered down a short hall to another room where there were lots of cabinets. He opened the first one. It seemed to hold containers in various sizes with names like garlic, salt, and pepper. Behind the next door there was a box, and a jar labeled peanut butter behind it. He pulled the box out.

"Cereal," he read. "Tastes great and good for you."

He knew the language. In fact his people spoke many dialects. He'd also studied Earth and their customs before he'd left New Symtaria. He knew they believed in free love. He frowned. Except he hadn't sensed that Callie wanted to mate with him. Then again, that had been during a different time period. Maybe they had changed their minds. A shame if that were the case.

He tore the top off the box and grabbed a handful of the cereal. After putting some in his mouth, he began to chew. Not bad. Not as good as a juicy steak, but it would appease his hunger.

As he continued to eat, he wandered through the rest of Callie's dwelling. There was a tall shelf that stood in one corner. He walked over to it. Cats of all shapes and sizes were arranged in a circle. Sitting in the middle of the little statues was a black jaguar. He smiled.

A bag sitting on a short table began to ring. He stepped closer, discovered how to open it, then brought out the object that was ringing.

It resembled one of the communication devices on New Symtaria. He flipped it open and it stopped ringing. Almost exactly like theirs.

"Yes," he said after he brought it to his ear.

"Hello?"

"Hello."

"Where's Callie?"

"Getting dressed."

"Getting dressed?"

"Yes, she was naked, but did not wish to continue not wearing clothes." His brow creased. "I don't know why. She has a magnificent body."

"Callie Jordon? We're talking about my best friend Callie,

right? She was naked in front of you? I mean, I don't have the wrong number, do I? As long as I've known her she's never had a man in her house, let alone one that spent the night with her. You did spend the night with her, right. In her bed?"

"Yes, we slept in the same bed, with our naked bodies pressed against each other."

"Maybe you'd better put Callie on the phone."

"Of course."

So the object was called a phone. He had thought they were larger, not as compact as this one. He carried it to the other room just as Callie came out.

"Phone," he said, handing it to her.

She looked startled. "Yes, that is a phone."

"She wants to talk to you."

Her face paled. "You weren't supposed to touch anything."

"It was ringing."

"It doesn't matter."

"I see."

"Tell whoever is on the phone I'm not here," she whispered.

"You want me to lie?"

"Yes!" she whispered, gritting her teeth again.

"But I've already told the woman we slept together last night with our naked bodies pressed against each other."

"You what!" she screamed, not even trying to keep her voice down.

Rogar had a feeling she was upset with him. He wasn't sure why. He'd kept the towel knotted at his waist. That was another thing. There was nothing wrong with his body. Everything worked. Why would she not want to look upon his naked form?

"DeeDee, hi. No, no, he's an old friend from . . . out of town."

Rogar noted her shoulders relaxed and she didn't seem quite as tense.

"Yes, pulling your leg. That's Rogar. Quite the jokester.

Nope, sorry, he's leaving town this morning. Only wanted a place to crash for the night. Yes, on the sofa. Okay, talk to you later. Bye-bye." She snapped the phone closed.

Callie glared at him. "You told her we slept naked together?"

"Did you want me to lie?"

"Yes, since I didn't invite you into my bed."

"Then I will lie next time."

"There won't be a next time because you're leaving today."

Rogar had a feeling getting Callie back to New Symtaria was going to be more difficult than even he had imagined.

She escaped to another room, returning a few minutes later with a long strip of white cloth that bore markings of some kind.

"You plan to bind me?" he asked. Not that it would do her any good. The cloth looked flimsy at best.

"That's not a bad idea, but no, I need to get your measurements so I'll know what size clothes to buy."

He nodded.

"Put you arms out."

He did as she asked, enjoying that she had moved closer. He liked the way she smelled. Not at all like a cat. No, this scent was clean and sweet. All too soon, she backed away to write his measurements on paper.

"Arm length, okay, got it," she mumbled as she jotted down numbers. Then she returned and wrapped her arms around his chest. Her gaze darted to his face.

Callie had beautiful eyes. They were green, but not just any green. They were a clear, deep green.

She stepped back, bringing the cloth together again. "I'm not Symtarian."

"You're from a proud and noble lineage."

"Then why was I left on the doorstep of the orphanage like someone's trash they were trying to get rid of?"

"I thought you said your parents were dead."

She glanced at him as she carefully wrapped the cloth

around his waist, trying not to come into contact with his skin. "I tell people my parents died because it sounds better than saying they dumped me on a doorstep." She looked at the cloth, then went back to her paper. "To me, they are dead."

"I'm sorry. This hurt you very deeply."

She shrugged. "It was so long ago that it doesn't matter now."

When she returned with the measuring cloth, he rested his hands on her shoulders. For a moment, she didn't move, then she looked at him, jutting that fierce little chin forward.

"I don't care about them anymore," she repeated and he wondered who she was trying to convince, herself or him? Callie's eyes practically dared him to challenge her words.

"Of course," he told her, letting the matter drop.

She knelt down, stretching the measuring cloth from his waist to his ankle. She dropped one end, though, and when she reached for it, lost her balance. She grabbed him for support, but only caught his towel, gripping it tightly as she landed on her bottom with a thud.

Rogar was once again very naked.

"Oh, God," she muttered as she stared at him.

She made a choking sound. He reached under her arms and helped her to her feet.

"I'm . . . uh . . . sorry," she stuttered.

He casually pried the towel from her fist, knotting it again at his waist.

"Your inseam . . . uh . . . oh, hell, I'll just guess." She raced for the door, stopped, then hurried back and grabbed the bag off the low table before rushing out. She returned a few seconds later, ran through the house, came back with the phone, then stopped at the door again.

"Don't touch anything."

"Of course not."

"Don't answer the door if anyone rings the bell . . . or knocks."

"I won't."

She nodded, then closed the door behind her.

She was very emotional, this part Earthling, part Symtarian woman. And very beautiful. He moved to the window, brushing the curtain to the side, and watched as she climbed into her vehicle. Rogar wondered how long it would take him to convince her that they should mate.

Soon, he hoped, because she already heated his blood.

You'd better think more about getting her home where she truly belongs rather than lusting after her, Balam's thoughts mingled with his.

Rogar frowned. *When I need your advice, I'll ask for it.*

You'd be better off if you asked for it more often. When have I ever steered you wrong?

Rogar snorted. *I can name a number of times. Remember when you suggested I mate with that pretty blond handmaiden my mother employed.*

I didn't know she was already joined with someone, he sniffed.

No, not someone. The man nearly beat me to a pulp.

I might have been wrong that once, Balam conceded.

And what about the time . . .

Enough! Trust me on this, if your mind is on mating, then how can you protect her? He's coming, you know. I can sense he's not far away.

Rogar sighed. *I know, I have sensed him, too. I won't let down my guard. Never fear, I will protect her with my life.*

And that is what I'm afraid of.

Chapter 3

Callie backed out of her driveway and aimed for the nearest clothing store. She didn't care about the cost, just as long as they came close to fitting him. She wanted Rogar, Prince of New Symtaria—yeah, right—out of her house and out of her life.

Besides, they wouldn't cost that much. She was going to a resale store that was nearby. She shopped there all the time. If he didn't like it, so be it, but she would insist he leave, no matter what. The guy was crazy.

She snorted.

An alien. Uh-huh, sure. And she was supposed to be one, too. She wasn't any more an alien than . . . than that light post on the corner. So what if she had always felt like there was something different about her and . . .

Her body began to tremble so hard she could barely steer. The community park was only a block away. As soon as she came to the entrance, she pulled in and parked.

By now her body was shaking so hard she could barely catch her breath. She shifted the car into Park, then turned the key off before bringing her hands to her face.

"Oh, God, this isn't happening. It can't be."

It wasn't so much about Rogar being in her apartment, as it was the fact that she'd always felt different from everyone else. Not because she was an orphan, either. She'd always known there was more to it. What if she was as crazy as him?

"No, no, no!" She laughed hysterically. Was she really going to buy his story that she was part alien? Really? It was too preposterous. There was no such thing as aliens from other planets.

Tap. Tap. Tap.

She screamed and turned so fast she almost got whiplash. Her heart pounded inside her chest as she looked at the uniformed officer standing outside her car.

Just a cop. She'd thought it might've been an alien come to whisk her off in his spaceship and poke her with . . . probes or . . . something.

He motioned for her to roll the window down. She nodded and turned the key until she had power, then pushed the button to bring it down.

"You okay, miss?"

She nodded. He reminded her of Ben, very fatherly, gray hair, and with concern on his face. If the officer continued being this nice, she would totally lose it.

He suddenly sniffed. "What's that odor?"

She sniffed.

Bleh! She knew exactly what it was. "Tuna fish," she squeaked, then cleared her throat, and in a clearer voice, continued. "I guess I forgot to take it out of my car." A few days ago.

He stepped a foot away from her car. "Do you mind stepping out of the vehicle?"

"Well, actually, I was just going to the clothing store . . ."

"Miss, it wasn't really a question as much as it was an order."

"Oh." She opened her door, and got out. "Is there a problem?"

His demeanor had rapidly changed from concerned officer to suspicious officer. She barely kept herself from sticking her arms in front of her and telling him to take her to jail. Just lock her up, and throw away the key. That's the way her day was going.

"Stand straight, then bring one finger to your nose, then repeat with the finger on your opposite hand," the officer told her.

It took her a second to figure out why he was asking her to touch her nose. As soon as it dawned on her, her back stiffened. "You think I've been drinking!" Oh, God, this was priceless.

"Miss, just do what I asked," he said the words slowly, as though he were talking to a child.

"Well, fine." She stood straight, touched one finger to her nose, then the other. She repeated for good measure. "Would you like me to walk a straight line, too? I can, you know."

Damn it! Could her day get any worse? She glanced toward the street. A gray land yacht was slowly going down the road. Oh, no, her landlady. Great! Just great!

"Your eyes are red-rimmed, and you were weaving before you pulled into the parking lot. It's called probable cause," the cop told her.

She sniffed, her bottom lip trembled. "Because I was crying, and I didn't want to run over anyone, so I pulled into the parking space here, and I just wanted to get myself together so I could go shopping because he needs clothes and . . ."

"Boyfriend?"

"Alien from another planet."

The officer frowned. "Yeah, some men can be jerks and you wish they were on another planet. I bet by the time you get home, he'll be ready to apologize. Most men usually realize they screwed up." He sighed. "My granddaughter just broke up with her boyfriend. 'Bout your age. You remind me a lot of her. She's pretty, too, and could do a whole lot better in the man department."

"You think I'm pretty?" She sniffed.

"Know so." His face reddened. "For a kid, that is."

Okay, she felt a little better. "Thank you."

"Dry those eyes now, and when you're out shopping for him, buy yourself something nice. If he doesn't straighten up and act right, just call me and I'll set him straight for you."

"Thank you, officer."

He walked back to his car and climbed in. She got inside her car, remembered the sandwich, and carried the brown sack to the Dumpster, dropping it inside. Ugh! It was pretty rank.

She kicked it into high gear once she was inside the store. She kept imagining Rogar causing all sorts of problems. He could destroy her things while she was gone. Not that she had that much.

By the time she arrived back home, which was still standing, and she would be eternally grateful for that, she had convinced herself that DeeDee was the prankster. Why else would she call early this morning? DeeDee thought sex was the cure for everything, and Callie needed to get more of it. Which Callie thought was crazy, of course. Not that she was a virgin or anything.

That was another area she knew she was different from everyone else. She would never admit it to anyone, but sex just wasn't that great. Everyone else seemed to enjoy the hell out of it, though.

Where was this fever, this uncontrollable passion everyone spoke about, or that she read about in her books? If it was out there, she certainly hadn't found it. She really had her doubts that she would ever have an out-of-control sexual encounter.

She turned the key off, and as soon as the car finished coughing and sputtering, gave its death rattle, then died, she grabbed the packages off the backseat and went inside.

All was quiet.

Too quiet.

Had he left? Maybe he hadn't existed in the first place. This might go back to her thoughts that insanity probably ran in her family.

An unexpected flash of disappointment swept over her.

He'd been really sexy, and it had been cool watching him transform into a powerful jaguar.

Right there, that should tell her something. No one could change form. She'd imagined the whole thing. And now she had all these men's clothes. Callie supposed she could donate them to the shelter. For now, she let the bags drop to the sofa, then walked to the bedroom. She glanced toward the bed. It had been a great fantasy.

She turned to go back to the other room just as the bathroom door opened. She screamed.

"I apologize for scaring you. I washed," he said. "It wasn't the same as standing beneath a waterfall and letting the water cascade over me, but it was pleasant."

Oh, right, she wanted that image in her head! She could see he'd taken a shower, his hair was damp. Rogar had no right to be this hot. Not when she knew what she had to do. Her line of charity had gone way past the limits of her comfort zone.

Not that it would be easy. A lock of his hair fell forward. It looked sexy lying on his forehead. Her gaze wandered down his body, the hard ridges, the six-pack abs. Thank God he had on the towel or she would be tempted to ravish him.

"I'll get your clothes." She hurried out of the room and grabbed the bags, taking them back to the bedroom. He still stood by the bathroom door looking like a friggin' god that had come to Earth to tempt mortal women.

She tossed the bags on the bed. "As soon as you're dressed, we need to talk." Without waiting for his reply, she hurried out of the room.

Callie paced the living room while she waited for him to join her. She turned when she heard his footsteps. It was so not fair that he looked almost as good with clothes as he had without them. The dark slacks fit him as though they were tailor-made. She'd chosen a maroon knit shirt and a size ten shoe. She'd guessed at the shoes.

"Do the shoes fit?" She pointed to his feet.

"Everything fits."

She drew in a deep breath. "Then you need to leave. You can't stay here."

He took a step nearer, his intense gaze studying her. "You would deny who you are?"

She turned and walked to the door. "I'm not who you think I am. I didn't come from another planet, and I don't think you did, either."

"Would you like me to change form again?"

"No!"

"But if it will prove to you that what I've told you is true . . ."

"I've seen magicians perform the same trick lots of times. It only proves you know magic."

"I'm the only one who can tell you where your ancestors came from, Callie. I know you have questions."

She did. How many times had she wondered who her parents were? Why they had abandoned her. Why they hadn't loved her enough to keep her.

A familiar, lonely ache engulfed her. All her life she'd felt rejected. No matter how often she told herself her parents were the problem, not her, she couldn't quite get past the hurt.

She drew in a deep breath and squared her shoulders. No matter how badly she wanted answers, she knew she couldn't be part alien. She stiffened her spine and looked him in the eye. "I think you'd better leave."

He was thoughtful for a moment, and she wondered if he might refuse to go.

"If that is what you wish. Good-bye Callie Jordon."

"Good-bye."

He went out the door.

At the last minute, she hurried to her purse and grabbed what little money she had left from her check—her last bill— a twenty. There went her lunch for next week. It would be PB&J sandwiches.

She ran out the door. "Rogar," she called.

He stopped and turned. "You've changed your mind?"

She shook her head, then shoved the bill in his hand. "You might need some money. I'm sorry I don't have more."

He studied the bill, turning it over in his hand, before stuffing it in his pants pocket. "Thank you."

"Good-bye."

He smiled. One of those crooked half smiles that sent her pulse racing. Before she did something foolish, like ask him to stay, she turned and hurried back inside, shutting the door firmly behind her. She closed her eyes and willed herself not to open the door to see if he'd really left.

After a few deep breaths, she went to the kitchen. There was an empty cereal box on the counter. Darn, that had been her breakfast for next week. At least she had coffee. She could live without a lot of stuff, but never her coffee.

Her cell phone began to ring. She hurried to the other room and unearthed it at the bottom of her purse.

"Hello?"

"Me again."

"Hi DeeDee."

"Did your friend leave?"

"Yes, why?"

"Just curious."

"No, I wasn't lying, and no, we didn't have sex."

"I didn't really think you had," DeeDee said, sounding disappointed. "But a girl can hope."

Callie laughed. "You know, the world does not revolve around having sex."

"It does if you do it right." She paused. "Come out with me tonight. It's Saturday. We'll go to a club and see what we can drum up."

Callie almost said yes, but then she remembered she was broke until next Friday. "I can't this weekend. How about next?"

"I can spot you the money."

Callie cringed. Her friend made a lot more money, plus her parents were loaded and doted on their only child, but Callie refused to borrow from DeeDee. She made her own way in this world. Always had. She wouldn't change now.

"Can I take a rain check? There are some things I need to get done around the house."

DeeDee's deep sigh came across the line. "If you insist."

"I'm afraid I have to."

Callie closed her phone a few minutes later, after DeeDee told her about the guy she'd met at a club last Saturday. DeeDee led an eventful life. Her motto was live while you're young. She also thought Callie was old before her time. Maybe she was. Sometimes Callie felt older than her twenty-six years.

The next morning Callie stretched her arms above her head and yawned as she came awake, then stilled. Cautiously, she glanced around the room.

No one there.

She'd half expected to see Rogar sitting on the end of her bed, legs crossed, and stark naked. She was almost disappointed that he wasn't. DeeDee was right, her life was definitely lacking male companionship.

The weekend dragged at a snail's pace. She cleaned everything there was to clean, and still found herself going to the window and looking out.

Was Rogar okay? Had he found another female more willing to let him crawl into her bed? One who was more willing to believe his far-fetched stories?

She was glad when Monday morning came so she'd at least have her job to occupy her mind. The petting zoo wasn't so bad. She enjoyed working with the baby animals. The kids that came to try to torture the animals were another matter.

If she was honest, most of the children weren't that bad. It was just that there was always at least one monster in the bunch who thought pulling the goat's tail was great fun.

Callie was tempted to visit Sheba first. Her place of Zen, gather her Chi, but she knew that would make her late so she headed in the opposite direction.

"Hi, Callie," Gail said as Callie joined her coworker.

"Morning."

Gail critically eyed her. "Rough weekend?"

She walked into the small enclosure that would hold the baby animals when they brought them out. "Do I look that bad?"

"Not that bad. You could never look bad. Just tired."

"I read a book I couldn't put down."

Gail nodded, knowing Callie was addicted to books. "Yeah, I get pretty caught up in them, too. Give me a sexy hunk over a boring rerun any day." She laughed.

The phone rang in the small building next to the enclosure. "I'll get it," Gail said.

Callie began to bring the animals to the enclosure. They had quite a few. A miniature horse, a lamb, a potbelly pig they called Morris, a duck, the goat, a very fat cat that wasn't really a baby, to name a few. They were sweet, but they weren't the big cats that she longed to take care of.

She looked up when Gail returned. "Everything okay?"

"You're being pulled."

Callie groaned. When someone didn't show up for work, she was the one who got pulled to do their job, and why not, she had done everything at the zoo, from driving one of the tour buses, to mucking stalls—oh, God, she hoped it wasn't that. She loathed cleaning the stalls, especially the elephants'.

She knew the only reason they had stuck supervisor on her name tag was so she would stay. The quarter an hour raise had helped, she admitted to herself, but it wasn't like she would get rich from it or anything.

"You're supposed to go to the main office."

Callie's smile was weak at best.

"The secretary said it had to do something with a private tour. Hey, don't feel too bad, we have three classes of first and second graders scheduled to go through this morning."

Callie was thoughtful for a moment, then she nodded. "You're right. Nothing could be as bad as that." She grinned, then made her way to the main office.

Still, she wasn't particularly fond of private tours. If someone could afford the cost of a guide, and an open minibus or Jeep, that usually meant their kids were spoiled rotten. The last time she had chauffeured one, she'd ended up with a giant sucker stuck on the back of her uniform, and cotton candy in her hair. The generous tip had only mildly soothed her ruffled feathers.

She went inside the air-conditioned private office.

"Go on in, Mr. Campbell is expecting you." His secretary waved her inside.

She took a deep breath. She always hated going inside his office. It wasn't that she disliked him. Okay, maybe she did. He was superficial and pretentious, nothing like his father. If it made him look good, then he was happy, no matter whose toes he stepped on along the way.

She opened the door and walked in. Mr. Campbell was seated at his desk. The office was done in dark, rich wood— only the best, of course, but it was rather like walking into a cave. It took a moment for her eyes to adjust. When they did, she saw the man who sat across from Mr. Campbell. From the back, he looked familiar. Dark hair brushed his shoulders, he wore a deep green shirt and dark slacks.

"Callie, come in, come in. I want you to meet Rogar Valkyir, you'll be giving him a private tour of the grounds. Mr. Valkyir, this is Callie Jordon."

Rogar stood, then slowly turned.

She tried to swallow, but couldn't. She choked instead. Rogar quickly poured her a glass of water from the pitcher on Mr. Campbell's desk, then handed it to her. She gulped half of it down as she pulled her thoughts together.

"Are you okay, Ms. Jordon?" Rogar's words were soft and silky, like a caress.

"Fine, thank you very much. I swallowed wrong."

"Miss Jordon." Rogar bowed slightly.

"Mr. Valkyir." She said between gritted teeth. She didn't know what the hell his game was, but she was damned well tired of playing!

"Callie is probably the one person who knows everything about the animals we have at the zoo," Mr. Campbell continued as though the temperature in the room hadn't suddenly dropped ten degrees. "He especially wants to see the big cats. I'd like for you to give him anything he wants." He didn't smile, he beamed.

"I'm anxious to see the park," Rogar said. "Are you ready?"

No, she wasn't, damn it! How the hell had he maneuvered his way in here and gotten Mr. Campbell to bend over backward and arrange for a private showing? And where did he get the new clothes? His clothes cost way more than the twenty dollars she'd given him. She had an awful feeling that she'd had the wool pulled over her eyes. Fury did not begin to describe the emotion she felt right now.

Don't make a scene, she told herself. "Yes, of course, Mr. Valkyir."

"Rogar, please."

Her blood pressure shot up a couple more notches. "Rogar." She smiled sweetly, trying not to bare her teeth.

Before she reached the door, he was there, opening it for her. The guy moved fast. Yeah, right, he definitely had some fast moves. Like convincing her he could change into a jaguar. Correction, almost convincing her. She hadn't realized getting laid had taken on this degree of finesse. The guy was a master at it. And to think she had almost fallen into his trap. God, she was such a moron.

"What are you thinking?" he asked as they walked toward the covered carport where they kept the zoo vehicles.

She wondered if his sexy accent was even real. And that name, Rogar Valkyir. It had to be phony, too.

She glanced his way, her eyes narrowing. "You don't want to know."

He put a hand out to stop her. She could feel his strength, his heat, through the cotton of her shirt. Against her will, tingles of awareness rippled over her.

"Yes, I do want to know. You look angry. Have I done something wrong?"

She snorted. "Angry? Angry doesn't even come close to what I'm feeling." She jerked out of his grasp, which wasn't difficult since his hold had been light.

"Then I will try to make it better. Just tell me what I need to do, anything at all, and I will do it for you." He smiled and for a moment she was lost.

She quickly cleared her mind. "You're going to be my hero, huh?" She drew in a shaky breath. He had the looks of a hero.

"Is that what you want? A hero?" His voice caressed her.

She aimed her thoughts down another road. "If you want to do something, tell Mr. Campbell you've changed your mind about the private tour, then go back where you came from. I don't need a hero, nor do I believe you're an alien either. Good line, though. It almost worked."

"Line?"

"Yeah, so you could have . . . sex . . . with me." She looked away as heat rose up her face.

"You think that was what I was trying to do?"

Her spine stiffened. "Weren't you?"

"Everything I told you was the truth."

"Sorry, I'm not buying it this time." She opened the Jeep's door and climbed in on the driver's side. "If you're going, get in." She turned the key, not waiting to see what he would do. Out of the corner of her eye, she saw him climb inside.

This was going to be a very long day.

She smiled to herself.

And she was going to make it just as boring and painful for him as he would be making it for her. She was going to hit every speed bump, take him past the area where the refuse was dumped . . .

He was going to be so sorry he showed up today.

Chapter 4

"That's where the monkeys are kept. Did you want to get out and look at them, too?" Everywhere Callie had taken Rogar, he'd insisted they stop and get out. He was only wasting his time because she'd made sure her answers were curt, and she refused to talk about anything except the animals.

There was no way she would lose her job if Rogar complained. What could he tell Mr. Campbell? Only that she'd pointed out the different animals, and given him details about them, which is exactly what she was supposed to do.

"Are you going to be mad at me for the rest of your life?" he asked, rather than telling her whether or not he wanted to get out.

"Yes." Okay, her smile might look a little snarly, but showing teeth counted as being friendly. Right?

She thought of something that had been bothering her. "And I want my twenty dollars back, too." She eyed his expensive clothes, trying not to look at the cut or how well they fit his muscled body, but rather the quality of the material, which wasn't easy. "Twenty dollars might not seem like a lot to you. For me, it means gas and lunch all week."

He reached in his pocket and pulled out a wad of bills. Her mouth dropped open. There had to be at least a couple of thousand there. When he handed her a twenty, she pursed her lips to keep from saying something she probably *wouldn't* regret, and grabbed it out of his hand.

"Did you want to get out and look at the monkeys?" She kept her gaze forward.

"No, I want to see the big cats."

She shifted into Drive, and took off, only slowing when she left a little rubber in her wake. By the time she had gotten to the area where the cats were kept, she was a little calmer.

Why should she let Rogar get to her? It wasn't as though she would ever have to see him again. And she would refuse another private tour if he was the one paying for it.

"We'll have to walk from here," she said as she parked close to the bridge. "We only have one jaguar right now, Sheba. The lion and her cub are a little farther away."

He didn't say anything, only climbed out. They walked across the bridge, and once more, she inhaled the scent of jasmine and ginger, and once again, she began to relax.

She also remembered the last time she had been here. The black jaguar had to be a pet of Rogar's, and he'd done a switch of some kind. Okay, maybe she did envy him for that. What would it feel like to be able to get that close to a wild animal? Everything she'd been taught in college, everything that had been drummed into her head, had leaned toward caution when working around the bigger cats. No one seemed to have told Rogar, though.

She still hadn't quite figured out how he'd gotten the cat in and out of her house, but he'd probably rigged it while she slept, and then moved the jaguar after she'd fainted. There was no other explanation, except that he was an alien who could change form, and she wasn't buying into that again.

"At night the cats are double caged over there." She pointed toward the cages. "If we go around to the front, you can see something that closely resembles a jaguar's natural habitat. We call it the pit."

Without waiting for her, he started in that direction. She didn't really have a choice, except to follow. The space was large, with trees that weren't close enough to the double fence that a cat could escape, but it provided an environment that was more like the animals' natural one. Sheba seemed satisfied. Callie hoped she was. Although Callie often wondered if she might be lonely. That was one reason why she made a point of visiting the jag. She knew all about loneliness.

As they rounded the corner, the blood drained from her face. There were four teenagers pushing each other and cutting up. That was pretty normal. What wasn't normal was the kid, who couldn't be more than fifteen, walking on the top ledge of the second wall. The one that protected the patrons. If he lost his balance, he could fall into the pit. If Sheba attacked, Mr. Campbell would have the jaguar put down.

"You aren't supposed to be up there," Callie said in a quiet, but firm voice. "Please come down."

"Hey, Gary, you got a hot chick begging you. That's a first." He guffawed and pushed one of the other boys. "You going to do what she says? You pussy-whipped like your old man?"

Gary looked as though he might have gotten down if his friend hadn't razzed him. Now he only looked undecided.

"I think you better do as the lady asked," Rogar said.

For the first time today, she was glad he stood beside her.

"Whatever." The kid shrugged and started to jump back to the fence closest to the visitors, but his foot slipped. His arms windmilled, then, as if in slow motion, he fell into the pit.

Callie sucked in a breath.

Sheba began to pace back and forth, getting closer and closer to the boy. The boy groaned and raised his head.

"Don't move," Callie called out, reaching for her cell phone. Oh, God, she really didn't want to see the kid ripped to shreds. "Everyone stay calm, and please be as quiet as possible." She glared at the other boys just to get her point across, then punched in the number of the main office. As soon as the secretary answered, she began to talk. "We have a situation at the jaguar pit. A boy fell in. Get someone here with a tranquilizer gun, and call an ambulance."

"I'm on it," Mr. Campbell's secretary told her.

Callie snapped her phone closed and glanced at Rogar. He'd taken off his shoes. "What are you doing?"

"Making sure he doesn't get eaten."

Her eyes widened. "You can't go in there!"

He grinned. "Watch me."

In one graceful movement, he jumped to the first stone wall, then across to the next. If she wasn't scared out of her wits, she would've admired his agility. He dropped into the pit as though it were only a few feet down, rather than fifteen. Oh, God, she was going to throw up.

She looked around. A crowd had gathered, but she had to say they were staying very quiet, other than a few collective gasps when Rogar had dropped to the ground.

"What are you doing?" She intentionally kept her voice low. Sheba was already pacing across her enclosure, eyeing the intruders.

Seemingly quite unconcerned, Rogar looked up and grinned. "I'm being a hero. Isn't that what you said you wanted?" He quirked an eyebrow.

For a moment, he made her forget where they were, and that he was in danger, but then Sheba's angry cry echoed through the compound, chilling Callie's blood.

"No, I don't want a hero."

He shrugged. "Too late."

She wanted to throw something at him, she wanted to . . . Her thoughts stilled as she watched Rogar turn and face Sheba. As he walked toward her, Rogar began to talk quietly in a tongue Callie had never heard. It not only had a hypnotic effect on Sheba, but also the small crowd of people.

He slowly moved toward the cat, then when he was a few feet away, he stopped, and dropped to his knees. Sheba opened her mouth, teeth bared, and cried out again, pacing back and forth in front of Rogar.

"What the hell is he doing in there?"

Callie jumped, whirling around, and came face to face

with a man wearing the same color uniform as hers. She didn't know the man's name, but he worked at the zoo, and he carried a tranquilizer gun.

"One of the kids was playing trapeze and fell into the pit. He's moved and groaned, but that's about it. We need to lower a basket, and a couple of men, while Rogar has Sheba's attention," she said.

"If he'll give me a shot, I can put her down, then we won't be taking a chance anyone will get hurt."

"And maybe we won't need to. He apparently has worked with big cats before or she would have already attacked."

He raised the gun. "I won't do anything unless I have to."

Four medics came hurrying around the corner with ropes and a basket. They worked quietly and efficiently lowering two men and a basket over the side. They didn't waste any time as they spinal packed the kid, then eased him into the basket. There were enough men up top to pull the basket back up. Both medics were next. They looked relieved to be out of the pit.

But most of the time, Callie kept her gaze on Rogar. Sheba had stopped pacing. Callie wondered if the cat had decided he'd make a good meal.

"Everyone is clear except Tarzan," the guy with the gun said. "If he'll move to the right just a bit, I can get a shot, and we'll get him out of there all safe and sound."

But Sheba padded closer to Rogar. Callie caught her breath when the cat suddenly rose on her hind feet, and planted her big paws on Rogar's shoulders.

The crowd gasped.

But then Sheba surprised everyone when she licked him on the face.

Shocked silence reigned over the crowd. Rogar began to pet the cat and laugh, as though Sheba was no more than an overgrown tabby.

The crowd began to chuckle, then clap. The guy with the gun lowered it. "What the hell?" He pushed his cap higher on his forehead. "In all my born days, I ain't never seen nothing like this. Who the hell is this guy?"

"He's a hero," she spoke softly.

Rogar stood. The cat twined around his legs. He patted her neck then leaned down and said something to her. She gave his hand one lick, then in just a few moves, climbed the nearest tree. Sheba stretched out on one of the limbs, purring from deep in her throat, as though she was totally contented at the moment.

Rogar didn't get in any hurry as he came back to the wall. Someone lowered a rope and he swiftly climbed it. As he joined everyone up on top, people began to shake his hand and slap him on the back.

"What did you think you were doing?" Callie asked when he was finally able to join her. "You could've been killed."

"Sheba would never hurt one of her own," he said softly.

Callie opened her mouth, then snapped it closed. She raised her chin a few notches. "I still don't believe that . . . that you're an alien who can change into a jaguar."

"Not even a little?"

She clamped her lips together and turned on her heel. "I think the tour is over."

"You didn't answer me," he said when he caught up to her, after putting his socks and shoes back on.

She didn't answer him because there was a part of her that did believe him, and if she believed him, then what did that make her? She knew what it made her—crazy.

She stopped and faced him, poking him in the chest with her finger. "You're a flesh and blood man, not an alien, and certainly not a jaguar."

"You have a guide who lives in you, too, Callie. Have you not felt her talking to you? She guided you to the zoo, to work where you would be most comfortable."

"My guide?"

"Yes, you share bodies with your guide."

"And I can share this animal's body that lives inside me?"

He nodded.

She laughed. "Bull!"

"I can teach you how to connect with your guide."

Was this guy for real? Yeah, he was a great magician, and it was obvious he'd worked with animals. She respected him for that, but she refused to be taken in again.

"The tour is over." She climbed into the Jeep. As soon as he was inside, she started the vehicle and aimed for the carport. Once there, she wasted no time pulling in and putting the Jeep in park.

"Let's not do this again." She got out and walked to the petting zoo without looking back.

But damn, she wanted to take one last look, embed him in her memory banks. She didn't.

"You're back," Gail said with obvious relief.

"Sorry it took so long."

Gail leaned against the fence, absently petting the cat that came out of hiding. "Did you hear about the kid that fell into the jag's pit?"

"I was there."

She straightened. "You saw it? I heard this guy jumped into the pit and saved the boy. He hypnotized the jaguar or something. Everyone is talking about it. Is that what really happened?"

"Pretty much," she hedged, wanting to drop the subject, but when Gail looked as though she wanted more information, Callie relented. "He's worked with big cats before. He's good."

Gail looked disappointed, but Callie really didn't want to talk about it anymore. Apparently, Gail finally sensed her reluctance, and let the matter drop.

The rest of the day passed quickly. Maybe because Callie kept getting lost in thoughts of how well Rogar had worked with Sheba. The jaguar hadn't been any more immune to his charms than had Callie.

And maybe Callie had been a whole lot jealous. How many times had she dreamed of petting Sheba?

She clamped her lips together. No, Rogar took dangerous chances that she would never be stupid enough to try. End of story.

When her shift ended, her feet were heavy as she trudged to the employee parking lot. She would probably never see Rogar again. That was a good thing, though. She certainly didn't want him in her life.

Her car looked forlorn, off to itself, as almost everyone had left for the day. She unlocked the door and sank into the cushioned seat, except it had lost any semblance of comfortable long before she'd bought it off the used car lot. Still, she was off her feet, and that was all that really mattered.

She inserted the key and turned it.

Nothing.

Not even a chugga-chugga.

She let off, counted to five, then turned it again.

Nothing.

This was so not happening.

She turned the key again and heard the soft purr of an engine. No chugga-chugga? Had her car miraculously healed itself? Cool. She frowned. Except the dash lights hadn't come on.

She looked up. There was a sleek black convertible sitting beside her car—Rogar was behind the wheel. A Jaguar, no less. Her dream car. The one she'd cut out of a magazine and put on her vision board that hung on the wall in her bedroom.

Rogar smiled.

She quite possibly hated him. He'd had the nerve to take the last of her money, then flaunt his fancy clothes and expensive car? Her some-day-in-the-distant-future car! She glared at him, but it didn't seem to faze him. All she wanted to do was leave, forget about him. She turned the key one more time.

Nothing happened.

Great, just freaking great. She grabbed her purse off the passenger seat and opened her door, slamming it closed after she got out. She didn't look at his high-dollar car or at him, but instead, marched past with her head held high.

A car door opened and closed, then his hand was on her arm, effectively stopping her. She turned and glared at him.

"Go away."

"You need a ride home."

"I'm not going anywhere with you."

"Why not?"

She stopped and stared at him. He really didn't get it. "Because I don't like you."

He frowned. "Really?" He looked genuinely puzzled.

A mental picture of how he'd worked with Sheba formed. What he'd done had taken courage. Rogar had probably saved that boy's life. "Okay, maybe not liking you is too strong—" she conceded, "but I don't care to be in your company."

"Then don't, but at least let me take you home."

She sighed. "But I'll still need to get my car at some point."

"I'll take care of that, too."

She didn't want to accept his offer. What she wanted to do was sit in the middle of the parking lot and bawl. Would she ever catch a decent break?

"Let me be your hero," he spoke softly, his words like a warm breeze drifting over her.

"I don't want a hero." She hated that her bottom lip trembled.

"But you do need saving right now. At least, let me do that."

What choice did she have? "Okay, you can take me home, but that's all."

He smiled.

Why did she feel as though he'd played her just as much as he'd played Sheba this afternoon? But then, what choice did she have? Right now, she really did need a hero.

They walked back to his car, and she slid into the passenger seat. Black leather cupped her body in pure luxury. This was what a real car felt like. God, it was almost an orgasmic experience.

Rogar got in on the driver's side and started the car. It purred to life. She could almost feel the car's energy, the sheer power under the hood.

He clutched and shifted, grinding the engine. She flinched.

"You do know how to drive, don't you?"

"Your vehicles are antiquated compared to those on New Symtaria, but I'm sure it won't take me long to have everything down."

"Well, la-te-dah."

He glanced in her direction. "We push a button and our mode of transportation takes us where we want to go."

"That sounds like loads of fun," she mumbled. Superior her foot. He didn't even realize what he was driving. The Jag was unsurpassed by any other vehicle as far as she was concerned. This was the car that made her drool, and he was grinding gears.

He pulled out of the employee parking lot, not even bothering to stop at the Stop sign.

"You do know how to read English, don't you?" she asked, sitting up a little straighter.

"Of course."

"You just ran a Stop sign."

His brow furrowed. "I don't know all of your rules."

Great, he was going to kill her with his driving. At least she would die in luxury. Not that she was quite ready to die. "There's a light coming up. You'll need to stop if it's red or orange, but you go if it's green."

He nodded.

"How did you manage to make it to the zoo?"

"People were nice enough to get out of my way."

She laughed. "I just bet they were."

He looked at her. "I like the way you laugh."

For a moment she couldn't breathe. No one had ever really complimented her. The workers at the orphanage tried their best, but there were so many kids, and just not enough hugs or compliments to go around. Most of the time, she went unnoticed.

She cleared her throat. "Better watch the road. My turn is coming up." But even after she pointed it out to him, he drove past. "You missed it."

"I'm hungry," he said. "There are places where we can get food."

"Restaurants?"

"Yes."

"You promised to take me home."

"Your stomach is making funny noises. You're hungry, too, and there wasn't much food at your dwelling."

He had her there. Besides, he did owe her for pulling all that crap on her about being an alien. It was time to make him pay.

She pointed him in the direction of one of the most expensive restaurants she could think of. So what if she wasn't dressed appropriately.

Chapter 5

Callie closed her eyes and savored the juicy piece of steak. This was so good and so much better than the PB&J sandwich she'd planned to have for dinner. She opened her eyes and met Rogar's gaze.

She shouldn't have let him talk her into going out to eat. Not that he'd had to do that much talking. She'd only justified her hunger with the fact that he owed her. But if Rogar thought he could suck her into his fantasy that he was an alien, he was sadly mistaken.

She laid her silverware across her empty plate. A waiter immediately appeared, almost out of nowhere, and removed it. Another brought a chocolate mousse in a crystal dessert dish and set it in front of her. It looked light as air, topped with a cloud of fluffy whipped cream and decadent swirls of dark chocolate.

"Are you regretting going to dinner with me?" Rogar asked.

She picked up her spoon and dipped it into the dessert. There was a creamy center. She took a bite, closing her eyes and savoring the bursts of cherry and chocolate flavors. She'd never tasted anything like this in her entire lifetime.

"Callie?"

She wanted to look him in the eyes and say yes, she regretted it with every breath in her body, but she couldn't make the words come out.

"If this didn't taste so damned good, then yes, I would regret it, but it does, so I won't lie. There, are you satisfied?"

He leaned back in his chair, looking full of himself. Sexy, but gloating. She'd throw the chocolate mousse at him if it weren't so delicious.

"Yes, I'm satisfied."

Before he could get too full of himself, she continued, "But I'm still not buying your alien from another world story, nor that I'm part . . ." She frowned.

"Symtarian," he supplied.

"Yeah, I'm not buying any of it. What are you? A bored trust fund baby? Too much time and money on your hands?"

"No."

"Then where did you get all that money?" Let him answer that one.

"I took the money you gave me and reproduced it."

The spoon she held clattered to the table, staining the white tablecloth with chocolate. She could feel the color draining from her face.

A waiter hurried forward, quickly cleaning the mess and telling her not to worry about it. As soon as he'd disappeared, she turned to Rogar. "You're a counterfeiter?" she whispered.

He was thoughtful for a moment, then his eyes widened. "Yes, that's what I did. I counterfeited the bill you gave me." He smiled, as though he was proud that he understood what she'd said.

"That's illegal." She furtively glanced around the room, expecting the police to pounce on them any second, but everything looked the same as it had a moment ago. God, how had she gotten herself into this? Not only was he a psychopath, but a criminal as well.

"Would you like coffee, ma'am?" The waiter asked, bearing a silver coffeepot.

"No, I'm finished. Just the bill." The waiter looked surprised that she didn't want to linger, but then he eyed her uniform as though he found her quite uncouth.

The waiter cocked an imperious eyebrow. "As you wish."

Ass.

"You don't find the restaurant to your liking?" Rogar asked.

"It's great." She would never be able to show her face in here again, though. Not that she could afford this place.

Oh, no, they knew she worked at the zoo since she still wore her uniform. When they discovered the bills were phony, they'd come to arrest her, and she'd never get to work with the big cats.

The waiter came back with a leather folder and placed it beside Rogar. She reached across and grabbed it. Maybe she could leave them an IOU. No, that would probably get her in bigger trouble. She opened it and looked at the total. It took her a second to catch her breath. She wanted to cry.

The wine they'd had with their dinner had been three hundred dollars a bottle. The meal was one hundred and eighty. Oh, good Lord! The mousse was thirty dollars! Thirty freakin' dollars for pudding? It didn't matter that it was decadent and exquisite—no dessert was worth thirty dollars.

The waiter pried the leather folder from her hands and handed it back to Rogar, who casually reached into his pocket and peeled off 6, one-hundred-dollar bills. Before she could snatch the folder again, the waiter scooped it up in his hands with a wide grin and bowed before making a hasty exit.

Rogar came to his feet, then waited for her. A waiter hurried over and nudged her chair. What could she do? She came to her feet as the waiter pulled the chair out for her. Rogar handed him a twenty.

Of course they would fall all over themselves to do his bidding when he flashed money at them. She was halfway to the door when she remembered something and hurried back to the table. The staff had already started to clear it. She marched over to the silver wine bucket and grabbed what was left of the three-hundred-dollar wine, hugging the bottle close to her chest. If she was going to jail eventually, then she was damn well going to enjoy the fruits of her criminal behavior.

Her gaze dared Rogar to say something when she rejoined him. He didn't.

The valet brought the car around. The young man lovingly caressed the side as he got out. She suddenly thrust the bottle of wine toward Rogar. "Here, I'm driving."

He shrugged. "It makes no difference to me."

He didn't seem to care if she could even drive a standard. This car meant nothing to him. The high-dollar meal probably hadn't, either. The injustice was almost too much to bear.

She scooted in on the driver's side, and the valet closed her door. For a moment she just sat there, eyes closed as she got the feel of such an exquisite piece of machinery. Then she opened her eyes and fastened her seat belt.

"Buckle up," she told Rogar. She was so going to show him what this baby could do.

"You can operate this vehicle?"

Now he wonders about his safety? She adjusted the seat to reach the pedals better. "Oh, yeah, I can drive it." An old boyfriend had taught her what a real car could do, and she'd been hooked.

After pulling out into traffic, she headed toward the outskirts of the city. As soon as the traffic thinned to nothing but an occasional vehicle, she glanced toward Rogar. "Hang on." For the first time, he looked a little nervous. He shouldn't, she knew what she was doing.

She downshifted, then tapped the gas, that's all it took with this baby, but she could feel the surge of power all the way up her arms. The wind blew her hair as a rush of excitement flowed over her entire body.

It had been a long time since she'd felt this free. No more problems, no more troubles. She was outrunning them. She didn't have to think about how many times she'd been passed over when it came to the animal keeper job or the crappy house she rented or never having enough money, always being caught between a rock and a hard place. No, everything was blown away like the wind through her hair.

Trees rushed past, buildings and businesses were replaced by pastures, which is why she chose this isolated area to test the car's speed. She laughed for the pure joy of it. But when she glanced at the gas gauge, she knew she'd have to turn around and go back or they would get stuck walking. The needle was almost on empty. It was fantastic while it lasted. She slowed, then pulled into a roadside park.

"Well, what did you think?" she asked after she turned the key off and slid around in her seat to face him.

"I think you know how to operate the antiquated machine," he said very nonchalantly.

"You're not fooling me for a moment." She grinned. "Admit it, you loved the ride."

He studied her, then before she could react, he leaned over, cupped her head with his hand, and brought her lips to his. She was just startled enough that she didn't stop him. But then his lips were brushing across hers, and the heat began to build.

His tongue delved inside her mouth, caressing, touching, at the same time his hand slid over the front of her shirt, unbuttoning it as he went, then cupping her breast, brushing his thumb across her nipple. She moaned, pleasurable sensations sweeping over her.

She had to stop him. She barely knew the guy, and what she did know, made her question his sanity. Maybe she should start questioning hers as well because it felt so good, and it had been so long since a man had touched her.

The headlights from a passing eighteen wheeler caught them for a brief moment, but it was enough to bring her back to her senses. She pushed on his shoulders. He stopped, but when she looked at him, she could see the effort written on his face.

"I can't," she spoke softly.

"Why? You enjoyed my touch."

He definitely said what he was thinking. Most guys would've tried to pull her back into their arms and attempt to kiss her into submission, or given up and tried again on another date, or moved on to greener pastures. They never asked why.

She took a deep breath. His gaze lowered. Damned full moon that left nothing to the imagination. She quickly buttoned her blouse. "I'm not ready to go that far with you." How prim and proper did that sound? Sheesh!

He moved back to his seat. "Then I'll wait until you're ready."

This guy was really full of himself. "And what if I'm never ready?"

"You were ready a moment ago, more than ready. You ached for more, and you were panting. You still haven't accepted what you are. When you do, then we will mate."

"Excuse me?" He really had his nerve.

She wasn't about to get into a conversation about how bad she might have wanted him. She frowned. Probably because he was right. She moved the topic to safer ground. "I won't ever believe that I can shift into an animal. It's a ridiculous notion. I think you're crazy." Had she actually just told him he was crazy while sitting at a roadside park, no one around to hear her scream while he killed her?

"I'm not crazy."

"Of course not." She attempted a friendly smile. "It was only a figure of speech. We'd better get back." She quickly started the car and pulled out onto the road, keeping the speed limit this time.

Maybe she didn't really think he was crazy. Not serial killer crazy, anyway. He had saved that boy's life. Killers didn't normally go around saving lives. But he was—different.

She knew he watched her for the first few minutes before he turned his attention back to the road. Rogar was quiet. What was he thinking?

Rogar closed his eyes, feeling the wind on his face. It was a feeling much like the one he had when he became one with the jaguar and they would run through the jungles on New Symtaria. It was the same kind of freedom.

He closed his eyes for a moment, frustrated with how things were going. He had to convince Callie of who she really was, what she could do. He opened his eyes, narrowing them as he scanned the passing scenery. The moonlight made it as bright as day, but there were still shadows all around them.

But were the shadows safe or dangerous?

Not all Symtarians thought it was a good thing to bring their people home if they had mixed blood. They thought it would weaken their race. These rogue Symtarians weren't willing to admit the purity of the Symtarian blood was killing who they were. They needed impures like Callie to ensure their survival.

Yes, Earth was inferior in many ways, but there were good things, too. He enjoyed listening to Callie's laughter, and watching her interaction with Sheba that first night. There was kindness inside her.

And he liked the way she immediately responded to his touch, pupils dilating, nipples hardening.

He drew in a shaky breath. Symtarians needed to mate often, needed the release that went with it.

A sign flashed, drawing his attention to the fact that they were back in the city. It wasn't good that he would become so lost in thought. Danger was still out there, still waiting. He had to remain alert. If for no other reason, he had to protect Callie.

Chapter 6

"Thanks for dinner, and letting me drive your car." She got out, leaving it running, and hoping he would take the hint and leave.

"Can I use your bathroom?" he asked.

Now what was he up to? That was the oldest line in the book. If he thought she would succumb to his charm, he'd better think again. No way was she inviting him into her bed.

She sighed. But he had given her a ride home and bought her supper—sort of. "But then you'll need to leave," she told him.

He reached over and shut off the engine, pocketing his keys before getting out of the car. She couldn't fault him for that. In this neighborhood it probably wasn't wise to leave a Jag running. Shoot, it might not even be wise to leave one in the driveway. Not that he would be here that long.

She unlocked the front door, flipped on the light, and they went inside. He started toward the bathroom, but turned, placing his hands lightly on her shoulders. Okay, here it was, his move to get her into bed. But he only looked deep into her eyes.

"You have the ability to change form. Your guide is there"—he tapped her chest—"in your heart . . . and in your soul, waiting for you to acknowledge her. You need her as much as she needs you."

Funny, she didn't feel afraid because he was talking crazy again. Maybe because she knew he really believed what he was telling her.

She might as well play along and humor him.

Yeah, sure, who was she kidding? She was beginning to buy into his fantasy . . . sort of.

She cocked her head to the side. "And exactly how do I change form?"

"You only have to close your eyes and think about your guide. Think about your other form. It will happen if you let it."

He moved his hands from her shoulders, taking his warmth with him as he walked out of the room.

What if he was right? What if she was part alien? She'd been about eight when she'd first heard the voice inside her. What if it had been her guide? Callie had been scared. She'd told one of the counselors and the next thing she knew, she was sitting in front of a psychiatrist.

Who would want to adopt a kid who heard a voice talking to her? She'd stopped listening, and eventually it went away.

Callie was so confused. Rogar had said to change form, she had to close her eyes and think about her guide. If she did this, and didn't change, that would prove to him, and her, that she wasn't part alien.

Before she could chastise herself for being as crazy as Rogar for even thinking she quite possibly could be part alien, she took a deep breath and closed her eyes, then exhaled. After a few seconds, she opened her eyes, and looked at her arms. They still looked like her arms.

Rogar had said she needed to concentrate. She took another deep breath, exhaled, and relaxed her whole body. She pictured fields of green grass waving in the breeze, and could almost feel the wind on her face. *Animal guide, are you there?* The sun raced across the sky. The moon came out. There was strength in the magical orb in the sky. She could hear people speaking, and knew it was her ancestors who had crossed before her. She felt her body changing.

What was happening? Was she dying? Had Rogar come back and killed her while she wasn't looking, and she didn't know she was dead yet?

Ridiculous, she wasn't dead. At least, she was pretty sure she wasn't, but she hurt. Her body ached in places she didn't know she could ache. And burned with an intensity she didn't know existed.

She tried to open her eyes, but she couldn't, and yet, she felt the damp fog surrounding her. Weakness enveloped her, and she slowly sank to the floor and curled into a ball as her heart began to race. The blood rushed through her veins. Her skin stretched, then tightened.

This wasn't funny. Stop!

No sound came from her.

Oh, God, she couldn't speak! She couldn't see!

She whimpered.

As she lay there, everything began to return to normal. She heard a dog barking outside. A car zoomed past. A neighbor called her children to come inside.

For a moment, Callie just lay on the floor, trying to catch her breath, letting the world catch up to her. The pain wasn't so bad now. At least, she didn't feel as though her body was going to explode.

Finally, she opened her eyes. Something wasn't right. She felt different. The room looked the same, only bigger. Why did everything look so big?

Her movements were disjointed as she made her way to the bedroom. Rogar better have some answers, and he'd better have them damned fast. She paused in front of the full-length mirror in the hallway, which was the only place she had space for it.

There was a rabbit in her house. Why was there a white furry rabbit in her house? And where was her reflection? She only saw the damned rabbit.

She had her explanation, Rogar was a vampire! They did exist. He'd probably bitten her that first night and now she was a vampire, too, and that was why she had no reflection. She'd never be able to go into the daylight again. Oh, God, no more Krispy Kremes.

Oh, great, the rabbit crapped in her floor. Black pellets were on her clean floor.

"You've changed form," Rogar said from her bedroom doorway at the end of the hall.

He was still talking crazy. Why didn't he just admit she was a vampire and now would be doomed to live forever? Never to know if her makeup was on straight because she had no reflection.

She thought about that for a moment. If she lived forever, she was bound to get the animal keeper job. But then, she couldn't go into the light of day. It might be kind of difficult to work only at night.

Rogar came toward her. Good, because she was about to lay into him. He would regret ever turning her. Bleh, she was not about to drink blood to stay alive.

He stooped and picked up the rabbit, except she knew he was picking her up.

"I know things are confusing right now, but it will all get easier in time."

What the hell was he talking about?

"You make a cute rabbit," he said.

Rabbit? Rabbit! She'd shifted into a freakin' rabbit? That was her guide? Hey guide, I don't want to be a rabbit. If I'm going to be anything, I want to be a sexy animal. Rabbits were anything but sexy.

Oh, this was fantastic. Didn't jaguars eat rabbits? Rogar had probably wanted her to change form so he could have a late-night snack.

She didn't want to be a rabbit. She wanted to be Callie again.

"To change back, you only need to think about who you were before the change," he said as if he sensed her thoughts.

Okay, she could do this because she damned well didn't

want to stay a friggin' bunny. What would that accomplish? That she could be the life of the party leading the bunny hop? That she could have hundreds of baby bunnies? That sex would be really quick—wham, bam, thank you ma'am? Actually, that pretty well summed up her sex life now.

Nope, she was changing back ASAP. She willed her eyes, the rabbit's eyes, to close. She thought about driving the Jaguar home and feeling the wind on her face, working at the zoo, how Mrs. Winkle would flip out if she realized Callie not only had a rabbit in the house, but a two-hundred-pound sleek muscled black jaguar.

I want to be Callie again, she thought to herself. *I want to be Callie. I want to be Callie.*

The fog once again rolled in and she began to change.

Everything went black.

Callie stretched her limbs. Her body ached. A burning sensation slammed her gut. She arched her back, moaning. There was pain, but not severe enough that she couldn't stand it.

She didn't hear the voices this time. Only soothing words coming from Rogar as he helped her to return.

God, she was so tired. As though she'd just run a ten-mile marathon.

"Callie?" Rogar whispered close to her ear.

She realized he was sitting on her bed, and she was on his lap. She threw her arms around his neck and buried her face in his shoulder. A myriad of emotions washed over her. "You weren't lying. I'm part Symtarian." She hiccupped.

"No, I wasn't lying to you."

"But I don't want to be a bunny rabbit. I want to be something exotic."

She could feel the rumble of laughter in his chest.

"It's not funny. And I didn't hear any kind of guide talking to me, either."

"Callie, you surprise and mystify me."

"I'm sorry."

"Don't be." He sighed. "I remember the first time I took another form. It terrified me."

"Yeah, well, it scared the crap out of me." She frowned. Literally, actually. That was so embarrassing. Rabbit pellets on her floor. "I still didn't hear my guide."

"It's because you haven't found each other yet. Sometimes it takes awhile for you to connect."

"Then I'm not a bunny?"

"Maybe."

"Maybe? What's that supposed to mean?"

"When you take the form of your guide, then you will have a more solid connection with body, mind, and spirit."

Good, she was glad she probably wouldn't be a bunny. It seemed rather demeaning. Not that she had anything against bunny rabbits. They were cute and cuddly—when they weren't dropping pellets all over the floor.

She sighed. "Shapeshifting hurts."

"Are you in pain?"

She shook her head. "Not anymore."

Callie could hear Rogar's heart beat through his shirt. It soothed away her fears. The warmth from the heat of his body enveloped her in a warm cocoon. It was cozy. She snuggled closer, feeling safe and protected for the first time in her life.

It scared the hell out of her.

A cool draft of air brushed over her from the bedroom window that she always left cracked open just a bit. Her eyebrows drew together as she realized something else.

"I'm naked, aren't I?"

"Quite naked."

Chapter 7

"It's all right," Rogar said.

"No, it's not okay that I don't have clothes on," Callie told him.

"But I've already seen your body. I've felt it next to mine. You should be proud of how you look." He still couldn't understand why nakedness bothered her so much. Right now, it bothered him, but in a whole different way.

She leaned a little away from him, attempting to cover her breasts. "Well, it does bother me, a lot. I hardly know you." She sniffed.

He tried not to laugh, but he lost the battle.

"It's not funny," she complained.

He sobered. "You're right, it isn't."

She was so beautiful. The moonlight was the only light in the room, but it cast her in mysterious shadows and wavering soft lights.

And he couldn't resist. He didn't even try. It was the nature of the beast inside him. He lowered his mouth to her lips, wanting to taste her one more time, then he would let her get dressed, as much as he hated the notion of her covering that magnificent body.

She stiffened, then slowly began to relax against him. Her lips were soft, then she shyly opened them; her tongue explored his mouth, cautiously caressed him. Her touch was innocent and bold at the same time.

One kiss, then he would stop.

But he'd forgotten about the heat that radiated from her lush body or that it would quickly ignite the flames of his desires. When she tangled her fingers in his hair, he knew he wouldn't be able to stop at just a kiss.

Callie gasped when he cupped her bare breast, but she didn't pull away or tell him to stop. He ran his thumb over her nipple. She moaned.

He ended the kiss, lowering his head until he could take her breast in his mouth. She cried out, arching her back, when he sucked, gently tugging her nipple with his teeth.

She was driving him wild with need. His body ached to fill her, to plunge deep inside, and test the heat within.

He laid her back on the bed. She scooted up farther, and he wondered if she would tell him to leave. By the ancient saints, by the gods and goddesses, it would drive him insane if she were to send him away without the release he sorely needed. Many a weaker man had been driven insane when they didn't get fulfillment. Their race was a race that survived only by controlling the warring emotions inside them, keeping their animal instincts reigned in. It wasn't always possible.

His eyes narrowed as he tried to read what she was thinking. Would she save him from going mad with lust, or cast him away?

Callie opened her arms. "Make love to me."

A low growl emitted from deep in his throat as his gaze moved over her naked body. He hadn't dared look too closely when he didn't know the outcome. What if she had turned away from him?

She was beautiful, her breasts full, nipples tight. The curls at the juncture of her legs hid what he wanted to touch, to taste, but not for long. Soon, he would part her legs. He would listen to her sweet voice beg for more.

He swallowed hard, and slipped off his jacket. She watched him, her gaze drinking in every one of his movements. He intentionally slowed as he unbuttoned his shirt, then let it fall to the floor.

She drew in a deep breath when he reached for the button on his slacks and pushed it through, then drew the zipper down. Her eyes widened in anticipation. He kicked out of his slacks, then hooked his thumbs in the waistband of his briefs.

Earth clothes were too bulky. On New Symtaria he wore loose robes until the climate turned cooler. But maybe wearing more clothes wasn't so bad because watching Callie's eyes widen, the way her chest raised and lowered when she began to pant, made him feel powerful, made him want her pleasure to be great.

He pushed his briefs down, then let them slide over his legs and drop to the floor as he straightened again. She bit her bottom lip, but not before a moan escaped. He'd known she had a passionate side. It ran through the veins of all Symtarians. Her Earth blood could not dilute it. He planned to see just how strong it was. He kicked the briefs away, then climbed on the bed, lying beside her.

"You're beautiful," she whispered.

He frowned. Women were beautiful. If anything, men were handsome. But never beautiful.

She tentatively lowered her hand and stroked down his length. His body jerked in response. Maybe it didn't really matter how she thought he looked. They were just words. Callie pushed on his shoulders and he gave in, moving to his back.

"You don't look like an alien," she said as she explored his chest.

"Our races are very similar in many ways. That's why our people were sent here when our planet was dying and we had to find another one." He'd read some about Earth's history and understood that women liked to talk before, during, and after sex. He didn't mind this need. Symtarian women were much the same. He liked listening to their voices. They were softer, and most of the time, sweeter than a man's voice.

But there were times when talk wasn't needed. He turned back to his side, brushing the back of his hand lightly over her body, moving between her breasts, over her abdomen, down to her hip, then her thigh, then repeated the moves as he journeyed back up her body. Ah, she was lovely to look at, to touch. Her skin was soft as the finest material.

When she moaned, he knew she wanted more. He'd have liked to hear it from her lips, have her tell him exactly what she wanted, but maybe it was too soon. He didn't want to push her, but some day he would have her telling him everything she wanted without embarrassment, and he would do the same until they knew instinctively what the other craved.

He leaned forward, drawing her tight nipple into his mouth and sucking gently, then gave equal attention to the other. His hand moved down her body. He ran his fingers lightly though her curls. Her body stiffened.

He leaned away from her. "Do you want me to stop?"

She shook her head. "More," she choked out.

He smiled. "Yes, that is exactly what I plan to give you." He fingered the fleshy part of her sex. She cried out, spreading her legs wider for him. He delved deeper, feeling her readiness.

His own ache grew stronger. He moved between her legs, spreading them wider. The moon bathed her skin in translucent light. "Beautiful," he whispered before lowering his head and running his tongue over her.

Callie cried out, raising her hips, knotting the sheets in her fists.

He slid his hands beneath her bottom, bringing her even closer to his mouth, sucking her inside, running his tongue over her until she quivered and cried out.

Rogar had been too long without a female companion, and the sounds Callie made were pushing him to the brink of his lust. He moved so that he could easily slide into her moist heat.

"Wait," she moaned.

"You would stop me now?' he croaked.

She turned and stretched until she could open a drawer in the table beside the bed. She brought out a small packet. He could see her face had turned a bright red.

"Condom," she said, then tore it open and handed it to him. "It's for your . . . you know."

He took it from her. Of course, he'd heard of this tradition. On New Symtaria, everyone took an injection to prevent any disease or children. When they were ready to have offspring, they took another. He would follow her customs.

Rogar slid the condom on, then slowly he sank inside, letting the rush of heat flow over him. He closed his eyes, and gritted his teeth at the sheer pleasure she gave him. This was good. He didn't mind so much the sheathing as he shifted his hips, and sank a little deeper.

Callie cried out, and he was lifted out of his fog of passion.

"Am I hurting you?"

"No, it just feels so damned good." To prove her words, she brought her legs up, wrapping them around his waist.

He sank deeper. Gasped as pleasure rushed over him.

"More."

Callie had gotten greedy. Not that he could blame her. He wanted more, too. He slid out, then plunged deeper. She rocked her hips. He knew he couldn't hold back any longer, and sank back inside.

His movements intensified until they both cried out at the sheer ecstasy of the moment. The world exploded around him into brilliant lights. He gasped for air as he rolled his weight off Callie.

Mating with Callie had been more than he expected. It had been wonderful, it had been . . .

The familiar ache began to burn inside him. He tried to stop it, but the burning sensation had already begun to consume him.

Callie watched the changing expressions on Rogar's face

and knew he'd experienced the same thing that she had. She'd finally had the earth-shattering orgasm that she'd always thought some fanciful author had made up while eating a chocolate bar or something. No, this was the real thing.

She turned on her side, watching him with more than a little wonderment. If there was ever a bumper sticker that read, ALIENS ARE A GALAXY ABOVE THE OTHERS, she was getting it. She'd never had sex like that. He was magnificent, superb . . .

He suddenly doubled up, groaning.

Oh, no, sex with her had been too much. She'd killed him. Been overly aggressive . . . or something. Was she doomed to never have another orgasm like the one she'd just had?

"Rogar? Rogar!" She sat up, grasping his shoulders as he seemed to struggle for air. A thick fog rolled across the room. His shoulders began to sprout hair. Oh, crap, he was shifting. Maybe making love wasn't nearly as good for him as it had been for her, and now he was going to eat her. Not good! Well, not when it was literal.

She jumped up and ran for the bathroom door, slamming it closed, and then fastening the latch. She'd never realized how flimsy the door was. She started to unlock it and hurry through to the living room, but she heard a deep throated purr and froze. Okay, maybe it wouldn't be prudent to leave just yet. She eased over to the toilet and plopped down on the lid.

The purring grew louder, as though the cat was right outside the door. Cold chills washed over her. Not just from being nervous, either. She glanced around, then breathed a sigh of relief when she spotted her white terry cloth robe on the counter by the sink.

Wrapping her arms around herself in an attempt to ward off the chill in the air, she tiptoed over and grabbed the robe. Pure bliss. Now if only Rogar would change back to human form.

She stopped in the middle of tying the belt. It was true. Everything he'd told her about being an alien was true. And what was worse, she was part Symtarian, too. She'd changed into a bunny rabbit.

A host of questions swarmed inside her. She nibbled her lip as she looked at the door. Was the black jaguar still in the other room? She really found it hard to think of the jag and Rogar as being one and the same.

If he'd changed to a bunny, she wouldn't mind opening the door. Bunnies couldn't really hurt anyone. They ate lettuce and dropped pellets on your floor.

Maybe he'd changed back and had fallen asleep. She'd felt tired when she'd changed back to herself. Well, until Rogar kissed her. After a few moments, she hadn't even been thinking about how tired she was.

But did she want to take that chance and possibly get eaten alive? Nausea rumbled in her stomach. She was a coward, so what.

She knelt in front of the door and peered through the keyhole. Damn it, she couldn't see anything. She lay down on the floor and moved her face as close to the crack at the bottom as she could get it, peering from underneath. Everything was black. She let out a deep breath. The blackness moved. There was a loud purr just on the other side of the door.

She rolled away, probably looking like a white tootsie roll with arms and legs. She didn't stop until her head banged into the side of the tub.

"Ow." She sat up, rubbing her head.

There was another loud purr.

Was the stupid jaguar laughing at her? She crawled into the tub, tucking her bath pillow beneath her head. It wasn't as good as her pillow on the bed. This was just one of those cheap ones that you inflate. It was an indulgence, but it had only cost a dollar.

She tried to get comfortable, but finally gave up. It was a lost cause. She sniffed. Her first major orgasm and what happens, the guy changes into a jaguar. She snorted. That was one for the advice columns. Maybe she should write Dear Abby. She could see it now.

Dear Abby,

What do you do when you have the greatest sex for the very first time in your life, and your lover turns into a jaguar? Is it a reflection on your performance?
Need advice ASAP!

Signed,
One Who Sleeps in a Bathtub

This was so not fun.

Chapter 8

What happened? Rogar's thoughts filled the jaguar.

Ahh, you're awake, Balam communicated the same way. *I had begun to wonder if you would ever regain consciousness.*

Where's Callie? Fear filled him. Rogar wouldn't be able to live with himself if he'd harmed her in any way.

We didn't eat her if that's what you're asking.

Then where is she?

I believe she's in the other room. She slammed the door and locked it.

Rogar felt relief wash over him. *I've never lost control like that before.*

Because you've never lost control at all. It was not I who initiated the change. This sometimes happens with the males of our species when passions rule. Don't worry, I have no desire to dominate.

Don't you? Rogar could feel Balam's amusement. Guilt filled him for even having those kinds of thoughts. Balam was a friend, not just his guide. *I'm sorry.*

You lead a more exciting life than I ever could. I don't mind living vicariously through you. There was a deep sigh. *Besides, our bond is stronger than most. It's when man and beast don't respect each other's needs that trouble begins.*

You're right.

Of course I am. The jaguar jumped to the bed. *You'd better go to her. I'm sure she didn't sleep well last night.*

Rogar flinched. *I doubt she'll be happy with me.*

She's very beautiful you know.

Yes, I do.

Rogar closed his eyes, felt the transformation begin, the damp fog as it began to roll in. He was used to it. The first time had been the hardest. At one point during the change, his thoughts were no longer entirely his. Rogar knew Balam experienced the same feeling. It was as though they stopped being two, and became one, if only for a moment in time. Never once had Rogar felt threatened—which made his guilt all the more harder to swallow. They'd always respected each other's identity.

He growled from low in his throat. It changed to a moan. A paw became a hand, a jaw that could crush a human head returned to human form, hair changed to flesh.

Rogar opened his eyes, blinking several times until the room came into focus. It was always the same—as if he'd walked from darkness into light. Tiredness washed over him in waves. He sat up, swinging his legs over the side of the bed, and waited for everything to come into focus. To catch up to being human again.

He finally stood, remembered he was naked, and quickly slipped on his briefs and slacks. Rogar wasn't quite sure if Callie would feel the same way about his nakedness as she did last night before they mated. And since she'd spent the night in the bathroom, he thought it might be wiser not to push his luck.

When he turned the doorknob and pushed, there was a catch that prevented him from opening the door all the way. He peered through the small crack, but he couldn't see Callie, nor did he hear her moving around. She might be sleeping. If he could manage to get inside, he would know for sure she was all right.

He looked around, spotting a card on her bedside table

that might work to unlatch the door. He picked it up, and slid it through the crack, then upward, unhooking the latch. He tossed the card on the bed, and opened the door.

She wasn't in the room. Had Balam lied and ate her after all?

I don't lie, Balam's voice interjected into his thoughts. *Try looking behind the curtain.*

Sometimes you pain me, Rogar told him. He knew Balam was smiling.

Rogar slid the curtain open, making very little sound, then grimaced. Callie was curled in the tub, her knees scrunched to her chest. He leaned over and shook her shoulder. "Callie."

She stretched, groaning. "Oh, Lord, I feel like death warmed over."

He wasn't sure what death warmed over meant, but from the pained expression on her face, he was pretty certain it didn't feel good.

Callie opened her eyes, then frowned. "Why am I in the bathtub?"

"We mated last night . . ."

She smiled. "I remember."

He felt heartened that her smile was full of satisfaction when she remembered.

Her smile quickly turned downward. "Was I so bad at making love that I had to sleep in the bathtub, rather than in bed with you?" she asked.

"You were magnificent."

"No," she said as if he hadn't spoken. "I remember now, you changed into a jaguar and I was afraid."

He nodded.

Her eyes grew round. "Oh, crap, it is all true. I didn't dream I was alien—I am an alien. I changed right before we made love—into a freakin' bunny which was so uncool." She quickly sat up, then grabbed her neck. "Oh, damn!"

"Here, let me help you." He practically lifted her out of the tub, then aimed her toward the bedroom. She held her neck as though it might snap in two at any second. More guilt washed over him. He helped her ease down to the side of the bed, then began to massage her neck.

"Oh, oh, oh that hurts . . . Ahh." She sighed. "Better." She leaned her head to the other side. "You have magical hands. I mean . . ."

When their gazes met, he saw her cheeks were a rosy hue. He couldn't stop his grin from forming.

"That's not what I meant, so deflate your ego," she said, one eyebrow arching.

"You didn't like when I touched you?"

She looked down, picking at the material of her white robe. "Yes, I liked it a lot."

Heat flared inside him.

Someone knocked on the front door.

Callie came to her feet, looked toward the door, then at him.

"Hide?" he guessed.

She nodded. "I'll get rid of them, then I have to get ready for work. Not all of us can make their own money." She paused briefly. "We'll talk about that later, too."

Callie hurried to the door, her movements stiff. That was something else they'd be talking about, too. The next time they made love, there would be no more changing form, and if he did, he would be the one sleeping in a bathtub.

She glanced at the clock as she passed by. Who would be knocking on her door this early in the morning? It was barely seven.

For safety, she peeked through the window before opening the door. Not that she had much to worry about. All Rogar had to do was shift into the jaguar, and whoever was on the other side would have a heart attack.

But it was her heart that pounded when she saw her land-lady's car in the driveway. Great. What did she want?

Callie unlocked the door, then opened it. "Mrs. Winkle, is there something wrong?"

The older woman raised her chin. "That's what I was about to ask you. I saw you with the policeman yesterday and it looked like he was doing a sobriety test."

The old busybody. Callie took a deep breath and smiled sweetly. "A bad case of allergies, that's all. Was there anything else?"

Mrs. Winkle glanced over her shoulder.

Damn, she'd forgotten about Rogar's car being parked out front.

Mrs. Winkle looked at Callie again. "I won't have any shenanigans going on in one of my rent houses. Mr. Abner, a few blocks over, didn't keep a close eye on one of his renters. I told him more than once that he had to keep up with what's going on, but he only laughed." She puffed out her chest. "The next thing he knew, they were throwing wild parties. I tried to warn him."

"I'm sure you did your best."

"So, did you get a raise? That's a pretty fancy car for someone who works at the zoo."

Callie gritted her teeth to keep from saying something she might regret, but before she could say anything, Rogar stepped into the living room.

No good could come from this. Mrs. Winkle would kick her out for sure, and houses this cheap weren't easy to find in a halfway decent neighborhood. At least, he'd put on a shirt, although he hadn't bothered to button it, and he was barefoot. She glanced at Mrs. Winkle. The woman's mouth had dropped open. The old battle-ax finally drew in a long, deep breath.

"You have a man in your house."

Rogar continued forward, took Mrs. Winkle's hand in his, and brought it to his lips. "Prince Rogar Valkyir, at your service."

Callie almost lost it. He hadn't lied. Did the man not know how? He was going to get her thrown out on her butt.

"Prince? Here, in one of my houses?" She drew her hand

out of his, her eyes narrowing, then sneezed. "Oh, excuse me."
Her brow puckered. "Is there a cat in the house? I swear, I
sneeze every time I come over."

"And each time I tell you, there are no animals," Callie
said with more than a little exasperation.

"I met Callie when she was attending college," Rogar interrupted. "We became friends. She was gracious enough to
let me spend the night."

Mrs. Winkle still looked skeptical. "You're a prince and
you stay here, rather than a five-star hotel?"

"No matter how lavish one's surroundings are, they can't
dispel the coldness of a hotel room. Only the warmth of a
friend's hospitality can do that, and I find the home Callie
rents from you is quite warm."

Mrs. Winkle's frown turned to a smile. Wow! Callie had
never seen her landlady smile. In fact, she was actually sim-
pering. Of course, why wouldn't she, Rogar had complemented
one of her rent houses. Couldn't she see they were practically
dumps?

"I do try to make the houses as nice as possible. My daddy
always told me that you could judge a woman's worth by the
property she owned." She sneezed. "Excuse me. It must be
pollen or something."

"You've done a splendid job making this home so exquisite, and Callie has told me more than once that she looks up
to you."

"I have?" Callie cleared her throat. "I have. I mean, you
are a businesswoman, after all."

"You have to run a tight ship," Mrs. Winkle nodded.

"It's the same way with a country, even one as small and
insignificant as mine. If you don't stay on top of everything,
you soon have wars."

Mrs. Winkle nodded. "Exactly." Then sneezed.

"But I'm sorry. I've interrupted your conversation. What
were you saying?" Rogar's gaze never left Mrs. Winkle.

"It was nothing, really. I mean, I don't actually let my renters have people move in with them, but since you won't be staying long . . ." She let her words pointedly trail off and Callie saw Rogar hadn't quite sweet-talked the old biddy.

"It's so peaceful here that I might decide to stay longer than I'd planned." He reached into his pocket. When he pulled out his roll of bills, Mrs. Winkle's eyes grew big.

Oh, yeah, give my landlady counterfeit money. Dig the hole a little deeper, why don't you.

He peeled off 5 one-hundred-dollar bills. "I believe this will cover the cost of Callie having a guest more than a few nights. If I should decide to stay longer, I'm sure we can come to an arrangement that will benefit us both."

Mrs. Winkle grabbed the money out of his hand, practically salivating. "I'm sure we can." She sneezed twice before stuffing the money down the front of her dress.

"And you won't mention that I'm here. The press can be quite annoying at times. I never seem to have a moment of peace when they discover my whereabouts."

"My lips are sealed."

"If you don't mind, I need to get ready for work." Callie looked between the two. It was nauseating watching Mrs. Winkle being reduced to a giggling schoolgirl as Rogar fed her ego and her bank account.

"Of course, dear." She looked at Rogar as if she hoped he planned on lingering.

"It was nice meeting you," Rogar said.

Mrs. Winkle held out her hand and Rogar kissed it. She blushed, then hurried back to her car, sneezing three more times before she got inside and drove away.

Callie thought she was going to be sick from all the sugar that had flowed between Rogar and Mrs. Winkle.

Bleh!

Chapter 9

"I need to get ready for work," Callie said when Rogar closed the door.

"You're really going to work? I thought you were lying to your landlady."

Now he'd confused her. "Why would you think I was lying? I may be half Symtarian, but the Earthling side of me still has to pay the bills."

"I have money."

She threw her arms in the air. "Counterfeit! It's illegal to make your own money. Which I've been meaning to talk to you about. You have to stop making money illegally. I'd rather not spend the rest of my life in jail as an accomplice, if you don't mind."

"Don't you want to know about your ancestors?" He conveniently changed the subject.

Now he'd hit a sore spot. "Of course I do. Everyone wants to know where they came from, what their relatives were like. I won't deny I've had questions over the years."

"Then stay with me."

"Ten years ago I might have jumped at the chance." She shook her head. "I've been on my own for a long time now and I've learned to make my way without any help. My job probably doesn't seem like much to you, but my dream has always been to work with the big cats. There's an animal keeper job opening up soon and I'm next in line. I've worked hard for that position, and I won't let anything jeopardize it."

"You're from another world."

"Only part of me, the rest is from right here on Earth." She tilted her head and studied him. "I've never shifted until last night, and I had to think about it before I could. Can I control it? Keep from shifting again?"

He took a step back and Callie knew she'd shocked him.

"You would give up that part of who you are?"

"Then it can be done?"

"You would be killing a part of yourself."

"Just like my parents killed off a part of themselves when they dumped me at the orphanage?"

"You don't know their reasons."

"And the next verse is, I don't want to know." She looked at her hands, gathering her thoughts. "What if the truth is worse than I could imagine?"

"What if it isn't?"

"Maybe I don't want to take that chance." A long time ago, she'd created a fairy tale in her mind that her mother and father had to leave her because they were dying of some horrible disease. The lies she told herself were so much better than facing what the truth might actually be—that she was dumped because she'd become a burden. She just wasn't sure she wanted to face the truth.

Rogar raked his fingers through his hair, clearly frustrated. "Let me explain what a guide means. At least, give me that."

Didn't he realize it wouldn't make any difference? She still wouldn't go back to his planet with him. She'd finally adjusted to this one, and she'd been born here! No, Callie didn't want to walk into the unknown and take a chance it was worse than Earth.

She sighed. But Rogar had traveled a great distance, and he was starting to grow on her.

"We'll talk after I get off work," she conceded.

He finally nodded.

She hurried from the room, more to get away from Rogar. She wanted to tell him that he could be waiting for her every night, but it wouldn't do him any good. It was as though all her life she'd been working toward this one job. The dream was as much a part of her as breathing, and she wouldn't let anyone or anything stand in her way.

Sometimes new dreams can become just as important.

She stumbled as she went inside her bedroom. Dizziness washed over her. It hadn't been her thoughts. It couldn't have been. She'd been dreaming of working with the big cats since going to the zoo on a field trip when she was nine. It was the first time she'd felt whole.

Damn it, Rogar was making her think things she didn't want to think. She brought her hands to her face. And feel things she didn't want to feel.

She grabbed a uniform out of the closet, and undergarments out of the drawer, then marched to the bathroom. She refused to think about anything to do with him, or shifting into another form. That was his world, and she wanted no part of it.

She showered, then dressed, before going to the other room. "I'll need a ride to work," she said. He'd changed clothes. He must have gone on his own little shopping spree with his counterfeit money.

He didn't say anything. Just walked to the door.

The silent treatment?

"I'm . . . I'm sorry that I'm not what you were wanting," she told him as guilt flooded her.

He turned around, his expression puzzled. "Not what I wanted?"

He ambled over to where she stood. She swallowed hard, looking everywhere but at him. He raised her chin and forced her to meet his gaze.

"Not what I wanted? How can you say that? You've been

everything I could imagine. I love watching the changes happening in you. I love when you laugh. I love mating with you."
He lowered his head, his lips brushing against hers before he deepened the kiss.

Heat flared inside her. He slid his hand down her back, cupping her butt, pulling her closer to his need. His tongue stroked hers, then sucking. Her pleasure centers exploded. She wanted him, she needed him. He pulled away, looking as shaken as she felt.

"That . . . that won't change my mind. I still won't go with you," she said.

"Then I'll stay just long enough to tell you the story of our beginning."

Would he really do that? Tell her the Symtarian history, then leave, letting her live her life as if nothing had happened? She studied his face, not quite trusting him.

"And you won't speak again about me leaving with you?"

"If that is what you want."

"It is."

He opened the door and she walked outside, feeling as though she was entering into another phase of her life.

"But it doesn't mean that we won't mate again," he said.

Oh, she was counting on that, but she chose to keep her thoughts to herself. This was all too new.

Rogar dropped her off in front of the employee entrance, and promised he would have her car back by the time she got off work, then he ground the gears as he shifted, and pulled away.

She felt torn about going inside. For a moment, she wanted to chase after him. That was crazy, of course. She might be part alien, but as she'd already told him, the other half was Earthling, and she planned on sticking with what she knew.

She clocked in and went straight to Sheba's cage. She just wanted to stop by for a few minutes. Sort of anchor herself to where she really belonged, but she would need to hurry.

"Hiya, Pete," she said. Pete was just closing the gate to Sheba's empty cage.

"Hey, Callie. You just missed Sheba. I've already turned her out into the pit."

"I was hoping I would get here before you did."

"Running late this morning?"

"Car trouble," she said without going into detail.

"Bummer."

"Yeah."

He strolled over to where she stood. "I heard you were around when the guy jumped down into the pit to save that kid. Man, I would've given my left . . ." He cleared his throat. "I mean, I would've given just about anything to have seen that. They say he was a hero, and he had Sheba acting like a spoiled housecat."

"That pretty much sums it up." Even though she was a little irked that Sheba had taken to Rogar so quickly, Callie couldn't stop the warm fuzzies from tickling her belly. Not that she had a right to feel pride in what Rogar had done. It wasn't as though she and Rogar were an item or anything. They'd mated—she frowned—they'd *made love* once. Yes, she liked him well enough, but that was as far as their relationship went. When he returned to his own planet . . .

Wow, it was really hard getting used to the fact he was indeed an alien, but she knew it was true.

"That's what we need," Pete said, and she realized she'd been lost in thought.

"What do we need?"

He brushed his hand through his unkempt hair. "Someone like him working with the cats. Maybe he could even do something with Sheba. Like walking around in the pit while she's in there, and maybe talking about the big cats. It would be a great draw, don't you think? More money for programs and all."

She stiffened. "Excuse me?"

"Huh?" Confusion knit his brow.

He really didn't get it, did he? "The next animal keeper opening is supposed to be mine."

"Oh, now I understand." He nodded. "But you could have the one after that."

"I don't think so." She said between gritted teeth, then turned on her heel. "I have to get to work."

"But I thought you liked working with the baby animals, and the kids who come through the petting zoo."

She didn't even bother to answer. Not that it mattered because Rogar wouldn't be staying. He wasn't a threat. The job had her name written all over it. Besides the fact, Mr. Campbell promised it to her.

Well, he hadn't actually come out and said the words, but his implication had been pretty strong.

She walked inside the building beside the petting zoo and grabbed the keys just as Gail hurried in.

"Sorry, I'm running late."

"Don't worry. I just got here myself."

"So, everyone's all buzzing about what happened yesterday."

"I've heard," she spoke dryly.

"Does he really have a sexy black Jaguar?"

Callie stilled. How could Gail know about Rogar's ability to shift?"

"I mean the car, not the cat." Gail laughed.

Callie relaxed as she walked toward the baby animal pens. "How would I know?"

"Didn't he take you home when your car wouldn't start?"

How the hell did she know about that? Did she also know they'd had wild passionate sex?

"Ben saw you leave with him," Gail explained. "It's so romantic. Like Prince Charming."

What would Gail think if she knew Rogar *was* a prince? Not that Callie would be the one telling. "There's nothing going on between us. My car wouldn't start. He was just leaving and offered me a ride home. End of story."

"Really?"

Gail looked so disappointed that Callie almost laughed. "Yes, really."

"Well, since you apparently don't want him, mind tossing him my way?"

Callie chuckled, but at the same time, a little flare of jealousy sparked inside her. Which was so totally ridiculous. She and Rogar were only friends—who'd made wild passionate love last night. No biggie. Of course she wasn't jealous. A touch of indigestion from all the rich food she'd downed last night was more plausible.

Gail and Callie didn't have a chance to speak again as they opened the gates and led the baby animals out to the big open pen. The little ones were more than eager to stretch their legs and greet the new day. Callie wished she could feel the same way. Her day was going downhill in a hurry.

She was leading the lamb out when the phone rang in the office. She glanced up, but Gail was already hurrying to answer it.

"Okay, Lamb Chop, off you go." She patted the animal on the back and it joined the others in a half-hop, half-walk gait that had her smiling. The young animals were cute. Kind of like being around puppies all day. But it wasn't what made her truly happy.

"Mr. Campbell wants you at the main office as soon as you can get there." Gail wiggled her eyebrows. "Maybe your prince has returned."

Only if he wanted to be a dead prince.

Chapter 10

If Rogar was on the other side of her boss's door, Callie might just lose what little sanity she had left. She opened the door and cautiously walked inside. No sign of Rogar. In fact, the only person she did see was Mr. Campbell.

Why the hell was she disappointed? Relief is what she should be feeling.

"Come in, come in . . . uh . . ."

"Callie," she supplied.

"Yes, Callie." He gave a short laugh. "My mind went blank."

She'd been working at the zoo for how many years? Had done every menial job that was thrown her way, and without complaint. Well, none that Mr. Campbell could hear. At least his father had known her name.

She sighed, wondering what Mr. Campbell could want with her this time. "Is something wrong?"

"No, not at all. On the contrary, it's absolutely wonderful."

Ohmygod, she was getting the animal keeper job. She'd be working with the big cats. Okay, technically, Mr. Campbell didn't do the hiring and firing, but he was aware of what was going on, so he made recommendations all the time. He called them *recommendations*, but it meant you had the job. Really, who was going to say no to the boss?

This was fantastic, the best thing that had ever happened to her . . .

Calm down. Wait for him to tell you the good news.

"Have you seen this morning's paper?"

Huh? "No, I haven't." She rarely read the paper. It was usually too depressing.

He opened it on his desk, running his hand down the crease. She walked closer, then swallowed hard when she saw the picture of Rogar with Sheba. The jaguar was rubbing against his legs. Above the article it read:

Mysterious Man Hypnotizes
Jaguar and Saves Child

"You can't buy PR like this!" Mr. Campbell grinned from ear to ear. "This is just great. Exactly what we needed."

She instantly deflated. So much for getting the animal keeper job. It couldn't be much longer, though. Mr. Campbell had practically promised the job to her.

She raised her chin. "How is the boy, by the way?"

He frowned. "Bruises, that's all, and a mild concussion. We're taking measures so that something like that won't happen again. Our lawyer said we were clearly not at fault. Even the newspaper article favored us rather than the kid."

"I'm glad he's recovering."

"Yes, but that's beside the point."

Mr. Campbell could be a real pain in the ass sometimes. "What is the point?"

"The public loves a hero. We all want more John Waynes, but these days they're few and far between."

"And that has what to do with me?" If he expected her to go into the cage with Sheba, he'd better think again. At least, not like Rogar had done. She had to admit, Rogar had a very special quality. And why shouldn't he, since he was part jaguar.

Part jaguar? Shared his body with one? She mentally shook her head. So confusing.

"I want you to find him," he beamed.

Her pulse began to race as dread filled her. "And why would you think I'd know where he was staying?"

"Because he took you home last night when your car wouldn't start."

Did everyone at the zoo know her personal life? "We met again purely by coincidence. He saw my car wouldn't start, and offered me a ride home. That's all there was to it."

Mr. Campbell's shoulders slumped. Good, let him feel what she felt when she realized she wasn't here to get the job she'd been wanting forever and ever.

"Why did you need to find him?" Surely a few photos wouldn't be that big of a deal. It had to be more than that.

Mr. Campbell puffed his chest out, regaining some of his excitement. "Picture this, Rogar working with the big cats."

There was a moment of silence. Enough for her to know she didn't like where he was taking her.

"You were there. You had to have seen the way he handled Sheba. The whole zoo is buzzing. Everyone tells me he was hypnotic, that he had the cat worshipping the very ground he walked on." He rubbed his hands together. "And they want more."

She could feel the color drain from her face. "But . . . but I was promised that job." She'd been passed over so many times, and yet, they would give it to a stranger?"

"There will be another opening, and I'll make sure you get that one, but think of what he could do in the way of PR, the extra funding for the zoo . . ."

And a substantial raise for Mr. Campbell from his father who still controlled the purse strings.

She squared her shoulders. "I'm sorry, I don't know where he is," she lied.

Mr. Campbell frowned, it was quickly replaced by a devious glint in his eyes that she had a feeling didn't bode well for her.

"You know, I'm sure we could add another animal keeper job working with the big cats. If you bring this man to me, and we hire him, then you could even start immediately."

Excitement flittered through her, then died a fast death. Rogar would never agree to stay. "Your idea won't work. The guy is super wealthy. He gave me a ride home in his Jaguar, and he paid for a private tour of the zoo. I even heard he might be a prince or something. He doesn't need a job."

"Oh." He sat down heavily in his leather chair. "You're probably right. Okay, then I guess you can go back to work."

There was no better time than now. "Mr. Campbell, about that job as animal keeper . . . for the big cats?"

He looked up as he folded the newspaper. "What about it?"

"Well, I am next in line for the first opening."

He tossed the paper to the side. "There isn't an opening, though, so why are we having this conversation? Besides, you know I don't do the actual hiring."

Ass. "Yes, sir." She turned on her heel and marched out of his office.

She was never going to get the job. She would be stuck with the baby animals for the rest of her life. The closest she would get to the big cats would be the fat stray that was in the petting zoo.

But if Rogar walked in right now, they would hand him the job on a silver platter. It wasn't fair. For a moment, a thread of anger at Rogar weaved through her, but just as quickly, she dismissed it. It wasn't Rogar's fault. Mr. Campbell was another matter.

She didn't notice that she was going in the opposite direction of the petting zoo until she was at the bridge that led toward the big cats.

Oh, who cared? She didn't. At least, not right now. She hurried to the pit. Sheba was resting in the shade of one of the trees. She purred from deep in her throat, welcoming Callie. At least, that's what Callie liked to think. And maybe Sheba was glad to see her. Could Sheba sense the animal inside Callie?

This couldn't be happening. It was too insane. First, Rogar tells her that he's an alien. Then he tells her she's part alien, too. And that she has an animal guide.

Now, Mr. Campbell is ready to hand over the job she's wanted most of her life, to Rogar, and her boss would put it on a silver platter if Rogar asked.

If she didn't know everything was true, she'd laugh. Oh, Lord, her life was screwed up beyond repair. She leaned against the concrete barrier and rested her chin on her hands. "Oh, Sheba, what in the world am I going to do?"

Callie should just quit. Her college education was going to waste. This was home, though. At least, the closest she'd ever been to having one. So what if her family consisted of a jaguar and a handful of zoo employees. She couldn't just leave, could she? She looked at Sheba, knowing they'd shared a bond from day one.

She sighed. Maybe it wouldn't be that much longer before she got the job.

A group of children came up the path, drawing her from her thoughts. She straightened, smoothing her hands over her shirt so she would look professional, then pasted a smile on her face.

Ten-year-olds. She could guess their ages within a few months. Three of them barreled up the sidewalk. One tripped, falling toward her. She instinctively grabbed and caught him, along with all of the soda and all the crushed ice that was in his very large blue cup. She sucked in her breath as ice went down the front of her shirt.

"She made me spill my drink," he screamed in her ear.

Great, now she was wet, cold, sticky, and had hearing loss. Would her insurance cover this? Hmm, not likely. She glanced at the teacher who already looked frazzled, and felt a moment of pity. They should double teachers' salaries. The woman clapped her hands together and the little boy stopped yelling.

"Kelvin, don't you think you need to apologize to the woman, then thank her for catching you?" the teacher scolded.

"My soda . . ."

"Kelvin?" The teacher gave him that look that works on every child, and most adults.

Kelvin kicked at the sidewalk. "Sorry."

Callie kept her smile bright and cheerful. "It happens a lot. Apology accepted."

"Can we go to the petting zoo now, Mrs. Cooper," Kelvin asked.

Apparently, he assumed his apology would automatically clear him of all wrongdoing. Callie smiled at the teacher and walked away. When she was a safe distance, she pulled her shirt out of her pants and shook the rest of the ice out.

"What happened to you?" Gail asked as Callie hurried inside their tiny office. If you even could call it an office. A small desk and a private bathroom.

"I was checking on Sheba and met up with a class that will be here in about ten minutes." She reached inside a bottom drawer and pulled out a clean uniform top. It always paid to have an extra one around here.

"The Wild Bunch." Gail groaned.

The next two hours were frantic as back-to-back classes came through the petting zoo. Kelvin didn't improve after he got to Callie's section. If anything, the sugar in the soda had only wired him more.

Kelvin pulled the cat's tail, then cried when Miss Kitty spat at him. The he chased the duck, until the duck turned and chased him, while he screamed and yelled. The kid had a great shot at being an opera star. He could already shatter eardrums.

Then the baby goat butted him, knocking little Kelvin on his keester, and Kelvin screamed and yelled some more. Before Callie could take a deep breath, they left, and the next group arrived. Little Kelvin morphed into little Julie, and everything repeated.

And then they were gone, and for a moment, there was

blessed silence. Until her cell rang. She reached in her pocket and brought it out, flipping it open.

"Hello?"

"Callie, DeeDee."

Gail made a motion of eating, then went inside. Callie nodded, and relaxed against the fence.

"What's up?' she asked.

"What's up?" DeeDee mimicked. "As if you didn't know, you sly fox."

"Have you been drinking?" It was early but . . .

"No, I did stop by your house, though."

Callie straightened. "Why would you do that?"

"I was dropping off your birthday present. Happy birthday."

Callie put her hand to her forehead and closed her eyes for a moment. With every thing that had been happening, she'd totally forgotten today she turned twenty-seven. Was that all? She felt so much older.

It was probably too much to hope that DeeDee hadn't seen Rogar. She swallowed past the lump in her throat. "Thanks. You . . . uh . . . shouldn't have."

"This is your friend from your college days, right? You told me he'd left. I'm hurt that you couldn't share all the juicy details."

So much for hoping. "He's not staying long."

Her sigh came across the line. "If I were you, I'd keep him as long as I could. Yum-yum."

"What exactly did you two talk about?"

"Not much. Oh, hey, I've gotta run. Big meeting in a few minutes and I'm a little late. I just wanted to tell you happy birthday."

"Thanks, but . . ." The phone went dead. She knew DeeDee well enough that this didn't bode well. They'd been friends a long time. The girl lived in a fairy tale of her own making. That wasn't to say she wasn't very astute when it came to business. DeeDee just believed in happily ever after.

Callie, on the other hand, had grown up in the real world.

The one where prospective parents came looking for a child of their own. They didn't want the odd kid. The one who lost herself in daydreams and heard voices.

Callie had eventually learned to tune out the voice inside her head, and not talk to her like they were best friends. But by then it was too late. New parents didn't want someone her age, they wanted babies. Cute little babies with their toothless smiles and that sweet baby smell. Not that she blamed them, but still, it might've been nice living in a real home.

Gail poked her head out the door. "You better eat while you can. June called to warn there's another class coming our way."

Callie straightened. Had she been lost in thought that long? Apparently.

The rest of the day went downhill. She was so exhausted that she didn't even stop by to tell Sheba good night. After finishing her paperwork, she and Gail walked through the employee's gate, and headed toward the parking area.

She glanced around, hoping Rogar would be inconspicuous when he picked her up, but he wasn't even there. At least, she didn't see him, or her junker car. But what she did see was a shiny new red Jaguar with an even bigger red bow on it.

Please, please don't let this be happening.

"Wow, now that's one fine looking car," Gail said.

"Yeah, it is." She was pretty sure she was going to throw up.

"Let's go see who it's for," she whispered, dragging on Callie's arm.

"Oh, no, we might spoil the surprise."

But Gail wasn't one to wait. She hurried over and walked to the back of the car. Her hand flew to her chest. "Callie, it's for you! There's a sign with your name on it. Hey, look everyone, Callie has a Prince Charming!"

Prince Charming was going to die a slow and painful death just as soon as she drove the car back to her house. She couldn't afford a taxi. But as soon as she got home, she'd throw the keys in his face!

But it was a really sweet car.

Chapter 11

This was her house, wasn't it? Callie slowed, but didn't pull in the driveway. It didn't look like her house. The ones on either side looked the same, but this didn't look like her house. Not even close.

Flowers bordered both sides of the driveway and the sidewalk. There was even a small three-tiered fountain with water splashing over the sides. A bench sat beside it.

It looked nice. She had a feeling DeeDee had something to do with all this.

Callie finally pulled into the driveway, parking next to Rogar's black Jag, and shifted into Park. Before she turned the key, she lightly caressed the steering wheel. The car was sweet. But she couldn't keep it.

Why not?

She closed her eyes for a moment and took a deep breath, willing the voice of reason to return, but it really, really didn't help when the new car smell filled her senses.

Rogar would probably tell her that her guide was talking to her, but that was so not true. It was the voice of greed asking why she couldn't keep the car.

What if the IRS came snooping around? Not to mention gift taxes, higher car insurance. No, she couldn't afford to keep the Jaguar. At least, not more than a week or so.

She got out of the car, then slowly walked to the front door, inhaling the strong fragrance of the colorful flowers. It was so pretty, she almost felt like skipping, well, except her feet were killing her. But everything was so nice, it sort of eased the ache.

The fountain played a peaceful melody as water overflowed from one tier to the next. More flowers surrounded the ancient oak, framed by stacked rocks. She could learn to enjoy coming home to this.

But it wouldn't last. Nothing ever did. Weeds would creep into the flowerbeds, algae into the fountain. Rogar would leave.

Her heart skipped a beat. No, she didn't want to think about that. No bad thoughts on her birthday. She wouldn't allow it.

She turned the doorknob. It was unlocked. She probably should tell him about locking doors when living in the city.

Once she stepped inside, her nostrils filled with the smell of cooking—really bad cooking. Her nose wrinkled. What was he doing? She was almost afraid to go into the kitchen, but she forced her feet to move forward.

Rogar had his back to her, and he was mumbling. She couldn't make out the words, but she recognized the tone. He didn't sound happy as he stood in front of the microwave.

Her gaze took in the rest of the room. It was a shambles. There was flour everywhere, empty boxes, plastic bags that held more food, some spilling onto the counter. Her stomach sank at the thought of cleaning the mess. She sniffed. It was her birthday, and she shouldn't have to clean.

But the table looked nice. It had been set with new dishes and stemware. In the center of a new red tablecloth was a pair of candlesticks with white tapered candles.

He was making her a birthday dinner. She sucked in her bottom lip as tears filled her eyes. The only person who had ever done anything special for her was DeeDee. This was so nice, so sweet . . .

Rogar stepped out from in front of the microwave. Sparks flew around on the inside like the Fourth of July. She rushed forward and flung the door open. "What are you trying to do?"

Something popped and hissed, then sizzled. She reached over and jerked the cord out of the wall. There was a grinding noise, then nothing. She had a feeling the sound had been the microwave's death rattle.

"It said place in microwave and cook five to six minutes," Rogar said. "Your machine malfunctioned."

Her machine? More likely he hadn't completely read the directions. It was a foil container. She turned on him, but before she could open her mouth to tell Rogar that she'd really liked her microwave, she got a good look at him.

He was streaked with flour, and something must have exploded because the flour was mixed with a blue liquid of some sort, and his hair stuck up at odd angles, as if he'd ran his fingers through it more than once in frustration.

Somehow, the microwave lost significance, and she began to laugh. His frown deepened, which only made her laugh harder.

"Why are you laughing?"

"Because you cared enough to attempt cooking." She walked close to him, started to hug him, then changed her mind, and simply smiled.

"You aren't angry because I destroyed your room?"

She shook her head. "It can be cleaned, but I'll have this memory forever, and it's a good one."

He smiled, then he lowered his head and kissed her. Warmth rushed through her. And at that moment, when his lips touched hers, she knew it was going to be hard to say good-bye to his touch, and everything he made her feel. Not when she wanted him so badly, not when . . .

Her nose wrinkled as the acrid smell of smoke began to fill her nostrils.

Smoke?

She pushed away. "What's burning?"

"Me. You set my blood on fire."

He reached for her, but she stepped around him. Oh, good Lord, what did he have in the oven? She opened the door. Black smoke barreled out.

"What are you cooking? A tire?" She quickly turned off the oven, and hurried to open windows.

"I did exactly what the directions on the box said. Bake for one hour. Apparently, this machine malfunctioned as well." He helped her open the windows.

"Let me get this straight, you can learn to drive a car, but you can't figure out how to cook?" She grunted as she attempted to raise a stuck window.

Rogar came up behind her and raised it with little effort. "I can pilot a space craft, one of your antiquated cars is not that difficult. Besides, we have similar vehicles where I come from."

She moved out of his reach. It would be better to keep a bit of distance between them. "You have vehicles, but you don't have a stove or microwave?" She didn't really buy that.

He straightened. "We have cooking devices which I'm sure are similar to yours but not as . . ."

"Antiquated?" She cocked an eyebrow. His supercilious attitude could be a little irksome at times.

"Yes, exactly."

"I take it you've never cooked."

"Correct again."

She shook her head. "Then how do you eat? Chase your food down, kill it, then eat it raw?"

His brow furrowed. "I have servants. You forget, I'm a prince of noble lineage. There are more important things for me to do than cook."

"You don't say."

His frown deepened. Damn, he was sexy when he frowned.

"I do say. I did say, that is."

"How are you in the cleaning department?"

"Cleaning?"

She walked back into the kitchen and surveyed the mess. It was worse than she'd first thought. He followed her inside. She was totally exhausted. The last thing she wanted to do was clean, especially on her birthday.

"We'll have to clean the kitchen. If it dries, it's going to be like cement, and I don't know how to run a jackhammer." She looked at him, hoping he understood the *we* part. She wasn't about to do it all by herself, and she didn't care if he was a prince or not.

"DeeDee said you were to celebrate your birthday. I don't think that includes cleaning."

"We do what we have to do."

He shook his head. "Go take a bath. It's ready for you. I'll clean the mess."

"But . . ."

"No. I've ruined your special day, but I'll make it better." He placed his hands on her shoulders and gently nudged her toward the other room.

She took one more look at the kitchen, and decided she would leave it all to him. She was too tired to argue. But as soon as she stepped inside the bathroom, she felt guilty.

There were at least a dozen candles glowing. The bathtub was half filled with water, and covered in rose petals. The scents filling the air were a lot better than the ones in the kitchen. She turned the hot water on and quickly stripped out of her clothes, and stepped in.

As soon as she slid her shoulders beneath the water, she knew this was the best birthday present ever. She didn't care about the mess in the kitchen, or young Kelvin and his soda spilling down the front of her shirt. All she cared about was the water lapping against her tired muscles.

The kitchen would probably be in an even bigger mess when she finished her bath, but she didn't care. Not right now, not at this moment in time.

She must've dozed because the next thing she knew, the

water had cooled. She climbed out, and after drying off, blew out the candles, and wrapped in her terry cloth robe.

The house was quiet. She made her way into the kitchen. Rogar was humming a strange tune as he cleaned the counter. The kitchen was back to normal. He'd lit candles and the scent of apples and cinnamon filled the room.

He turned, then smiled. "Better?"

And he'd apparently washed up a little himself, because he was no longer streaked with flour. She smiled. "Much better." Her stomach rumbled. She hoped he wouldn't be serving whatever had been burning earlier.

"I used your phone to have food delivered."

"Is that how you created the pretty flowers lining the drive?"

"I have my database, and DeeDee showed me the Yellow Pages."

She nodded. "A marvelous wonder, the Yellow Pages." She'd never heard of a database, but it sounded techy, and she wasn't much into that kind of stuff.

"Do you like the car?"

"Very much, but I can't keep it."

He stopped midway to the sink with the dishcloth. "Why not?"

She opened her mouth to try to explain, but she had a feeling he wouldn't understand about taxes and insurance. "It's complicated. Besides, you're really going to have to stop duplicating money."

The doorbell chimed. "Food." He went to the door and opened it.

Callie covered her mouth to keep from laughing. A young boy stood at the door with two boxes in his hands. Rogar had ordered pizza.

"Two supremes and a bottle of soda comes to twenty-seven fifty."

Rogar took the boxes and soda, setting them on the coffee table, then reached in his pocket for money. The kid wore a dumbfounded look on his face when Rogar handed him a bill.

"I can't change a hundred, sir."

"I don't need it changed. Here's another for your trouble. Will that suffice?"

"Yes," he squeaked. He cleared his throat. "Thank you, thank you so much! Bitchin' cars, too." He took off running. Callie wondered if the kid thought Rogar would change his mind.

Rogar scooped up the boxes and carried them to the table. "I hope you like pizza. The yellow pages said they were voted number one."

"I love pizza."

He opened the box and inhaled. "I think I will, too." He put a slice on each of their plates, juggling it because it was hot. He motioned for her to sit, then twisted the cap off the soda, sticking it toward her.

Now he'd confused her. "What?"

"Do you want to smell it?"

"Why would I do that?"

"That's what they did at the restaurant."

She took the lid and waved it under her nose. "Two thousand nine, a good year." Then she tried really hard to keep a straight face. He may have adapted to a lot of Earth's ways, but there were things he just didn't get.

He poured some of the cold soda in each of their glasses before he sat across from her. She raised hers to her lips and took a drink. "Very good."

He smiled. When he reached for his fork, she shook her head.

"There's only one right way to eat pizza." She picked up the wedge and took a bite, swirling the cheese around her finger and poking it in her mouth. "Good." She nodded her head as she chewed.

He picked up his slice and took a bite. She laughed when his cheese stretched out and he couldn't get to the end of it.

"Just pinch it with your fingers," she told him. "Don't you have pizza on New Symtaria?"

He shook his head. "We have other delicacies that you would like, although your pizza is very good."

She took a drink of soda, then set her glass back on the table. "Tell me about your planet. Are there trees? Oceans?"

"Our planet is the polar opposite of Earth so they are very similar. We have oceans and mountains, green grasses and trees."

"What happened to the other Symtaria?"

"Pollution. We killed our planet."

That sounded all too familiar. "What's to keep the same from happening to New Symtaria?"

"Everyone learns from their mistakes—eventually. Now we're careful to protect our new home."

"In the meantime, you dumped most of the people onto other planets."

He cringed. "Not dumped. When our planet was dying, my grandfather was one of the rulers. He made the decision to relocate most of the people, while the rest searched for a new home. It took many years."

"And now you're trying to bring everyone back."

"Yes."

"Why? I'm sure most have new lives. They've created their own roots in new lands."

"It doesn't matter. We need them to come back."

"Need? What does that mean?"

He reached for his glass and she wondered if he was going to answer her question. Why did they *need* everyone to return?

Chapter 12

Rogar had blundered and he knew it. He stalled by taking a drink of the liquid Callie called soda, then choked and coughed as it burned his throat. This soda did not go down as smoothly as the wine. He brought his napkin to his mouth as he tried to bring his fit of coughing under control.

Callie's birthday celebration was not going well. At least, not as well as DeeDee had said it would. He and Callie should be in bed making love. DeeDee told him that women appreciated when men made an effort to cook a meal. They wanted the fairy tale, the romance. When he'd looked up fairy tale on his database, it had shown a picture of flowers along a walkway. It hadn't been difficult to find someone to come out and provide the landscaping. He'd offered lots of money, and they'd immediately done his bidding.

Nor did it take much to have a food store deliver ingredients for a gourmet meal. He'd thought the instructions for the preparation were self-explanatory, but apparently not.

When he'd researched romance, he'd come up with candlelight, presents, a rose-scented bath, and making love. It seemed everything had to be in that order. Not that he'd minded, as long as the last one on the list didn't get forgotten. He had a feeling because the first two had been disasters, the last might not happen.

The bath with candles and petals was a good idea. That

one seemed to work very well. The stress was gone from Callie's face and she looked more relaxed. Maybe that's why he hadn't guarded his words as well as he could have. He'd make sure he was more careful in the future.

"You okay?" she asked when his breathing returned to normal.

"The drink is strong and made bubbles in my nose."

"But you're okay?"

"Yes."

"Good, then tell me why you *need* the people to return. You said needed, not wanted."

"Maybe I chose the wrong word. Your Earth words sometimes carry a meaning I don't wish to convey." He'd lied. But it had been for Callie's own good. Now he was starting to pick up her bad habits.

She smiled. He breathed a sigh of relief.

"Not buying it," she said, still smiling.

He frowned.

"You might as well tell me."

He tapped his fingers on the table, then finally spoke, choosing his words more carefully. "Our blood has become too pure. If we don't mix with impures, we will destroy ourselves. Our children cannot be of pure blood."

"So mix with another species. Problem solved."

"It's not that easy. You should know that. There are certain consequences that go along with being Symtarian."

"Like changing form."

"Yes." He picked up his glass, then set it back on the table without taking a drink. "People have been locked away, driven insane, when they heard their guide speaking to them. Or worse."

"Worse?" Her eyes widened. "What could be worse than that?"

"Actually shifting. Changing into animal form, then changing back. Not knowing what happened to them."

"And there's no one to explain?"

He shook his head. "The Symtarians left on Earth adapted the best way they knew how. They were told to blend with this new society, so they hid who they were, even from their offspring, thinking they were probably doing the right thing."

"Why didn't your people come for them sooner?"

"The old leader died, my grandfather, others took his place . . ." he hedged.

"You forgot about them?" One eyebrow quirked upward.

"Yes." He hated to admit it, but that was exactly what happened.

"And now you want everyone to come home so there will be mates with less than pure blood so the Symtarian race will continue."

"Yes."

"And what happens if I decide to stay here?"

Maybe it was best that she knew everything. "Then your life will be in danger."

Callie closely watched Rogar's face. He looked serious. "What do you mean, I'm in danger?"

"Some want to keep our line pure. They don't like the thought of mixed bloods, and they're trying to destroy every one of them."

She shot out of her chair. "You mean there's someone out there who wants me dead?"

He nodded.

"But I didn't do anything to this other person."

He grimaced. "You were born."

The room suddenly tilted and she had to grab the edge of the table to steady herself. "Is that what happened to my mother? Was she murdered by this monster?"

Rogar looked away. He knew more than what he was saying. All this time, and he hadn't told her what she so desperately needed to know, to understand.

"You know, don't you? You know what happened to my parents. Why they left me at the orphanage, don't you?"

"I didn't want to upset you needlessly."

She slowly sat down in the chair. "Tell me. I have the right to know."

He didn't look happy. "I have very little information. The last known whereabouts of your parents was Kentucky. That's where your father was . . . found dead."

She hugged her middle. "How . . ." She swallowed past the sudden lump in her throat. "How was he murdered?"

"Isn't it enough to know he died? He has no more pain. His sleep is peaceful."

Her gaze didn't waver from his. "How was he killed?"

"The report said his heart was ripped out of his chest, his skin shredded. They thought a wild animal might have killed him."

"And my mother?"

"No one knew what happened to her. A neighbor said she was far into her pregnancy."

Callie closed her eyes for a moment, then took a deep breath. "Do you think she might have been protecting me? Is that why she left me at the orphanage? Maybe she didn't leave because she didn't want me?"

He stood, coming around the table, and gathered her in his arms. She rested her head on his shoulder, and realized her cheeks were damp.

Rogar led her to the sofa and sat down, pulling her onto his lap. "Symtarians bond very strongly with their children, from the moment of conception. More so than any race I know. Your mother wouldn't have left you because she didn't love you. I'm certain she cared for you very much."

"And this person who killed my father, is he still out there?"

"I'm afraid so. His name is Zerod. He was son to one of the elder rulers, born later in life. He was against mixing our blood. But we had no choice. Our blood had become so pure that it's harder to control our guides. Zerod lost control of his, and now his guide rules his head."

"And that's dangerous?"

"You should be one with your guide, a blending, so to say. The natural instinct of the guide is to hunt, to kill, but always to protect the human side. When the guide begins to take over, then those natural instincts are stronger. But Zerod has the blood lust on his human side as well. That makes him an even greater danger. And there are those who follow him."

"And he wants to kill me."

"Yes. That's why it's imperative we bring everyone home. Zerod is searching for you even now."

She closed her eyes and breathed in Rogar's scent. For the first time in her life, she felt protected.

The real world quickly closed in around her. Rogar wouldn't always be there to protect her, and she couldn't leave the only thing she'd ever known to step into the unknown.

He lightly began to caress her arm. She doubted he even realized what he was doing, but she did, as heat spread through her. She bit her bottom lip. Sensations swarmed over her, and her body tingled to awareness. It would be so easy to let him continue to touch her, raise her face so that he could brush his lips across hers. How much more difficult would it be to say good-bye if they grew even closer?

She came to her feet, putting distance between them. "What can I do to protect myself?"

He blinked, as though he'd also been lost in thought.

"I can do something to protect myself, can't I?" She sounded a lot braver than she felt.

"Not without your guide."

"The bunny?"

He shook his head. "That wasn't your guide."

It was a good thing because she really doubted a rabbit could protect her from anything, except maybe a giant carrot.

He stood and came toward her. Not stopping until he was barely a foot away. She could feel the heat emanating from him. Her nipples tingled as he awakened her body to awareness. But he didn't touch her.

"Close your eyes," he told her. "Take a deep breath, then exhale."

She did as he asked, but caught his scent again. It tickled her senses. Tempted her to step closer.

"Free your mind," he said, breaking into her thoughts. "Let it go blank."

Not easy with him standing this close, but she tried, until a car went barreling around the corner, apparently on two wheels the way it screamed. That was followed by a horn honking and an obscenity being yelled out. She wondered if she should pull at least one of the Jags into her tiny garage. The red one maybe. Anything could happen . . .

"You're not concentrating."

She opened her eyes. Not good. Now she was staring at him. Rogar was really handsome. "Easier said than done with all the noise."

"That's how you ended up as a bunny. You didn't concentrate."

"I'm not exactly the kind of person who gets into all that meditation stuff."

He cocked an eyebrow.

"Okay, I'll try again."

She closed her eyes. What should she think about? Maybe an elephant. Then she could squash anyone who got in her way. It would be kind of hard to hide if she was an elephant, though. A horse could run fast.

Her red Jag had a lot of horsepower. She'd felt it the moment she'd turned the key. Unleashed power that she'd had complete control over.

"Are you concentrating?"

She glared at him. "Yes, if you'd quit interrupting me. Sheesh." She closed her eyes and forced herself to think about an animal. She'd love to shift into a jaguar, like Sheba.

There was a knock on the door.

She opened her eyes. "This isn't going to be that easy. If

DeeDee is on the other side, she's got a lot of explaining to do about filling your head with happy birthday ideas."

She marched over to the door and flung it open, but a man she'd never seen before stood on the doorstep.

"Oh, I'm sorry, I thought you might have been someone else."

He smiled. The man was handsome with light brown hair, just a touch of silvery gray at the temples, and gray eyes. It was what she saw in his eyes that made her go cold. There wasn't an ounce of warmth. It was almost as though he was dead. He looked behind her and his smile widened.

"Rogar." He held up a newspaper. "You take a good picture, but then, you are my cousin so I would expect no less."

"Cousin?" She looked at Rogar, and knew by the glare in his eyes that there was no love lost between these two.

"I lost you for a while in Kentucky." His gaze turned to Callie. "You look much like your mother." He reached out and twined a dark curl around his finger.

Cold chills of dread swept over her. "You knew my mother?"

"Leave," Rogar said with barely controlled anger. "You're not welcome here."

"But I'm not here for you," his words were silky.

Rogar stepped closer, moving Callie behind him. "I won't let you harm her."

"She's an impure," he spat. "Not worthy to breed and produce weaker versions of herself. It would be an abomination to our society!"

And then she knew for sure. This was Zerod, the man who'd murdered her father, and stolen her childhood. For the first time in her life, she wanted to kill someone.

Chapter 13

Rogar hated Zerod with a passion. He killed because it was something he loved to do. But Rogar wouldn't let Zerod harm Callie, not while there was breath left in his body.

"You killed my parents," Callie said, stepping from behind Rogar.

Zerod grinned, and walked inside the house. "Only your father. He distracted me long enough for your mother to escape and give birth to you. Then she disappeared. Clever woman. If she isn't dead, I'll find her."

"You bastard!" she hissed.

"I mated with a human, you know," he said, turning back to Rogar, as though Callie was merely an annoying insect. "It was pleasurable, in its own way, but then I had to kill her, of course. I enjoyed hearing her scream, during both experiences. Watching her die was even more pleasurable." His eyes glazed.

"You're sick." Rogar was disgusted they shared even one drop of the same bloodline. "Someone should have killed you long ago," he told him.

"But then, you and I know it's forbidden for one Symtarian to kill another. No excuses. It would mean immediate death to anyone who dared break the king's law." He smiled. "I wonder how the king would feel if he had to kill his eldest child. I think it would drive him insane, don't you?"

Rogar growled from deep in his throat. "Don't push me or I'll be tempted to see."

Don't trust him, Balam's thoughts joined with Rogar's.

Never.

"I know you too well. Your family is important to you." Zerod laughed. "I know you hate to admit it, but we are related. Join forces with me."

"And murder innocents."

He shrugged. "The impures are a different story. There is no law against killing a half-breed."

"On New Symtaria maybe, but on Earth we have a different set of laws," Callie spoke up.

Zerod didn't acknowledge her. Instead, he stretched his arms out to the side, growling low in his throat. The air grew heavy and damp.

He was changing form, but Rogar knew Zerod well and anticipated his treachery. He and Balam were ready.

"Hide in the bedroom." He shoved Callie to the side, and closed his eyes, not waiting to see if she obeyed, only praying she would.

His change came seconds after Zerod adopted his guide's form of the tiger—seconds in which Zerod slashed one claw across Rogar's thigh. Rogar fell back, kicking out, connecting.

Balam.

I'm here, and he will not harm us again.

Rogar breathed a sigh of relief, felt the blending of their souls, saw through Balam's eyes.

Zerod's animal guide paced, stopped and turned, then launched himself across the room. Balam jumped sideways at the last moment, but not before he slashed the tiger's muscled shoulder. It screamed in pain, but quickly turned and crouched, then sprang back, knocking into Balam. Balam grunted when he fell against the sofa, his head hitting the wooden rail across the bottom.

For a moment, Rogar was stunned, but Balam recovered

quickly, and moved out of the way, anticipating the tiger's attack. The animal hit the table instead, knocking it over, the lamp crashing to the floor.

The tiger turned, his eyes menacing, spitting anger because Rogar and Balam were still alive to protect Callie. He opened his mouth, and roared his frustration and fury, then ran through the open doorway.

Balam sank to the floor, knowing neither Zerod nor his animal guide would return tonight. The jaguar's breathing was labored. His wound bled freely.

Thank you, old friend, Rogar told him.

Not so old that I couldn't whip Zerod.

True. You've always been my protector against the evils that plague me, and once again, I owe you my life.

You can't stay here. She's still in danger.

I know.

Fog rolled across the room. Rogar closed his eyes, letting the change take place. When he became himself once again, he was sitting on the floor. He groaned as the burning in his gut was replaced by the searing heat from the wound that stretched across his thigh, from his knee to his hip.

"Rogar, you're hurt," Callie said as she knelt beside him. "I need to get something to staunch the flow of blood."

She was gone before he could say anything. He scooted against the back of the sofa until he could lean against it for support.

"I thought I told you to stay in the other room?" he asked.

She laid a towel across his thigh, pressing against it. He sucked in his breath as pain shot down his leg.

"I have to stop the bleeding."

"I know." His energy was quickly draining. "Why didn't you stay locked in the bedroom?"

"It got too quiet. I figured if you were dead, then I wouldn't stand a chance anyway. If you were still alive, then you had to be hurt or you would have called out that it was safe."

She moved the towel. He saw the bleeding had slowed.

"And I was right. You are hurt," she said.

"A scratch." He attempted a smile, but couldn't quite force his lips to curve upward.

"Duh, that's pretty much a gimmie. It's the length and depth of the so-called scratch that has me worried."

He frowned. She was beginning to remind him of his sister, who could be quite annoying at times. But Callie was taking care of him, and that gave him a good feeling.

"I have bandages and gauze. I think you need stitches. Probably a tetanus shot."

"This will be sufficient," he told her. She didn't look convinced. "Symtarians heal faster than other species. Besides, your doctors would ask too many questions."

"You're right. It would be kind of difficult explaining you were mauled by a tiger." She cleared her throat. "Thank you for saving my life."

"It's a life worth saving." He watched as she blushed, then quickly set about bandaging his leg, but the higher she went with the gauze, the more flustered she became. He glanced down and saw the cause of her embarrassment. He was naked. He gritted his teeth and moved his leg, then raised it slightly so she had better access to his wound.

"Yeah, right," she mumbled, but she placed the bandages over his wound, then began to wrap his leg the rest of the way, careful not to get too close to anything other than his wound.

Her touch was warm and gentle. He rather enjoyed that she was taking care of him. It had been a long time since anyone had done so. He could get used to it. If they had more time, that is, which they didn't. "We can't stay here. You're in danger."

"I know," she said.

He clasped her hand, felt the trembles running through her body. "Come back to New Symtaria. You'll be safe there."

"I can't." She bit her bottom lip and shook her head. "I know someplace we can go where we'll be safe."

"Zerod will still be around, and there are others who believe as he does."

"That's why you have to teach me about who I am so I can defend myself."

And maybe he could teach her to love her other self as well. Enough that she would leave with him. "We'd better go then. Zerod will be nursing his wounds as well, but he will return."

"I'll just get some things."

Callie hurried back to her bedroom and began to toss clothes into a case, noting that her top drawer contained men's briefs and socks. When she opened the closet, Rogar's clothes hung beside hers. She should be furious he'd been so presumptuous. Except, if he hadn't been here, she'd be dead right now. A sick feeling rumbled in her stomach, and she had to sit on the side of the bed until it passed.

Had her mother felt the same way as Callie did right now? No, it had been worse for her mother because she'd watched her husband die, barely escaping with her own life. And she'd been pregnant. All the anger Callie had harbored over the years drained from her. She still didn't quite understand the reason her mother had left her at the orphanage, but she had a feeling it was a good one.

Callie wished just once she could tell her mother how much she loved her, and how it must have taken a lot of courage to do what she'd had to do. Maybe some day she would get that chance. Zerod had said she'd gotten away. She could still be alive.

Callie went back to the living room. Rogar was once again dressed in the clothes he'd worn before he'd changed form. His face was pale, and his hands trembled.

"Why didn't you wait? I could've helped you get dressed."

"I managed. Ready?" he asked.

"One more thing." She ran back to the bathroom and filled a bag with painkillers that she'd been given when she sprained her ankle a few months ago and had never used. It had healed really fast, but she'd paid for the pills, and she damned well wasn't going to throw them out.

She hurried back to the living room and grabbed the first aid kit. "I am now."

He started to reach for the suitcase, but she shook her head. "I've got it. Just let me take it out to the car, then I'll come back and help you." She only wished she'd kept the crutches, but they would've been too short anyway.

"I'll manage."

"Uh, I don't think so. Just stay put until I return."

She noticed his forehead was beaded with perspiration. *Don't go superman on me.* He finally nodded. She quickly went to the red Jag and stowed the stuff in the trunk, then hurried back to him. "Lean on me."

"I don't need to lean on anyone."

"Yes, you do, so stop being so blasted stubborn." She tucked herself under his arm and felt some of his weight shift to her. She got her balance before they made their way slowly to her car.

After he was safely in the passenger seat, she went to the driver's side. It was almost as though she could feel eyes watching her. Any minute she expected Zerod to pounce, but then, Rogar said he'd be nursing injuries as well. She hoped the SOB bled to death.

"Where are we going?" he asked as she backed out and started down the street.

"To DeeDee's. She owes me big-time for putting crazy ideas in your head." She cast a look in his direction and saw the corners of his lips had curved upward. The man was devastatingly attractive. It was so not fair that anyone could look as good as he did.

He closed his eyes and she could see the strain on his face. He was in pain, but he tried not to show it. Men. It seemed it didn't matter if they were an alien or not.

But he had saved her life. Damn it, she'd told him she didn't want a hero. Heroes only existed between the pages of her romance novels. It was so not fair that like the heroines in her books, Rogar was making her fall in love with him.

No, no, no! She couldn't be falling in love with him. He'd only come to Earth to collect her so he could take her back to New Symtaria. For breeding purposes at that. Not that she had minded making love with him.

Still, he was a prince for God's sake, and the only person she knew who'd married a prince was Cinderella. It only happened in fairy tales.

She was just reacting to someone who had showed they cared, someone who'd given her the best orgasm she'd ever experienced, and someone who'd saved her life. She had a touch of hero worship, but that was all.

She hit a pothole, he moaned. "Sorry. We'll be there soon. Only a few more miles."

DeeDee lived in a gated community. Her parents foot the bill, although DeeDee would've been just as happy living next to Callie. DeeDee's father was the CEO of a large company, and her mother was a photographer. She didn't take just any pictures, though. No, she shot the stars and their homes, and freelanced for magazines like *Vogue* and *Cosmo*. If that wasn't enough, they also spent time with their only child. Real quality time.

Callie often wondered why DeeDee was her friend. DeeDee had once told Callie that she was real, and the world needed more real people. Callie hadn't been quite sure what she'd meant, but they'd become friends.

She turned in at the entrance, stopping long enough to punch in the code. The gate opened, and she drove through.

DeeDee's house was more like a mini mansion sitting on half an acre. Callie usually hid her car in the garage, not that DeeDee had ever asked her to, but this time there was no need. It felt good driving a red Jaguar. Lord, maybe she was more materialistic than she'd thought.

It wasn't that late, only eight, but it was already dark. The lights were on so maybe DeeDee was home. Callie should've called. "I'll be right back so stay put," she said as she opened her door and got out.

She hurried past the bubbling fountain that sat in the middle of DeeDee's landscaped yard, barely giving it a glance, even though she loved the fountain. Hmm, was that where Rogar had gotten the idea? Probably.

Callie hurried up the three steps and rang the doorbell. A few minutes passed before the door was flung open. DeeDee stood there in a pair of baggy gray sweats and a faded T-shirt that once had the name of a football team on it, but was missing letters.

"What's wrong?"

"Nothing. I'm fine."

"Then why are you here. You hardly come over to my neck of the woods so something has to be wrong. Do you want me to call my dad? He can get you out of anything—trust me."

"It's Rogar . . ."

"Do you want me to hire someone to beat him up? He seemed nice, but if he hurt you, then you should retaliate . . ."

DeeDee had always been protective of her for some odd reason. Callie had never been able to figure that one out. It wasn't like she needed protecting. She figured DeeDee just felt sorry for her because she was raised in an orphanage.

"Callie, you're scaring me!"

She returned to the present. "No, it's not me, and Rogar didn't hurt me. He saved my life, but he's hurt, and we need a safe place to hide."

"Where is he?"

"In the car." She took a deep breath. This was the one time she'd actually asked for DeeDee's help. Would she give it? "Can you help us?"

"Of course. I can't believe you would ask."

"Even if it could put you in danger?"

"I'm your friend, and that's what friends do. Now, let's get Rogar into the house."

DeeDee left the door open, and they hurried to the car.

"How did he get injured?"

"He was mauled by a tiger."

DeeDee stumbled. "A tiger?"

"Long story. Can I tell you once we're inside?"

She nodded. "Yes, and I'll want to know every detail of this one."

Maybe she shouldn't have said so much. She could've lied and told her that he'd been in a fight or something, which he had, and not even brought up anything about the tiger.

She opened the passenger door. Rogar looked to be in a bad way. He was sweating a lot. His clothes drenched.

"Maybe I should've taken him to the emergency room." She bit her bottom lip.

"I'll be all right," he said as he opened his eyes. "I just need to rest."

"Let's get him inside," DeeDee said.

They eased his legs around until his feet were on the concrete driveway. Rogar only groaned once, but it was enough that she knew he had to be in a lot of pain.

With an arm across each of their shoulders, they took it slow and easy as they made their way into the house. The steps were a little tricky, but they managed to get him up them and inside the house.

"We'll take him to my room," DeeDee said. "I don't even want to try to get him upstairs to one of the guest rooms."

Good, because Callie had a feeling Rogar wouldn't make it up the winding staircase. The longer they walked him, the heavier he got. DeeDee only let go long enough to pull the cover back.

Rogar sighed as he fell back against the pillows, and immediately passed out. That's when Callie saw the blood had soaked through his pants. Oh, Lord, he was going to die. Why the hell hadn't she taken him to the hospital?

Chapter 14

Rogar opened his eyes when he felt someone tugging on his clothes. Callie's face swam in front of him. He'd known she wanted his body. He smiled, then frowned. Something didn't feel quite right. He was almost certain mating was out of the question. He shook his head. "I'm not sure I can mate, Callie. Maybe later?"

Someone snorted. He turned his head a fraction and saw a young woman. It was the same one who'd come to the house yesterday. The one who'd told him it was Callie's birthday. Except he hadn't quite pulled off the surprise he'd planned for her.

DeeDee, that was her name.

"Hello again," he said.

She smiled. "Hi. It looks like you've gotten yourself into quite a fix. Callie said you saved her life. When I said women liked fairy tales, I didn't mean you had to be the hero."

"I like being Callie's hero." Now it was coming back to him. Zerod had found Callie. They weren't safe. They needed to leave. His gaze took in the room. He vaguely remembered getting into the vehicle, and Callie driving them somewhere. He'd known she was smart.

"Everyone needs a hero," DeeDee continued. "Callie more than anyone I know."

"Do y'all mind not talking as though I'm not in the room? Besides the fact that Rogar could possibly be dying from the amount of blood he's lost."

"Sorry," DeeDee mumbled. "I think I have bandages."

"Good, then I'll save mine."

DeeDee hurried from the room.

Rogar studied Callie. Worry etched her face. It made him feel good that she cared so much, but he didn't like that his injury scared her. "I'll be all right. It will heal."

"We have to get the bleeding stopped or you won't be all right. You'll be dead. It would have been a lot easier explaining you were mauled by a tiger, and letting a doctor fix your leg, rather than trying to explain a dead alien."

DeeDee returned with a basket almost overflowing. "I just grabbed what I thought you might need." She glanced at Rogar's injury. His leg was partially uncovered. DeeDee turned a little green, then shoved everything toward Callie. "I can't . . ." She slapped a hand over her mouth and hurried from the room.

Callie didn't waste any time grabbing scissors out of the basket. With her lips clamped, she resolutely began cutting away the rest of his blood-soaked bandage. He closed his eyes and enjoyed the feel of her warm hands against his cold skin.

"Are you okay?"

He opened his eyes and looked at her. She was the most beautiful woman he'd ever seen. Her skin was a light golden brown from the sun's kiss. And her eyes—he didn't think he'd ever seen eyes so intense with emotion.

"I heal fast," he said, trying to alleviate the worry on her face. He never wanted her to be worried about him.

She nodded, then removed the rest of the bandage. One part stuck, pulling the hair on his leg. He sucked in a breath.

"I'm sorry. I should've taken you to the ER and let a professional look at this. I've only bandaged a few animals at the zoo. I don't have enough experience." She glanced down, then grabbed the bedpost when she weaved. "You really need a doctor."

"No doctor. He would ask too many questions. You know that could cause me a lot of trouble. Promise, no matter what happens, no doctor. You only pulled the hair on my leg, that was all. Look, the wound isn't as bad as you think. And it has already stopped bleeding. It only needs bandaging again."

"You're so brave," she whispered. Her eyes widened. "I have something that will help." She covered his wound with a clean towel. "I'll be right back."

He rose on one elbow and watched her as she ran from the room. His blood stirred. This was not a good time to think about mating. He lifted himself a little higher in bed. Weakness swept over him. He closed his eyes and took a deep breath, then opened them, and looked under the towel.

Three deep cuts slashed across his upper thigh down to his knee, but he could already see it was beginning to close. In two days' time, no one would be able to tell that he'd ever been hurt.

Symtarians healed rapidly. Right now, he had to admit it looked pretty gruesome, and the wound had weakened him considerably. His only consolation was that he'd given more than he'd gotten, at least, Balam had.

And he had Callie to tend his injuries. He admired her for showing grit when taking care of him. She had the strength of her ancestors' blood running through her veins.

He dropped the towel in place as Callie hurried back into the room. She carried a glass of water and something in her other hand.

"Why are you sitting up?" She stopped in her tracks, frowning at him.

He started to move back down in bed.

"No, wait. I have something for you to take."

She hurried the rest of the way over and helped him to sit

a little straighter. As she cradled his head against her chest, she poked something into his mouth.

"Don't chew," she spoke softly.

All he could think about was the way it felt to rest against her, hearing the steady rhythm of her heart. He rather enjoyed the idea that she was seeing to his needs.

She brought the glass to his lips and tilted it. "Swallow."

He did, feeling the object slide down his throat. "What was that?" He was only mildly curious. He knew she would never hurt him.

"A pill that will help with the pain."

He started to tell her he wasn't really feeling that much pain, but then decided he could just as easily tell her later. Besides, he might not be in any pain, but he was incredibly tired, which was normal for the healing process to begin. He closed his eyes.

Callie quickly put the fresh bandage on, then made sure he was tucked in, but as she brought the cover up to his shoulders, he grabbed her with more strength than an injured man should have. He looked deeply into her eyes, then slowly brought her closer, until his lips could brush across hers.

Heat immediately swept through her as his tongue caressed hers. His hand slid under her blouse, then under her bra until he cupped her naked breast. She moaned when his thumb brushed across her nipple. It immediately peaked as a swirl of sensations rushed down to settle between her legs.

Then he was falling back onto the pillow, eyes closed, his hand still on her naked breast. "Thank you for taking care of me," he mumbled.

She drew in a deep, ragged breath. Reaching under her blouse, she took his hand, but instead of removing it, she pressed it against her breast, holding it there for a moment. Then she tucked it under the cover, and straightened her clothes.

It was going to be so hard to tell him good-bye. Maybe she

should find a way to end this now . . . but no, she was doing exactly what she was supposed to do. As long as Zerod was out there somewhere, she could do no less. She walked out of the room. DeeDee was just outside the door pacing, but stopped when Callie came out.

"Is he going to live? His wound looked horrible." She dragged her fingers through her hair. "Some friend I am, running out on you and all. I just couldn't . . ." She visibly shuddered.

Callie wrapped her arms around her friend. "It's okay. And it doesn't look as bad as I'd first thought." She frowned, wondering about that, but then decided she was more used to seeing it, and it did look pretty awful still. "He's sleeping now."

DeeDee sighed. "Good."

"You let us in when you could've just as easily turned us away, and you did so with no questions asked."

"Yes, I did, didn't I?"' She cast a sideways look at Callie. "And now you can answer a few of them for me."

Callie closed the bedroom door. "Have you got something to drink?"

DeeDee nodded and started toward the kitchen.

"Stronger than soda . . . or wine," Callie said.

DeeDee raised her eyebrows. It was unusual that Callie ever drank anything stronger.

"It's that bad?'

"You might want to pour yourself a strong drink, too. A double."

DeeDee led the way to the less formal living area. There was a big screen television on one wall. A cream-colored sectional sat across from it. A plush beige carpet covered the floor, and in one corner was a mahogany bar. Behind the bar there were shelves of glasses and bottles of alcohol. Callie suspected DeeDee bought the liquor for the pretty bottles rather than the alcohol they held.

DeeDee walked behind the bar, tapped her finger against

her chin, then reached inside the small refrigerator and brought out the Margarita mix.

"When all else fails, grab the tequila." She rimmed the two glasses in salt, added ice, then mix, and two generous splashes of tequila. "Bottoms up." She handed Callie her drink, then went to the sofa.

Callie followed at a slower pace. How much should she tell DeeDee? They had been friends for a long time. Each one knew the other's secrets. Callie knew DeeDee hated pain of any kind, calling herself a wuss. That she'd lost her virginity when she was sixteen, and it had been the worst experience of her life. DeeDee had fallen in love at least a dozen times, and Callie also knew, no matter what, DeeDee would be there for her, but would this be pushing things too far?

Callie took a drink, then wrinkled her nose. "Wow, that'll open the sinus cavities."

DeeDee shrugged. "You said you wanted the hard stuff."

"Yeah, I know." She took another drink for courage, then set her glass on the coffee table. She leaned back, grabbed a pillow, and scrunched it against her chest. "Rogar brought news of my parents. That's really why he's here. That, and to take me home."

DeeDee was just taking a drink. She choked and coughed before she caught her breath and sat her glass down. "Do you think you might have led up to this just a little?"

DeeDee had always been just as concerned about Callie's past as Callie. She shouldn't have just blurted it out. "I'm sorry."

DeeDee's shoulders slumped. "You've known about this since Rogar came to town, haven't you?"

She nodded, wanting to take away DeeDee's hurt, and feeling incredibly guilty. How could she have told DeeDee any sooner when Callie was still coming to terms with it herself?

"You didn't tell me," DeeDee's words were filled with pain.

She would never intentionally hurt her friend. "I think I

needed for it to soak in, to know that it was real. It's complicated."

DeeDee suddenly sat forward, oblivious to the fact she sloshed some of her Margarita over the side of the glass. "You know your past!" She jumped up, set her drink on the coffee table, and ran to Callie, drawing her into a bear hug that nearly stole Callie's breath.

"DeeDee . . . air," she gasped.

"I'm sorry, sweetie." She laughed and clapped her hands as she sat down. "This is fantastic news."

"Yes, I know." Callie smiled.

Suddenly, DeeDee frowned. "I don't understand any of it, though. How did Rogar get mauled by a tiger?"

How much information should she give DeeDee? DeeDee wasn't just a friend. She was her *best* friend. Callie took a deep breath. "My blood isn't pure. I mean, I'm mixed blood." She twined her fingers together. "Some . . . uh . . . people in Rogar's . . . uh, country . . . want all mixed bloods dead. They think we're an abomination. Zerod, he's the leader, is . . . I mean has, this tiger. That's how Rogar got hurt." She let out a deep breath. That had sounded plausible. Maybe?

"You're from another country. I always suspected as much. I mean with your coloring, plus you have those hypnotic green eyes."

Callie brightened. "You think my eyes are hypnotic?"

"Duh, yes."

"Thanks."

DeeDee's spine stiffened. "Hey, wait a minute. You said someone was trying to kill you? That's crazy! We should call the police."

"No, I don't want to get them involved."

DeeDee slowly nodded her head in understanding. "Rogar is here illegally. An illegal alien."

Callie breathed a sigh of relief. "Yes. Well, sort of." It was almost the truth. He was an alien, and he was here illegally, so that pretty much made him an illegal alien.

"What is he—Greek?"

Now it might get a little tricky. "Symtarian. From New Symtaria."

Her forehead wrinkled. "Symtarian? I don't think I've ever heard of them."

"They're not well known in the States."

Callie reached for her drink and took a gulp to keep from meeting DeeDee's gaze. The alcohol burned her throat and made her eyes water. Bad move. She was already starting to feel a little light-headed.

DeeDee leaned back against the cushion and studied her. "You're not telling me something. I've known you way too long not to guess when you're leaving something out. You might as well spill everything."

Callie carefully set her drink back on the coffee table. "Really, there's nothing else to tell."

"Maybe I should look this New Symtaria up on my computer. What country did you say it was near?"

Callie should have known she wouldn't be able to get away not telling DeeDee the whole truth. She took a deep breath.

"You'll have to keep an open mind," Callie told her.

"I can be very open-minded."

Okay, DeeDee had wanted the truth. Callie only hoped she could handle it. "New Symtaria isn't on Earth. It's another planet. Rogar is an alien from another planet."

Chapter 15

DeeDee jumped from the sofa, went back to where she left her drink, and gulped it down as though she was suffering from a bad case of dehydration.

Callie had been afraid DeeDee wouldn't take the news well. Maybe she shouldn't have told her friend quite so bluntly. Lead up to it. Something like, hey, seen any flashing lights in the sky lately? Speaking of aliens.

DeeDee began to pace.

Now her friend was starting to scare her. She'd pace for a while, then she would turn and stare at her. Callie didn't think she had grown a second head or anything.

"My father has a friend who's a psychiatrist," DeeDee finally said. She hurried back to the sofa and took Callie's hands. "I won't let them lock you in a nut house. You've been under a lot of pressure at work. I know this animal keeper job is important to you, and you're always talking about Sheba as though she's your baby, but . . ."

"I'm not going crazy," Callie spoke slowly and distinctly.

DeeDee sucked in her bottom lip and was thoughtful for a moment. "Then Rogar has filled your head with a lot of nonsense. He's probably using this as a line to get laid. Guys are like that." She patted Callie's hand. "You're such an innocent."

"I'm not that innocent, DeeDee." Sheesh, did her friend

think she was that gullible? "At first, I thought Rogar was pulling a fast one."

She nodded. "See, that's all it is then."

"Until I saw him change form. Symtarians are a race of aliens who shapeshift. They take on the animal form of their guides." She frowned. "Or another animal until they truly meet their guide."

DeeDee leaned a little away from Callie. "Wow, and you believed all that crap? You are naïve."

"But it's true. He really did change into a jaguar, and he's a prince on his planet."

DeeDee fell back against the cushions laughing. "Okay, where's the camera?" She glanced around the room. "This is a great Halloween prank, and I have to admit, you had me going there for a bit. Great makeup on Rogar's leg."

She shook her head. "This isn't a prank. It's the truth. I'm part Symtarian. And Rogar was really attacked. There are Symtarians who think the mixed bloods should be destroyed, that we taint the race. Zerod murdered my father, and now he wants to kill me as well, and any other mixed blood Symtarians."

DeeDee looked skeptical. "Okay, maybe I do buy that he was attacked because I don't think you would make that up, but come on, tell me how he really got hurt? You don't have to lie and say it was aliens. If Rogar was goofing off around your precious Sheba, and she hurt him, I won't tell anyone."

This was going to take longer than Callie had expected. "I am telling you the truth."

DeeDee was thoughtful. "Let me get this straight. You're part alien?"

Finally! "Yes."

"So that means you can shift into an animal."

"Yes, well, I've only done it once, and I wasn't very good at it. Rogar said the bunny rabbit wasn't my true guide. We have to sort of find each other."

"A bunny rabbit?" She cocked an eyebrow in disbelief.

Callie nodded, knowing how lame everything sounded.

"So change form, then I'll believe you."

"But . . ."

"Like I said, this is a good prank."

"I'll do it already! But remember, I don't know what form I'll take because I haven't found my guide."

"Fine with me." She leaned back against the cushions and crossed her arms.

Was that a smirk on her face? Callie really hated when she wasn't taken at face value, and DeeDee should know she would never lie. If she wanted proof, Callie would give it to her.

She closed her eyes and concentrated. Nothing happened. Maybe she should chant or something. No, Rogar said she only needed to concentrate.

"You still look the same to me," DeeDee commented.

Callie opened her eyes and glared at her friend. "I need complete silence."

DeeDee zipped her fingers across her lips, then pretended to turn a key and throw it away. Smart ass. Well, she would soon make a believer out of her.

Callie closed her eyes again, suddenly feeling very self-conscious. She had to relax, being tense would only make things harder. She inhaled, then exhaled as she let her mind go blank. A familiar swirling began to churn inside her.

Breathe in, breathe out.

A familiar fog began to close around her. Her arms and legs began to ache. She gasped and curled into a ball, then stretched her limbs. Vaguely, she heard DeeDee cry out, telling her to stop whatever the hell she was doing, that she was scaring her, but it was too late for that now.

The world around her went dark. Every bone in her body ached. This was worse than when she'd changed into a bunny. Her skin and bones were being stretched beyond what she could stand.

She couldn't breath. Was she dying? She was too young to die.

Everything suddenly stilled. The pain went away.

Callie blinked rapidly. As before, it was as though she was looking through someone else's eyes. DeeDee was sprawled across the sofa in a dead faint.

It was DeeDee's own fault. She had certainly done everything she could to convince her friend that she was part alien, but had she believed her? Nooo . . .

Callie frowned. She didn't think she had shifted into another rabbit. She came to her feet, or whatever they had changed to. The sofa creaked and groaned, then crunched. Two pillows that had been right beside her flew across the room.

Not a good sign.

She lumbered over to the mirror on the wall, accidentally bumping a side table on the way and sending the lamp crashing to the floor. Good grief, she felt as though she'd put on a ton of weight. She felt more bloated than when she PMSed.

She stopped in front of the mirror.

Well, hell.

Life was so not fair. A rhinoceros? This was no longer fun anymore. She didn't want to be a big hulking beast. She wanted to be something sleek and exotic.

She glanced behind her. Wow, talk about having a big ass. No diet would help this one. Nope, she wanted her own body back. She was pretty sure this wasn't her guide.

Now to change back. If poor DeeDee roused, she'd probably have a heart attack this time.

Callie closed her eyes and let her mind go blank. She began to ache, to burn as though someone had set her on fire. The damp fog did nothing to cool her. This wasn't good. Why did it hurt so much this time? Rogar would have some explaining to do. He'd said it would get easier, but this was a lot harder than last time. Maybe because she was so big.

Oh, Lord, what if she didn't change back to herself. Would

DeeDee still be her friend? Would she take care of her, feed her? Ohh, don't drop any pellets or she wouldn't.

Pellets? Yeah, right!

Her pulse suddenly quickened and she found it was all she could do to take a deep breath. The world spun around her as she sank to the floor. She stretched her limbs, then drew them back close to her, curling into a ball.

She blinked, everything was fuzzy. She closed her eyes and just concentrated on breathing. Letting the change happen.

Things began to calm. When she ran her hands over her arms, she knew she had shifted back. Oh, thank God. Not that she had anything against the rhinoceros. It was a lovely animal, she just didn't want to *be* one.

"Callie?"

She opened her eyes and saw DeeDee. Good, she was afraid there for a minute she had gone blind. "I'm okay. Just give me a moment." She closed her eyes.

"Are you sure you're okay?" DeeDee asked after a few more seconds passed.

"That one took a little more out of me than changing into a bunny." She didn't want to scare her friend more than she already had, and attempted to sit up.

DeeDee grabbed Callie's arm when she started to stand and stumbled, then helped her to the sofa. Callie frowned when she saw it was broken down on one side. "Sorry about that."

"It can be replaced." She grabbed a throw, draping it over Callie's shoulders.

Callie pulled it closer, then watched as DeeDee drained her drink. "I know, I felt the same way when Rogar told me everything."

"You really are an alien, aren't you?"

"It would seem that way."

"And this Zerod creep is trying to kill you."

She nodded.

DeeDee went behind the bar and made herself another

drink. Callie shook her head when DeeDee raised her glass, silently asking Callie if she wanted a refill. She needed to stay sober so she could take care of Rogar through the night. She wanted to make sure his condition didn't worsen.

DeeDee returned, plopping down on the sofa, then wrinkled her nose. "It smells like rhinoceros in here."

"Sorry about that, too."

DeeDee nervously began to light scented candles. Was she avoiding talking about everything that had happened? DeeDee was obsessive about her scented candles so it could be anything.

Callie suspected it was more that DeeDee was trying to decide how to act around her, now that she knew Callie was part alien. "It's okay. I'm still the same person."

DeeDee laid the lighter down, then looked at Callie. "Except for the fact you can change into . . . into an animal."

"But none of that matters. Not really. I'm still the same person you met ten years ago." She had to grit her teeth to keep from crying out. She didn't want to lose the only friend she'd ever had. She would give up knowing anything about her parents, who she was, and where she came from, if it meant she would keep DeeDee in her life.

DeeDee suddenly smiled. "I remember the first time we met. Your date had taken you to the Blue Bayou. I used to love that bar. They had the best jazz band on Saturday nights."

"Ugh, Mark Lemons. I remember him. He *was* a lemon!" She still had no idea why she'd agreed to go out with him. He'd been a groper.

"You pushed him away, but he grabbed you and dragged you right back, then he tried to kiss you," DeeDee said. "My friends told me not to get involved, but I took one look at your face and knew I couldn't stand by and watch while you tried to fight him off."

"I'm so glad you didn't." By herself, she hadn't been able to get away. "But you waltzed over with your drink and tossed it in his face. He was furious. I thought he was going to hurt you."

DeeDee laughed. "I think he would have if I hadn't showed him the lighter I held."

Callie grinned. "And told him if he didn't want to become a human torch, he'd better leave now."

"Good thing he didn't push his luck. As far as I know, water with lemon is not flammable."

"It did work, and you were very brave to come to the aid of a stranger. We need more people in the world like you." DeeDee had given her a ride home, and they'd been friends ever since. The princess and the . . . alien.

"And I'll be there with you through this, too."

"I know."

"Get dressed, then we'll form a plan of action." She stood, then left the room to give Callie some privacy.

Callie was just buttoning the last button on her shirt when DeeDee tapped on the door.

"I'm decent," Callie called out.

DeeDee walked back inside the room. "By the way, does that always happen?"

"What?"

"You change back and find you're naked."

"Yes."

"I bet they have a lot of sex on New Symtaria." She stopped. "Wait, didn't you say you changed into a rabbit."

Callie could see the wheels turning. "Yes," she said slowly.

"I'm assuming Rogar was there."

Oh no. She had a feeling she knew what was coming. "Yes."

"Not going to tell me, are you?"

"No."

DeeDee grinned. "It's about time you got laid."

"DeeDee!" She glanced around as though Rogar would appear any second and she would be even more embarrassed.

"It's okay, I won't push for details."

"Thanks."

"Not right now, but later, look out."

"DeeDee!"

She shrugged. "Well, he is an alien. Of course I'm curious."

"Can we get back to the matter at hand? After all, I am being chased by a crazed Symtarian who thinks it's his destiny to destroy all the impures."

"You'll need a place to hide out, and I have the perfect one, the camp. You remember, *Camp in the Pines.*"

Callie fell against the cushions with a groan.

"It's the perfect place. My parents have a nice cabin. You remember."

"And the camp is crawling with bluebloods."

DeeDee stiffened. "Excuse me? I just happen to be one of those bluebloods you're referring to."

"You know what I mean. I went there with you once and it was quite enough. They were so snobbish."

"But you have to admit, the cabin is great, the view is spectacular, and you had a fabulous vacation."

She and DeeDee did have fun when they didn't need to play the social card. There were all sorts of activities. It wasn't like she had a long list of choices, either. "Okay, we'll go, and thanks so much for helping. You didn't have to, and I really appreciate it."

"Yes I did. You're my best friend." Her smile embraced Callie. "You can take my Hummer, but don't scratch it."

"We can't leave the Jag here. If Zerod comes snooping, I don't want him to find anything connected with us."

"No problem. I have vacation coming up. Mom and Dad have been after me to join them. Now would be a good time. I love Colorado in the fall. I'll have someone pick the Jag up, though."

"Then it's settled." She hoped.

"Looks that way. Want to tell me how it was with Rogar now?"

Callie surreptitiously glanced around. He'd probably kill her for gossiping, but, well . . .

"Oh, Lord, it was the best sex I'd ever had, DeeDee. I mean, unbelievable." She hugged her middle. "I never thought it could be like that. Rogar was fantastic. He was . . ." She laughed. "Out of this world."

DeeDee didn't say anything. Callie thought her friend would be more excited for her. Damn, she was kind of disappointed.

DeeDee crossed her legs. "You've fallen in love with him."

"Pffttt, of course I haven't."

"He's the guy in black leather."

"I think you've had a little too much tequila."

DeeDee shook her head. "Think about it, Rogar is the guy who swaggers into your college classroom wearing a black leather jacket. The bad boy. Except Rogar is even more dangerous now."

"He's not at all dangerous. He would never hurt me. I mean, the guy saved my life."

"I don't mean dangerous that he would harm you, no, it's even worse. He's made you fall in love with him."

"You're crazy." She barely knew the guy. Having a fantastic orgasm didn't equal falling in love with someone.

"Think about it. The guy comes from another planet, he's dark and mysterious, then you have fantastic sex, and if that wasn't enough, he saves your life. It's the hero syndrome, and you've fallen head over heels in love. I can tell by the look on your face when you talk about him."

Callie opened her mouth, but closed it when no words came out. She couldn't be in love with Rogar. He was a fling, that was all. He wanted her to drop everything and run off to another planet, and that wasn't going to happen. No way, no how. Earth was her home. And she was so close to having her dream job. It would be stupid of her to even consider going with him.

But just the thought of him leaving without her sent a queasy feeling rumbling in her stomach.

Life sucked.

Chapter 16

Callie was not in love with Rogar, infatuated yes, but not in love. She hadn't known him long enough. He was hot, sexy, and yes, he'd been her hero. Dark, dangerous, and mysterious. She was sure he had some flaws somewhere, other than his cooking.

"You're so in love with him," DeeDee said.

"Am not."

"Are to."

"Callie," Rogar bellowed from the other room.

She jumped to her feet. "Crap, I gave him one of my pain pills. It should've knocked him out and let him get a few hours sleep. He must be in excruciating pain."

DeeDee raised her eyebrows. "You gave an alien a pain pill?"

Callie frowned as she hurried to the bedroom. "It never hurt me. I'm part alien." Now that she thought about it, she'd never taken anything stronger than a Tylenol. There had never been a need. At the edge of the doorway, Callie skidded to a stop.

Rogar stood in the middle of the bed weaving back and forth, wearing only his briefs, and the large white bandage. At least it wasn't blood soaked. "Where's my weapon? How can I protect you if I don't have a weapon?"

"It's okay, we're safe at DeeDee's. Zerod won't find us here."

He seemed to think about that for a moment.

"You need to lie back down before you fall off the bed and hurt yourself," Callie spoke softly so she wouldn't startle him. From now on, no more pain pills.

"She's right. Sit down, Rogar," DeeDee told him as she came in behind Callie. "Apparently, he's feeling better."

In one movement, Rogar's legs went out from under him and he plopped down on the bed, then laughed uproariously when he bounced. When DeeDee chuckled, Callie cast a glare in her direction.

DeeDee shrugged. "He's funny. Besides, *you* gave him the pill, not me."

"I didn't know it was going to make him act all . . . goofy. What if his wound starts to bleed?"

"Callie, sweetheart, come lie beside me. I want to mate with you. I want to hear you cry my name out in ecstasy again."

"Oh, this is serious if you cried his name out," DeeDee commented.

Heat crawled up Callie's face. This was not happening in front of DeeDee.

"I think I'll leave you to get him settled back down," DeeDee whispered. "Just do me one favor."

"What?"

"Don't have sex in my bed. It's not a visual I want right before I go to sleep."

Callie groaned as the door closed. Then she looked at Rogar, who was sitting in the middle of the bed, with a silly grin on his face.

"You need to get some rest," she said.

He patted the bed. "So do you."

She cocked an eyebrow. "I have a feeling sleeping is not what you have in mind."

"You don't trust me?"

"No."

"Then I'll stay up with you." He swung his legs over the side of the bed.

"No! You could start your wound bleeding again. I'm surprised it isn't now. Besides, you're not that steady, and if you fall, I doubt DeeDee or I could get you back up again."

She hurried over when it seemed he wasn't paying a bit of attention to her. It didn't take much effort to get him to lie back down. Again, he patted the mattress beside him.

"Please?"

"Okay, but we're not making love. I won't have you bleeding to death, and me feeling guilty for the rest of my life." She crawled in beside him and lay back against the pillow.

Rogar rose on one elbow and stared down into her face. "You're so damned beautiful."

"Since when did you learn our curse words?"

"Database."

"Huh?"

"It's like one of your computers, but much more technically advanced, of course. I can find out anything I want to know. It can do a lot of things that your computers can't."

She barely paid attention to what he said. She was mesmerized by his eyes, and the way he was intently watching her. When he began to lower his face toward hers, she closed her eyes, anticipating the touch of his lips, the heat that would follow.

But his head landed on the pillow beside her, his arm plopped across her chest like an anchor. She coughed as her air supply was cut off. This was not good. She wiggled out from under his weight.

He snored.

It was not fair to make her want his kiss, then fall asleep.

Except he was going to suffocate if she didn't get his face out of the pillow. She pushed until he rolled onto his back. Chest heaving from exertion, she fell back onto the bed. The man was big.

When she could breathe normally again, she pushed up on one elbow and stared down at him. A lock of dark hair fell across his forehead. She didn't hesitate to brush it back, her fingers lingering on his forehead, then smoothing across one cheek, and over his lips. She leaned down, and for just a moment, pressed her lips against Rogar's. His were warm. She reveled in the fact she could show how she felt without being just a little embarrassed.

Then it hit her, and she jerked back.

Oh, no, DeeDee was right. She was falling in love with Rogar. How could it have happened so fast? But she knew. It was just like DeeDee had said. Callie had a bad case of hero worship. She moved off the bed and quietly left the room. She found DeeDee in the family room.

"Oh, DeeDee, what am I going to do? I think I've fallen in love."

DeeDee laughed.

"That's not exactly the reaction I was hoping from you."

"It's all right to fall in love, Callie." She patted the cushion beside her. "Tell me what's bothering you."

Callie walked over and sat beside her friend. "He wants me to go to New Symtaria with him."

"Would that be so bad? You would get to know your people."

This conversation was not going in the direction she'd expected. Didn't DeeDee care enough about their friendship to want her to stay?

"I know what you're thinking."

Callie studied her face, but she only saw the friendship that had always been there. Still, she had to ask. "You'd want me to leave?"

"What I want isn't important. Besides, I have a feeling we would still see each other on occasion. What's important is that you're happy. It should never be a choice between me and the man you fall in love with. Do you think you might be more afraid of the unknown?"

"I think another planet is a little more than the unknown."

She chuckled. "Yeah, I guess it is. But look at the adventure you'll have."

"What if I don't want an adventure?"

She patted Callie's hand. "If you think about it, you'll see that I'm right. You've never left this town except when I dragged you to my parents' cabin."

"It was a little more than a cabin. More like luxury enclosed in a log structure."

"Don't tell Mom and Dad that. They like to think they're roughing it."

Her parents were really nice, but they didn't have a clue about how it felt to scrimp and save. Their idea of roughing it was slower Internet service.

Callie shrugged. "But he doesn't love me. He only wants to make love."

"I don't know, he looks like he might care about you more than you think."

And if that were the case, could she go on an adventure like Rogar was asking her to take? Give up any chance for the job she'd worked toward getting most of her life? Leave Sheba. The jaguar had become a part of her life as much as any beloved pet.

But if she stayed, could she learn how to protect herself from people like Zerod? So many questions, and she didn't have a clue what the answers were.

"I'm beat, I think I'll go to bed." She stood, knowing she would stay in the room with Rogar. Apparently, so did DeeDee because she didn't ask if she wanted one of the other bedrooms. If Rogar needed her during the night, Callie would have to be close enough to hear him.

"See you in the morning."

There was a light blue chaise in the master bedroom. That would probably be safer than the bed. She took one of the pillows off the bed, and the blanket at the foot, then made herself as comfortable as she could. The chaise was meant for reading. It had a high back on one end and it was open on the other. It wasn't long enough for someone to stretch out on so she would have to curl on her side. It was only one night, and Rogar had saved her life.

As she punched her pillow, she was pretty sure she wouldn't be getting a lot of sleep tonight. Some birthday this had been— an alien called Zerod had tried to kill her. Now that would be a story to tell the grandchildren. Not that they would believe it, except they would be part alien, too.

Oh, Lord, how would she explain that if she married some-one from Earth? No, honey, of course we didn't get a cat. That's your daughter.

Or, worse, what if her animal guide was really a rabbit? Would that mean there was a possibility she would have twelve or more children at one time?

She shouldn't have drunk the Margarita. Alcohol always went straight to her head.

Maybe she would be destined to stay single for the rest of her life. She certainly didn't want to freak out her husband in the delivery room when she dropped a dozen or more kids.

Did they even have maternity clothes that big?

Oh, cripes, what if she delivered a baby rhinoceros? Ouch! That was so not going to happen. She would definitely insist on a c-section.

Her lids fluttered downward and she yawned. She didn't want to think about anything else tonight. She only wanted to sleep, and stay safe.

But her dreams were filled with Zerod chasing her, except he was a tiger. Right before his teeth clamped down on her head, the dream changed. Now she was in the delivery room with some guy who she knew was her husband, but he looked like a complete doofus, and was white as a sheet because this doctor kept catching all these babies that were flying out of her body.

She sat up with a start, drenched in sweat. The soft glow of morning light had started to creep inside the room. She sat on the side of the chaise, stifling her groan. She felt as though she'd run a marathon—or delivered a dozen or so kids.

She stretched to get the kinks out, then stood and stretched some more. After a quick check on Rogar, who looked as though he was having great dreams, she dug a pair of sweats out of her bag and headed toward the shower. A shower, then coffee.

Less than half an hour later, she was in the kitchen with a pot of coffee started.

"I thought I heard someone up and moving about," DeeDee said as she joined her. "Good, you have the coffee going."

DeeDee wore a flowing caftan and looked positively radiant. "How do you do it?"

"What?"

Callie waved her hand toward DeeDee. "Look this good first thing in the morning?"

"Bad night?"

"Miserable. I do not recommend sleeping on your chaise."

"There are spare guest rooms upstairs."

"I needed to be close."

She raised her eyebrows.

"It's not what you're thinking. Rogar saved my life so it was the least I could do." She glanced toward the glass pot. "Coffee's ready." And it was a good thing. It was way too early to get into a conversation about her love life.

"What time are you planning to leave?" DeeDee asked as she sat at the table with her coffee.

"I want to get out of town as soon as possible. And you?"

"I'll call Mom this morning to let her know I'll be joining them after all. I'll leave the same time as you."

"Good, I don't want you here if Zerod comes looking for us, and I'd guarantee he will."

"Are you scared?"

She nodded. "But I feel safe with Rogar."

"And I'll keep you safe," Rogar spoke from the doorway.

She jumped up and hurried to him. "What are you doing up? You don't want to start your wound bleeding again." She rested his arm across her shoulders. He moved his hand a few inches, and as they made their way across the room, she realized how close it was to her breast. In fact, it was brushing the side. By the time she had him in a chair, her nipples were tight and aching for more than a gentle caress.

"Are you feeling better," DeeDee asked, apparently she didn't notice the sexual undercurrent.

"Much better, but groggy." His gaze fell on Callie. "Did you give me something? I had a crazy dream that I needed to save you again, and couldn't find a weapon. Then your lips were touching mine and your hands . . ."

"Most of it was a dream," she quickly inserted.

"Callie . . ." DeeDee began.

"We didn't. I swear."

"Didn't what?" Rogar looked between them.

"Nothing. Would you like some coffee?" She could feel the heat rising up her face.

"Coffee?"

"It's a morning drink," DeeDee explained.

"Yes, I'd like to try coffee."

Callie poured Rogar a cup, then carried it to him. He took a drink, then coughed and sputtered before turning accusing eyes on her.

"Are you trying to kill me?"

"I guess it's an acquired taste."

She poured him a glass of orange juice instead. He seemed to like that much better.

"We can't continue to stay here," Rogar told them when he'd finished his juice.

"That's why you're going to my parents' cabin," DeeDee said. "Zerod won't think to look for you there."

He stiffened. "You know about Zerod?" He looked at Callie.

"I had to tell her, Rogar. I mean, your wound, and everything. I didn't want DeeDee to think we were criminals or something."

"I swear I won't say a word." DeeDee crossed herself—not that she was Catholic.

"It could be dangerous if you did."

She quirked an eyebrow. "That, and my parents would probably send me to a shrink."

Rogar sat straighter. "You can shrink people?"

"She meant psychiatrist. Someone who tries to help crazy people." Callie hated to put it that way, but it was the only way she thought Rogar would understand.

"Oh, you mean people with emotional problems," he said.

Callie frowned. "Yeah, that's one way to put it." She ignored DeeDee's smile.

"You will come with us?" Rogar asked. "It won't be safe here."

DeeDee shook her head. "I'll stay with my parents. My cousin is getting married in a couple of months. They'll be visiting them in another week so it's an extended vacation. I like her, even if her fiancé is a jerk." She curled her lip.

"Fiancé?" he asked.

"When two people fall in love, they get engaged. Her fiancé is the man she's going to marry. They plan to spend their life together."

He nodded. "Lifemate."

Callie's heart tripped at the way he said the word, then looked at her, as though he'd already staked his claim. She wondered what it was going to be like over the next few days living with Rogar. If he continued as he was right now, she had a feeling her heart was going to be in deep trouble.

She jumped up from her seat. The room felt as though it was suddenly closing in on her. "I need to call Mr. Campbell. When all this is over, I'll still need my job." She met Rogar's gaze. She was sure he caught her meaning. Leaving everything she had ever known was not an option.

Chapter 17

DeeDee had said they would be going to her parents' cabin, that it would be safe there. Maybe they would be out of danger long enough that Rogar could find where Zerod was hiding.

Rogar grit his teeth against the sudden flare of anger. He would kill Zerod, even if it meant death if he ever returned to New Symtaria. His family would ostracize him, as would the people. But he would do it for Callie. He would do it to keep her safe.

Why?

His forehead wrinkled. She was stubborn and obstinate. Her customs were odd, at best. She knew nothing of her true heritage, and furthermore, the only reason she was willing to meet her guide was so she could protect herself against Zerod. Not that she would defeat Rogar's more experienced cousin.

His hands curled into fists. She would never be able to take care of herself, even if she eventually accepted her guide. Her guide had been dormant too long. It would take years to gain what had been lost. No, Callie was too inexperienced.

He glanced across the seat at her. She drove the boxy vehicle with ease, he would give her that. There were some things she could do better than him, although he could've easily learned the functions. Size was the only difference between this vehicle and the Jaguar.

She adjusted the temperature setting on her side, then ran her hand along the wheel that steered the machine. Her touch was light, almost like a caress. He closed his eyes, remembering the way she had touched him.

Maybe that was the reason he'd become infatuated with her. She had a nice touch. But then, she was also very beautiful—more like a Symtarian than someone from Earth. The Symtarian women were beyond comparison.

She was more emotional, though, and her feelings often showed on her face. He knew when he'd pleased her or angered her in some way. He knew when she was content. Like now, she seemed relaxed.

Just as suddenly, her expression changed, and she began to nibble on her lower lip.

Was she thinking of Zerod? She shouldn't worry, because he would protect her, and when he left, she would come with him. He wouldn't give her an option, but he would give her a little time to get used to the idea. That was the only solution. There were others like Zerod, and he couldn't protect her every second.

"You're awake," she said.

He had been for a while, but he hadn't wanted her to know he studied her.

"How are you feeling?"

"More alert. Better."

"Yeah, sorry about giving you a prescription pain pill. I didn't realize it would have such an adverse reaction on you. We'll stick with the over-the-counter medication from here on out." She shifted in her seat. "It won't be long now. As soon as we arrive, I'll get you tucked into bed. Your leg must be killing you."

He opened his mouth to tell her that it should be completely healed by now, but when she cast a concerned glance in his direction, words failed him. There was such a wealth of sympathy and love in that one look. When she squeezed his hand, he decided he would be better off not explaining that very few Symtarian wounds were life threatening.

Instead, he quickly spelled cabin on his database. A picture popped up of a small log structure. Beneath it he read: cozy one-room cabin with few amenities. Often used by hunters when trapping or killing game.

Rogar liked the thought that she would be tucking him into bed inside a secluded, but rustic cabin. They would spend their nights making love. During the day, he would be showing her the path to her animal guide, and eventually the way back to New Symtaria.

All he had to do was tell her about the wonder and the beauty that New Symtaria had to offer. The wide streams, the green valleys, the highest mountains. The landscape was much the same as that of Earth, except better, so the transition wouldn't be that difficult for her. He only had to convince Callie to return with him. Since he'd have her all to himself, that shouldn't be a problem. He'd never had any trouble convincing a Symtarian woman to do his bidding.

When his body began to react to thoughts of just how he would convince Callie that it would be in her best interest to leave with him, he decided to change the direction of his thoughts.

"Did Mr. Campbell understand when you told him you were taking a few days away from work?" He rather hoped she'd been dismissed from her duties. Guilt flooded him. He didn't want her unhappy.

"There wasn't any problem getting time off."

That surprised him. "Mr. Campbell didn't seem the type who would be so generous."

She chuckled. "He isn't, but I tempted him."

Rogar didn't think he liked the idea of her tempting her boss.

"I told him that I was trying to convince you to come back for a few weeks," she said. "The bribe worked."

"And what will you tell him when that doesn't happen?"

"That you're a rotten person and refused to cooperate."

He wasn't sure he liked that solution any better.

"We're here," she said.

He sat straighter, and looked around. They were just passing under a wooden arch that proclaimed this was *Camp in the Pines*. They met a tiny vehicle with sticks poking out of bags in the back of the small conveyance. The man and woman smiled and waved, but Rogar thought their smiles were only pasted on their faces.

"There are many small vehicles here," he said as more passed them.

She laughed lightly. "They're called golf carts. You don't play golf on New Symtaria?"

He pulled out his database and punched in some letters. A video popped up on the screen of a man swinging one of the sticks at a small white ball. He connected with the ball and it sailed through the air. Then he walked back to his cart and drove to where the white ball had stopped. He hit the ball twice more until it went into a small hole.

Rogar looked at Callie. "No, we don't play golf. It seems like a pointless game."

"You might not want to say that too loudly around here. They take their game very seriously."

"Odd."

"Welcome to the blueblood society."

"Their blood is blue?"

"An expression. Their blood is actually the same color as mine, not that they would ever admit to it."

He punched in some more letters. Blueblood: an expression used to differentiate classes of people in Earth's societies. Bluebloods are wealthy, and believe themselves above other people. They always run with their own crowd, and consider mingling with the lower classes beneath them.

"It's a good thing we won't need to interact with them because I doubt I would enjoy it."

"We'll see a lot more of them than we want."

She pulled in front of a log home. This dwelling was set farther back than the others, and surrounded by tall trees.

"This is it," she said as she turned the ignition key and opened the door. "Stay put and I'll come around to help you." She climbed out and hurried to his side of the vehicle as he input the word cabin into his database again.

Callie opened the door. He shook his head and showed her the screen. "This place is not what my database has shown me."

She grinned, and for a moment, as he stared at her, he completely lost his train of thought. The spell broke when she glanced at the screen.

"The rich never do anything like the rest of us," she said.

He scanned the area. The house was shielded on both sides by trees. It wasn't as secluded as he'd hoped, but he supposed as long as he had a chance to talk to Callie about New Symtaria, and other things, then it would do.

"Come on, let's go inside," she said.

He eased himself out of the vehicle, even though he was certain his leg was now completely healed. There wouldn't even be a scar as a reminder of what had happened.

"Three steps, do you think you can make it?"

"I'll try." It felt good to have Callie this close to him. The heat from her body was like a soft touch. As they moved toward the cabin, it became more than a touch as she inadvertently rubbed against him.

Thoughts of her naked body pressed against him filled his head. A moan slipped from between his lips as he remembered what it felt like to sink deep inside her body.

She gripped him a little tighter around the waist. "I was afraid the drive would be too long, but this really was the only choice we had."

She thought his pain was from the wound. If she only knew, but he wasn't going to tell her. He rather enjoyed that she was so concerned about his health.

"As soon as we get inside, you can stretch out on one of the beds."

He nodded, gritting his teeth for effect when she glanced up at him.

"Then I'll get that bandage changed. I only hope it's not soaked with blood."

He stumbled on the last step.

"Careful."

If she changed his bandage, she would see the wound had healed, and he had a feeling she wouldn't be happy he'd taken advantage of her kindness. In fact, he had a feeling she'd be very angry with him. That wouldn't endear her to the Symtarian race. He'd just have to think of a way to keep her from seeing his leg.

They made it inside. Callie was right, these bluebloods lived differently from other people. He had a feeling if he downloaded an image of the room, it would come up under the title of luxury at its finest.

"It's a lot to take in, I know, but DeeDee's folks are actually really nice. Not quite as stuffy as some of their friends. And all this?" She shook her head. "This is their idea of roughing it—no formal dining room. It's an open floor plan."

"Strange people."

"Let's get you in bed. I can't believe I'm standing here keeping you on your feet."

They made their way to the back of the spacious cabin, and into a bedroom that housed another large bed. The beds on New Symtaria were not quite so large. Couples liked to be close to their mate, even in sleep.

With Callie's help, he made it to the bed and laid down, exhaling an exhausted sigh for effect. When she smoothed the hair off his forehead, he took her hand and brought it to his lips, inhaling the light scent of the sweet fragrance she wore, before letting his lips brush across her palm. He felt the shiver that went through her, and knew that his touch affected her as much as hers did him.

"I want to mate with you," he whispered.

She inhaled a sharp breath, tugging her hand free. "Your leg . . . we . . . uh . . . can't."

He almost blurted out that he was healed, but then remembered that Callie would kill him if she knew the truth. And she might not accept his help. He was stuck in a cage of his own making. He now had to decide what was more important, mating, or teaching her the skills she might someday need.

It was tempting to throw caution away, but those same skills might be the only protection she would have if Zerod or one of his followers discovered where they were. He couldn't risk her life.

"I'll just fix us something to eat."

She hurried out of the room. Rogar was left staring at the very opulent bedroom. There was a mirror above the bed. Why would anyone need a mirror above their bed? Earth people were strange.

Callie leaned against the wall so she could catch her breath. Rogar had said he wanted to mate with her. She trembled all the way down to her toes with need. When he'd spoken those words, a picture flashed across her mind of his naked body pressed against hers.

She tried to swallow, but couldn't, and finally pushed against the wall, and went to the kitchen. There were sodas in the refrigerator. She pulled one out, and popped the tab. As soon as it stopped fizzing, she brought it to her lips and took a long drink. The bubbles tickled her nose, but she was just grateful for something cold and wet.

There would be no mating, she thought to herself as she set the can on the counter. At least, not until his leg healed, and maybe not then. She would have to be careful to keep her distance. She was here to learn, to find her animal guide so she would have some measure of protection from Zerod. She had to keep Rogar at arm's length.

She rested her elbows on the counter and stared out the window into the woods behind the cabin. She was not in love with Rogar. It was only infatuation, temporary insanity, nothing more.

But he would be easy to fall in love with. He was really hot. And she'd never had sex like that before. Her nipples tightened just thinking about when they'd made love. A deep, yearning ache settled in her lower regions.

She quickly came back to her senses and pushed away from the counter when someone knocked on the door. With a deep sigh, she walked over. She'd wondered how long it would take for someone to stop by and see who was staying at the cabin. Instead of neighborhood watch, they should call these people neighborhood snoops. She pasted a fake smile on her face and opened the door.

"Yes?"

A tall, thin woman stood on the other side and with her was an equally tall, thin man.

"Oh, we expected the Jacksons." She raised a lofty eyebrow. "And you are?"

"Ms. Crane, don't tell me you don't remember me?"

The woman's brow knit.

"DeeDee's friend, Callie Jordon."

"Ohhh . . ." Her shoulders stiffened as though rigor mortis had set in. "I'm surprised that . . . uh . . ." Her look was more than a little condescending as her words trailed off.

"What? That they would let someone like me use their cabin?"

Ms. Crane's husband wore an expression similar to that of his wife. "Of course we weren't thinking that."

Callie hoped her smile was just as insincere as she felt right now. "Of course you wouldn't think that. Why that would make you both snobs, now wouldn't it? Forgive me if I gave that impression."

"Certainly." Ms. Crane sniffed. "It has been a long time since you've been here."

"Yes, it has."

She looked around the room. "And you brought a man with you. Did you get married?" she continued to grill.

Callie smiled. "No."

Her eyebrows shot up. "Oh, you're not married?"

"Callie, I thought I heard voices," Rogar said as he limped toward them.

Great, what was he doing up? He should be resting. She looked at the Cranes, who weren't even trying to hide their curiosity. More fodder for their tight little group. She'd bet they would run straight to everyone and have a field day telling them about how the Jacksons were letting just anyone, and everyone, stay at their cabin in their exclusive little resort. She wouldn't doubt they would have a get together to ban this from ever happening again.

Oh my God! What if she actually started dating one of their sons? Or befriending one of their daughters?

They were as bad as Zerod. It would seem she was considered just as impure here as she would be on New Symtaria.

"And you are?" Ms. Crane asked, looking down her very straight and narrow nose.

"Rogar Valkyir."

Their condescension didn't lessen, in fact, it seemed to increase. Callie realized it must be his accent and his name. Not only was he staying with Callie, but he was also a foreigner. Oh, they were going to have a good time relating the gossip they would gather today.

Rogar suddenly bowed at the waist. "Prince Rogar Valkyir, at your service."

The Cranes' mouths dropped open.

Callie could feel the color draining from her face. This was so not good.

Chapter 18

"You're a prince," Ms. Crane said, her hand fluttering to her chest.

"A prince?" Mr. Crane looked a little more skeptical than his wife.

"A small country." Rogar held out his hand to the other man.

Callie was grateful he'd at least said country, rather than telling them he was from another planet.

Mr. Crane hesitated, then apparently decided if Rogar were telling the truth, he didn't want to offend him. They shook hands. His gaze dropped to the medallion Rogar wore.

Rogar noticed his interest and looked down. "My family's crest. A trinket my mother insists I wear as the eldest child." He held it up for a moment. The sun caught the diamond and other stones, creating a prism of beautiful colors on the wall.

Oh, Lord, Rogar was playing his royal card.

"Can I see that?" Mr. Crane asked. "If you don't mind. I mean, it's very unusual."

"Of course." Rogar slipped the golden chain over his head, then handed it to Mr. Crane. Mr. Crane reached into his pocket and brought out his jeweler's loupe and closely examined the medallion.

Ms. Crane gave an embarrassed laugh. "My husband is in the jewelry business."

Rogar raised an imperial eyebrow. "Oh, he works for a living."

Ms. Crane's cheeks turned rosy red. Callie barely restrained her snort of laugher. It was about time Ms. Crane got a dose of her own medicine.

"Very unique," Mr. Crane mumbled as though he hadn't heard Rogar's remark. "The diamond is the most perfect I've ever seen. The clarity is outstanding. The other jewels are equally beautiful. It's probably worth millions." He slipped his loupe back in his pocket, and handed the medallion to Rogar. "Beautiful workmanship, Your Highness."

"Thank you."

Ms. Crane perked up when her husband called Rogar, Your Highness. Apparently, since he was wealthy, it stood to reason he would also be telling the truth about who he was, a blueblood like them, and worthy to be accepted into their ranks. It would seem she had forgiven him his earlier comment.

"We're having a dinner party of sorts tomorrow night if you'd like to come," Ms. Crane said, her gaze fixed on Rogar. Callie had no doubts the invitation did not include her.

Rogar put his arm around Callie and pulled her close to his side. "I'm afraid my fiancée and I won't be able to attend. We want to share this time together before we have to return to the castle."

Ms. Crane's eyes rounded. "Fiancée? Castle? Oh, my."

Callie was going to kill him.

"Maybe we can join you another time. I leave most social decisions to Callie, so check back with her. Now, if you'll excuse us."

"Certainly, Your Highness." They backed up, and Rogar shut the door in their face.

Callie heard Mr. Crane admonishing his wife for her nosiness, and Ms. Crane telling her husband it had been crude to examine the prince's medallion, then she asked if it was really genuine and worth millions.

Their voices drifted away as they got in their golf cart. As soon as it started, Mr. Crane floored it. Well, as much as you could speed away in a golf cart. Callie's ears were already burning.

She turned away from the window, planted her hands on her hips, and glared at Rogar. "What the hell did you think you were doing?"

"I heard them when they were talking to you. Even I could tell they weren't nice people. They needed to be put in their place. Aren't you happy I treated them as inferiors?"

"They deserved everything they got, but we're supposed to be keeping a low profile. They'll tell all their friends."

"We're safe from Zerod while we're here."

"Yes, but you just encountered a far worse predator—the Cranes. And how do you know about castles?"

"I looked up romance on my database on your birthday. Cinderella went to live in a castle with her Prince Charming."

He suddenly grimaced, reaching toward his injury.

Damn, what could she have been thinking? "We need to get you back in bed. Is the pain bad?"

"I can tolerate it."

She'd noted his hesitation so she was sure he must be in excruciating pain. "I told you, I don't need a hero, so quit coming to my rescue."

"Sometimes I think you are more in need of a hero than even you know."

"Well, you'd be wrong. I've been on my own for a long time. I work better without a partner."

"Then it's a good thing you have DeeDee. I'd hate to think you'd never had anyone to call friend."

"Only because I couldn't beat her off with a stick." The corners of her mouth turned down. DeeDee had come to her rescue, too, and then had hung around for the last ten years. She usually brought little care packages containing specialty foods, teas, and chocolates.

Wow, she must seem pretty pathetic to people.

"Like I said, I don't need a hero." She helped him onto the bed, and turned to leave, but he grabbed her arm.

"Don't go."

She hesitated. His hand was warm against hers. Maybe she needed the touch of another human being more than she had thought. But no, she couldn't stay. She felt vulnerable right now, and if she stayed . . . No, she couldn't.

"You said you wanted to learn more about New Symtaria, and how to protect yourself. We can start now." When she didn't say anything, he hurried on, "I'll go stir crazy alone in this room."

She knew the feeling. Sometimes she felt as though the four walls inside her house were closing in on her, and if she didn't get out, she would go bonkers. More times than not, she would find herself back at the zoo. Sheba was a great listener.

"Okay, I'll stay."

He scooted over, then patted the bed beside him. She laughed. "I don't think so Casanova." She dragged a comfy chair closer to the bed, and sat down, then saw that he held the small machine he called his database. When he looked at her, he was smiling.

"What?" she asked.

"Casanova?"

"What about it?"

"You think I'm the world's greatest lover. I accept your compliment." He bowed his head toward her.

"That's not what I meant! It was only an expression." Her brow furrowed. "He was also a womanizer."

Rogar raised the database again. "Yes, I see that now." He glanced at her. "You think that I would"—he looked again at the screen—"taste the charms of many women, never content with just one?"

She threw up her arms. "I didn't mean it literally."

"So you didn't enjoy when we mated."

"Yes, I did. Very much."

He smiled again. She could feel the heat rise up her face. "Could we just get started?" His gaze became more intense as it lingered on her. "Teaching me how to protect myself," she quickly added.

"If you're positive that's what you want to do."

"I am," she said, keeping her voice firm in case he thought otherwise.

He sighed. "I'm not sure where to begin."

"Why not start at the beginning, when you shipped my ancestors off to Earth." That had come out a little more sarcastic than she'd planned, but she felt as though their own people had dumped them. Much like she'd felt all those years at the orphanage.

He plumped a pillow and leaned back against the headboard. "I wasn't born yet, Callie, but I stand by what they had to do for survival. I wouldn't call it shipping them off, either, as much as I would say it was saving their lives, and the lives of others. They voluntarily decided to go."

"Why?"

"It was a dark time for our people. The planet was dying. The air had grown thick with poisonous gases. I've heard that staying outside without protection for any length of time could be lethal. The specialists conducted tests, and knew it was only a matter of time before the planet imploded.

"They took very little with them. There were only so many space crafts. They were lucky that everyone escaped."

"What happened to the planet?" she asked. "Did it die?"

"They say it did. Once I tried to find it using the old coordinates but there was nothing there, so maybe it did."

She leaned back in the chair and crossed her legs. "I can't imagine how that would feel. I mean, it would be hard leaving Earth in search of a new home, and knowing that the old one was dying."

"Sometimes change is good, though. The leaders found New Symtaria, and once again the air was clean and pure. There are oceans, like you have oceans on your planet. There are valleys, and mountains so high they are capped with deep snow."

"You know snow?"

"We have changes in climate, just as you."

"How many of my ancestors did they . . . volunteered to leave?"

He reached for his database. "We can look. Give me your finger."

Her gaze narrowed. "What are you going to do?"

"I won't hurt you. Trust me."

She wasn't so sure about trusting him. He was just too sexy. Okay, so maybe she trusted him, but maybe not so much herself.

She stood, walking nearer to the bed, and stuck her thumb out. When he reached for it, she jerked it back. "This won't hurt will it? I mean, you're not going to draw my blood or anything, are you? I hate needles." Yes, she was a coward, and she knew it.

"No, I'm just going to do a thumb analogy of your ancestry."

"You can do that? I mean, like looking at my family tree?"

"It's not that difficult."

He didn't know how hard she'd tried to find information on her birth mother, but to no avail. But now, he could tell her about some of her family. Did she want to know? They could be mass murderers. Or like Zerod, for all she knew.

"It will be okay, Callie."

She studied his face for a moment and saw the truth of his words. Maybe she would only discover they were animal keepers or something mundane. Oh, what the hell. She stuck out her hand.

He pressed her thumb down on the screen. "That should do it." He punched in numbers. "Here it is."

She leaned closer, as he turned the screen toward her. Staring back at her was an older version of herself. The woman had the same color eyes, even the same smile. Wrinkles lined her face, but it was almost as though she could feel the woman's warmth reaching out to her. Shock washed over her. She gasped, and took a step back, as tears filled her eyes.

"You didn't tell me the database would do that. You didn't warn me. I thought it was going to be a name or something." She turned and ran out of the room, not stopping until she stood in the kitchen. She took deep breaths as she tried to slow her pounding heart.

Rogar came up from behind, and wrapped his arms around her. "What is it? What did I do? Please, know that I would never hurt you."

She sniffed, then turned and buried her face against his chest. She immediately felt peace as she leaned against him. "I didn't expect to see a picture. It was just a shock, I guess. For so long I've wanted to feel a connection to someone. Even if that someone was already gone."

"I'm sorry," he whispered, brushing his hands over her hair.

"Oh, no, don't be. You've given me a wonderful gift."

"I just never realized how much it would mean to you, or I would have shown you sooner. Forgive me for not thinking."

He'd apologized for being a man. She smiled. "It was just the surprise of seeing her picture. We look a lot alike. Who was she?"

"According to the database, she was your grandmother." He pushed a button and handed the device to her. "Just touch the screen and slide your finger to scroll through what it has to say about her. I'll be in the bedroom when you're ready to continue."

"Thank you." She was glad he was giving her this time alone to read about her grandmother.

As soon as he left, she went to the sofa and curled up. For a moment, she just stared at her grandmother's image. The eyes seemed to be smiling back at her. Callie instinctively knew she would have liked her a lot.

With a sigh, she began to scroll down, reading the history of her grandmother. It told about her grandparents, and their parents. How her grandmother had taught others how to connect with their guide. Then her husband had died. That was why she'd volunteered to travel to Earth with her daughter.

Her grandmother had been excited about her journey. It still must have been hard to travel to a new place. Callie admired her grandmother's courage.

It's inside you as well. The same blood runs through your veins that ran through hers.

"Who are you?" she whispered.

Silence.

Had that been her spirit guide talking to her? But if it was, then why didn't the guide just tell her?

God, this was so damned frustrating. She felt as though she was being pulled into so many different directions. She'd wanted a background, a history, but she'd gotten more than she'd bargained for.

Aliens, her father brutally murdered, someone trying to kill her, a mother who might still be alive. An animal guide.

Or was the voice in her head just a sign of insanity?

Maybe none of this was real.

She jumped off the sofa and went to the window. The sun was shining. A couple of golf carts passed. Callie noticed they slowed just a little as they drove by.

Everything appeared peaceful, serene, but she knew somewhere out there a man wanted her dead because her blood wasn't pure enough to suit him.

What would happen if she opened the door and left? Just got into DeeDee's Hummer and took off. Not tell anyone where she was going. Rogar had cash. She could take it and sneak away. It would be enough to start a new life.

That was probably what her mother had done. Left Callie at the orphanage, then took off to God knew where, hoping like hell she could escape Zerod and save her child in the process.

Could Callie give everything up and assume another name? Always looking over her shoulder?

There was another solution, though. Fight back. She squared her shoulders and marched toward the bedroom, picking up Rogar's database as she walked by.

She kind of liked the idea of fighting back. Could she beat Zerod in a one on one? Probably not, but she'd studied tigers enough that she knew a lot about their habits. She wouldn't be going into this blind. Besides, she had good motivation— revenge. If he hadn't murdered her father, then she might have had a normal childhood. Zerod stole that from her.

It was payback time.

Chapter 19

Rogar raised his eyebrows as Callie marched into the bedroom, and silently breathed a sigh of relief. He'd been afraid she would walk out the door, get in her friend's vehicle, and drive away.

Callie's world had been turned upside down over the last few days. It was a lot to take in. All her beliefs had been challenged. But looking at her now, it would seem she was ready to fight back. There was a very determined set to her jaw.

"What do I need to do?" she asked, raising her chin a fraction.

He smiled. She was feisty. He liked her determination and attitude. Maybe her animal guide was a wolf. One of his brothers had a wolf guide. They were both very tenacious when they set their path in a certain direction.

"You need to understand your animal guide before you can connect with her." He finally told her. "Until that part of you is awakened, you are not complete. You've heard her, I'm sure."

Her expression changed to confusion. She sat back down in the chair. "I started hearing a voice when I was about eight." She looked down at her hands, twining her fingers together. "I told the head mistress. They sent me to a doctor. He asked all kinds of questions, then told the head mistress I had created an imaginary friend, which wasn't unusual. Ms. Barry said I'd better be careful telling anyone because they might think I was crazy and lock me away.

"I stopped listening to the voice because I'd heard older girls talking about the insane asylum. I didn't want to end up locked away. Eventually, I stopped hearing the voice."

Rogar gritted his teeth. It was a wonder Callie had survived not connecting with her guide. There had been instances that he knew about when a Symtarian chose not to acknowledge their guide, but it hadn't ended well. They were like lost souls wandering through life with nowhere to go. The loneliness had to have been unbearable. He sighed. Maybe it had been different for her because she was part Earthling.

"Can we find her?" She raised her head, met his eyes.

He didn't know, not positively, but he couldn't tell her that. He couldn't take away the hope he saw in her eyes. Besides, she might still find her guide. "It may take awhile, but yes, we'll find her."

"Sometimes I think I hear her talking to me, but then other times, I think it's my own thoughts."

That was a good sign. "She may be trying to protect herself. You can choose not to accept her. She may be afraid of scaring you in that direction."

"Then what do I need to do to find her again?"

He swung his legs over the side of the bed, and began to pace as he thought.

"Deep meditation. There are rituals that can be performed. They are very old and were once practiced in ancient times when it wasn't as easy for our people to connect with our guides.

"For centuries, our guides hid from us because they were afraid. As the years passed, they learned to trust, and our souls merged. I'll see if the information is stored in the database." He stopped pacing, and noticed she was staring at him. "What?" Had she changed her mind?

"Your leg. You're not limping."

He'd forgotten that he was supposed to be injured. He

might as well tell her the truth. "Symtarians heal quickly. I believe my leg is better." Not exactly the truth, but close enough.

She came to her feet, crossing her arms in front of her. "And how long has it been healed?"

He could continue to hedge. From the expression on her face, it might be prudent if he did, but she would eventually discover the truth. "Since this morning."

"This morning?"

"Yes."

"Why did you pretend it was still bothering you?"

He walked closer, his steps slow and purposeful. His eyes held an intensity that she had seen before. Her body tingled to awareness.

He stopped a mere breath away from her. "I enjoyed the way you hovered over me. It was stupid, I apologize, but I liked having you near me."

Something inside her began to crumble, maybe because she knew exactly what he was feeling. She'd been denied so many things in her lifetime, why should she deny herself the time that she could spend with Rogar. Yes, he would leave her, go back to New Symtaria, but damn it, she was going to take pleasure in what he so willingly offered.

"Kiss me," she said before she could chicken out.

"What?"

"Kiss me. Please."

He growled from low in his throat before pulling her against him and lowering his mouth to hers. She sighed, knowing she needed this as much as Rogar.

She was bolder than she'd ever been, stroking his tongue with hers, tasting him. She reached between them and began to unbutton his shirt, but her fingers fumbled in her haste.

Hell, he had plenty of money, even if it was counterfeit. He could buy a new shirt. She jerked, buttons popped, pinging on the hardwood floor as they landed. Then she was touching him, feeling his sinewy muscles, kneading his flesh.

How long had she dreamed of this? But she knew the answer. Since the first night they'd made love. She'd wanted him so badly her body had ached for more, but she'd refused to give in to her cravings. No more.

She shoved his shirt off his shoulders, her fingers lightly scraping down his back. He moaned, then nudged her away. She whimpered, but when he grabbed the hem of her T-shirt, her pulse sped up.

Slowly, he pulled it up, pressing the material against her breasts, over her already sensitive nipples. She gasped, but it was lost in the cotton material as he pulled it over her head. He let it fall to the floor, then reached behind her and unhooked her bra. Embarrassment flooded her. She'd never made love in the light of day. She covered her breasts as he tugged her bra off.

"Why do you shield yourself? I won't hurt you."

"No, it's not that." She was going to die of embarrassment right here, right now. When DeeDee and her parents came to the cabin, they would find her lifeless body decaying on their beautiful hand-hewn wood floor.

"Then what is it?" He lightly stroked her arms.

She swallowed hard, then looked at her feet. All the boldness from a moment ago had disappeared. "I've never been naked in front of a man in daylight. I mean, I'm not a virgin or anything." Her brow knit. "But, of course, you already know that. It's just that . . ."

"You're very beautiful. I love looking at your body. You are like the goddess Aricepta."

"You have a goddess?"

"We have many gods and goddesses that we worship. Aricepta is the goddess of beauty—you have been touched by her hand."

"I have?"

He gently tugged away her hands. Her face was so warm that she was afraid it would start glowing any second. But she didn't cover herself again.

"Your breasts are perfect. High-pointed, with dusky nipples. I love running my tongue over them, sucking them into my mouth."

She trembled, the ache between her legs grew stronger. He brushed his fingers across one taut nipple. She sucked in her bottom lip, arching toward him.

"I like seeing the need on your face. It matches the one I also feel inside me." He took her hand and placed it over his erection.

She lightly squeezed, he sucked in a breath.

She'd never really looked at a naked man. At least, not up close. DeeDee had stuck a magazine of sexy naked men in one of her so-called care baskets to Callie, then called her up to ask what she'd thought. Callie had reprimanded her, then mentioned she'd thought the pictures were . . . uh . . . enhanced, but right now, she was thinking maybe not.

Looking at pictures, covertly looking at Rogar when he'd been naked, was just not enough. She wanted more. Maybe it was time she became more assertive. She unfastened his pants, then tugged the zipper down, letting his slacks slide down his muscular thighs, and onto the floor. He stood there before her in only his briefs.

She glanced down. That was a really big bulge, but then she already knew he was built rather large. Oh, Lord, just thinking about him buried deep inside her made her want him all the more.

"Your turn," he said.

"I'm not finished. You still have your briefs on." She reached for the waistband."

He grabbed her hands. "Your pants next."

She stepped closer, letting her nipples graze the hair on his chest. "Don't you want me to touch you? To run my fingers over your swollen penis." Had she really said that? She had, and it felt damned good, as though she were superwoman—powerful and strong.

"You first."

He tweaked her nipple and spasms of pleasure swept through

her. Rogar had found her kryptonite. She guessed it didn't make any difference if she removed her pants. They would both be naked in a few minutes anyway.

She stepped back. "You win."

He smiled.

"This time."

His smile dropped, but then she thought he wasn't paying a whole lot of attention to what she was saying as she slid her sweats down, ever so slowly. The way she thought a stripper might perform. Then all of a sudden, she didn't feel quite so shy. She wanted to turn him on with her body.

When they were around her ankles she kicked them away, then slid her fingers under the waistband of her panties. She slowly lowered them, then halfway down, lost her nerve. Maybe it was the way he was looking at her. There was so much need in his expression.

"Don't stop," he said, words husky, but to ease her fears, he hooked his thumbs into the waistband of his briefs and tugged then downward.

Her mouth went dry. He was big, and this time she wasn't looking away. When she reached to take him in her hand, he stopped her. Turnabout was fair play, she supposed. She removed her panties, kicking them out of the way.

"Magnificent," he breathed.

She blushed, and looked away as she felt the heat crawl up her face . . . again. She was being ridiculous. It wasn't like there was anything majorly wrong with her body. She was a size six.

She let her gaze roam from his head downward. Broad shoulders, six pack abs, tanned—and no lines that she could see, and she looked closely.

But her gaze slowed when she came to his erection. Now that was magnificent. Thick, sensuous, made to give a woman pleasure. Made to make her cry out in ecstasy. She'd already experienced firsthand how it had felt to have him inside her, and it had been wonderful.

Her gaze rose, meeting his eyes. "You're not bad your-self." This time when she reached toward him, he didn't stop her. Good thing, too, because they would've had to have a se-rious talk if he'd stopped her exploration of his body.

She encircled him, and slowly slid down the foreskin. He jumped. She jerked her hand away. "I'm sorry. Did I hurt you?"

He took her hand and put it back on him. "It felt good. Don't stop."

Tentatively, she rubbed her thumb across the tip of his penis. It felt different than what she'd expected: soft, rub-bery, and a little damp. She watched his expression. His eyes were closed and his breathing ragged.

She reached lower with her free hand and cupped his balls, then began to lightly massage. When he groaned, she knew whatever she was doing, she must be doing right. Only prob-lem was, she was getting even more turned on just watching him. And she wanted more.

Leaning forward, she licked across one tight nipple. He sucked in a breath. She gave as much attention to the other one.

More. She wanted more, but before she could figure out exactly what she wanted, he placed his hands on either side of her head, and brought his mouth down to hers.

She tasted his need as his tongue aggressively explored her mouth. Then his hands were sliding down her back, she wrapped her arms around his neck, drawing him closer. He cupped her butt, pulling her against him. This was good. Right there. He'd found the spot that needed scratching.

She couldn't stand much more. She thought she might burst into flames any moment. She stepped away and quickly went to the suitcase. More heat flooded her face when she pulled out a handful of condoms.

DeeDee made sure she had plenty since Callie had forgot-ten to pack any. She grabbed one, ripping it open as she hurried back to Rogar. Her hands trembled, but he let her roll it down his length. God, she liked how he felt.

Rogar picked her up and slid into her. She gasped with pleasure as he slowly began to fill her. She tightened her arms around his neck. No one had ever made her feel this way.

She clenched her inner muscles. He cried out and drove deeper.

"More," she said.

He thrust inside her.

Faster. Harder.

She tightened her legs around his waist.

He thrust again and again.

Faster. Harder.

Yes, this is what had been missing from her life. It felt so good. He slid in, then slid out. Stroking her, filling her completely.

Her body felt as though it was on fire as the heat inside her began to build. Higher and higher.

"Now," she cried. "Oh, God, now!" Her body tightened, convulsing into spasms of pleasure.

Rogar growled from low in his throat, then flung his head back as he came. The growl became a roar, and then they were both falling on the bed, their ragged breathing filling the room. She couldn't talk, she couldn't think. Not that she wanted to.

He moved, and her body jerked and quivered again. She grasped his shoulders then relaxed. That had been so good. No, better than good. It had been fantastic. Better than even the last time. It had been . . .

Rogar suddenly pulled away from her, rolling onto his back. His arms stiffened as he stretched out, then curled into a ball.

What the hell was happening?

A gentle fog drifted across the room. Crap!

He was shifting form again. She scrambled out of bed and aimed toward the bathroom, then remembered the last time, and how uncomfortable it had been sleeping in the tub, and made an abrupt about-face.

She firmly shut the door and ran naked into DeeDee's bedroom, slamming the door behind her when she heard the deep purr of the jag. She leaned against the door and took deep breaths until her head stopped spinning.

Then she frowned. This was so going to have to stop. Not the sex part. That had been great. But cuddling with a black jaguar was not on her list of things to do. Sure, she loved the big cats, but snuggling with one—she wasn't that naïve.

She walked to the closet and flung the door open. At least DeeDee had left clothes. Her friend's taste usually leaned more toward the provocative, though. Rogar should love that since she didn't have much of a choice. Her suitcase was in the other bedroom.

Callie grabbed underclothes, a pair of shorts, and red T-shirt that she was certain would show most of her midriff, then headed for DeeDee's bathroom.

Yep, this could get old in a hurry. She was thoughtful as she walked into the bathroom. Maybe it wasn't too bad. The alternative was really bad sex, then snuggling with someone who snored or had bad breath, or worse, both.

Maybe she could put up with not snuggling.

She smiled as she turned on the shower. She had a feeling she could put up with just about anything, as long as Rogar made her feel like he had a little while ago.

She stepped under the spray, marveling that her body was still so sensitive. The water lightly pelting her nipples made her want to have sex again. She squirted gel on her washcloth, thinking that she and Rogar would definitely need to have a long talk when he shifted back to human form.

A long talk, then maybe more sex. Her smile was very self-satisfied.

Chapter 20

Rogar stretched and yawned, then looked around. For a moment, he didn't know where he was, then it all came back to him.

"Damn," he muttered as he swung his legs over the side of the bed and sat up.

You've been using that word a lot, Balam said. *What does it mean?*

I'm not exactly sure. It wasn't in the database. It's a curse of sorts, from what I gather.

You curse me? It's certainly not my fault you get so . . . involved emotionally that you change form.

I'm not cursing you, he said as he came to his feet and went into the bathroom. He marched over to the tub. Empty. He walked out, looking around. *Okay, where is she?*

She left.

Rogar quickly pulled on his slacks, his heart thundering inside his chest.

Your heart is pounding rather fast. Are you all right, Rogar?

I'm fine. I just need to find Callie.

She means that much to you?

He raked his fingers through his hair. *Yes, she does.*

Could she be your lifemate?

It doesn't matter if she is or not, if I can't convince her to travel to New Symtaria, now does it? And if I keep changing form, she'll be too scared to go anywhere with me.

They say some Symtarians go crazy if they don't have their lifemate with them.

Thanks so much for reminding me.

This affects me as well as it does you. I certainly don't want to end up like Zerod. You'll have to convince her to stay with you.

He left the bedroom and started down the hall. *And how do you propose I do that?*

You have to introduce us.

Seriously?

I won't eat her, sarcasm dripped from his words.

I don't know. But it was an idea. If Callie met one on one with Balam, she wouldn't be so terrified. She already loved the cats—as long as they were behind bars. *I'll think about it.*

Rogar walked down the hall, and opened a door. It had a bed in it, but the room was empty. There was an open door inside the room that he assumed led to another bathroom. He could hear Callie mumbling, and breathed a sigh of relief. A few moments later, she walked out, not noticing he was in the room. She was trying to tie her shirt just below her breasts.

"This is scandalous. I can't go around wearing this. I'd get arrested," she mumbled. "I look like what's-her-face from *The Dukes of Hazzard*. Verrry slutty."

Rogar leaned against the door facing, crossing his arms. He liked what she was wearing. The undergarment she wore pushed her breasts up, and the top she had on was cut low enough that the curves were exposed. A great deal of her abdomen showed, too.

Then she faced away from him. The shorts were cut high, and exposed just a little of the cheeks of her butt, enough that he was starting to react.

She turned, and screamed.

He straightened. "I'm sorry, did I frighten you?"

"What do you think?" She planted her hands on her hips.

His gaze slowly roamed over her. "I think I want to scoop you into my arms and carry you back to bed so we can mate again."

"I . . . uh . . ." She shook her head. "We cannot lie around and make love all the time."

"Why not? Don't you like mating with me?"

"Of course I do . . . Wait, we've already had this conversation before. I'm here to learn everything I can about New Symtaria, and my animal guide, so I can protect myself if I have to."

"Then we will mate tonight, after we go to bed."

"I . . . uh . . . need to get my own clothes. DeeDee's are too revealing."

She started to walk past, but he took her arm and pulled her against him, brushing the back of his hand over her breasts. She looked into his eyes, and for a moment, he saw passion flare.

But she was right, he needed to teach her everything he could, just in case she had to defend herself someday. There was one thing he did want.

"Don't change. I'll be the only one you see today."

She swallowed hard, then nodded.

"Let's get started." He wondered why he'd asked her not to change. The temptation would be excruciating. But sweet just the same.

"Not in there," she said as he started into the bedroom.

He smiled. "I can make love to you in any room, *la seba*. It does not have to be just in the bedroom."

"La Seba?"

"Sex goddess."

"Living room," she choked out.

"Then I will join you in a moment," he said before going into the bedroom.

Callie continued on to the living room, but after a few moments, she wondered what exactly he could be plotting now.

She strode to the bedroom door. No Rogar. Could he disappear, as well?

When she moved across the room, she heard the shower running in the bathroom. For a moment, she pictured him standing beneath the spray, water cascading over his sinewy muscles.

A swirl of heat spiraled downward, settling between her legs. What would happen if she opened the bathroom door and walked inside, taking off her clothes as she went? She snorted. As if she didn't know the answer to that one.

She clamped her legs together as a familiar ache began to build inside her. She jumped when the shower stopped and she hurried out of the room.

Her cell phone was on the counter ringing and vibrating all over the place like a really pissed-off bumble bee. She ran over and picked it up, flipping it open at the same time.

"Yes?"

"Callie, DeeDee. I just wanted to make sure you made it to the cabin okay."

"Yes, no problem whatsoever."

"You sound out of breath."

Silence.

"I hope you're staying in my parents' room," DeeDee said. "I really don't want that visual."

"So you told me," Callie interrupted. Now might be a good time to change the subject. "And you? Did you join your mom and dad?"

"I'll be there in about an hour. It was a boring plane ride, but I'm in a rented car now. How'd the cabin look?"

"Fine. The Cranes have already stopped by."

"Bleh! Nosey snobs."

Her feelings exactly. "I'm afraid Rogar took offense with their snobby attitude, and told them he was a prince. I just hope his admission doesn't come back to haunt us."

"I doubt it will. No one would ever find you there. If they do, then sic the Cranes on them."

"That's an idea."

"You take care, and if you need anything at all, I'm only a phone call away."

"DeeDee?"

"Yeah, sweetie?"

"Thanks. I don't know what I did to deserve you, but I'll be eternally grateful."

"Ahh, Callie, someday you're going to realize that I needed you just as much as you needed me. You're the one friend I know who treats me like a real person." There was a distinct sniffle. "You just make that big alien take care of you."

"I will." She slowly closed the phone, then looked up. Sensing he was in the room. He had a presence about him that called everyone's attention.

He'd changed clothes and wore a pair of dark brown slacks, and a casual hunter green top. He looked so delicious she could eat him up. Now that was a thought.

"If you keep looking at me like that, we might be in trouble."

She cleared her throat. "Do you want something to drink?" She hurried behind the bar, and opened the refrigerator. She got out a soda.

"That sounds good."

She set a couple of them on the counter. When she covertly glanced his way, she saw he was still watching her. If he kept this up, she'd be the one jumping his bones. She turned her back to him, and began to rummage in the cabinets. A sigh of relief escaped. This was exactly what she was looking for—junk food. The cure-all for not having sex.

She loaded her arms down with tortilla chips, bean dip, salsa, and chocolate cream-filled cookies, then managed to carry it all to the table without dropping anything. He brought the sodas. They each pulled out a chair.

But they couldn't live on junk food alone. Not and keep up their strength so before she took her seat, she grudgingly cooked them each a grilled cheese sandwich.

"Okay, tell me when you first knew about your animal guide," she said, after she set their plates on the table. She ripped open the bag of chips, then removed the lids from the dips. He followed her example and opened the cookies, but when he reached for one, she took it away. "Sandwich first. Chips and dip. Then cookies."

"Why? These look better."

"I cook a mean grilled cheese, I'll have you know. Besides, the bean dip has protein, and the salsa has veggies . . ." She held a chip up and studied it. "And the chips have corn."

He pointed toward the cookies. "And those?"

"Sugar and chocolate. They're for after a meal."

He nodded, followed her lead, and dipped a chip into the bean dip. He took a bite, then slowly chewed. "I like it."

Great, she was getting him hooked on junk food. "Do you have stuff like this on New Symtaria?"

"We have better, but this will do."

She rolled her eyes. "Of course." Bet they didn't have chocolate. They ate in silence for a few minutes.

She moved a chip around on her plate. "Were you scared when you found out you shared your body with an animal?" she finally asked.

"I knew about my guide from the instructions that we are taught. It did take me a while to distinguish between my own thoughts and that of my guide. It was as though we hadn't formed the separation that was needed."

"How old were you?"

"Ten years."

"I was eight when I started hearing the voice. What did you do?"

"I listened. I asked questions. At some point we began to make the distinction between our personalities."

She slid the chip through the dip, but didn't take a bite. "What's your guide like? I mean, you say he has his own personality."

Rogar leaned back in his chair, his forehead wrinkling in thought. "Balam? He's aggressive, like most animal guides."

"Unless you're a rabbit," she said with more than a touch of sarcasm.

"True."

Great, he didn't tell her that the rabbit might not be her guide, but then again, which would she rather be? A rabbit or a rhino? She thought the rabbit would be better.

"Balam has also been a good friend and protector."

"Balam," she repeated. "I like his name. Can you feel him inside you? Does he understand what I'm saying?"

"Everything."

Heat flooded her face. "What about when we . . . uh . . ." This was so embarrassing.

"When we make love?"

She nodded.

"Balam is like a shadow when we are in human form. You would not be embarrassed with thoughts in your head," he said, guessing her dilemma.

Since he put it that way, she guessed it wouldn't be the same, but there was still a lingering feeling that she was in the middle of a ménage à trios.

"He wants to meet you."

Her head jerked up. "Meet me?"

"Yes."

"Me? In the same room with a jaguar. I mean, you said you both had distinct personalities. What if he decides to eat me?"

"He won't."

"You're sure."

"I'm almost positive."

She leaned back, crossing her arms in front of her. "Almost is not the same as positive."

"I trust him." He sighed. "I thought you wanted to work with the big cats?"

She jumped up, and walked to the window. "I do, but my training taught me that even if you love something, even if it's a beautiful animal, that doesn't mean it isn't dangerous." She turned from the window and met his gaze. "Leaning on the side of caution is always a wise choice."

But how many times had she yearned to reach out and pet Sheba. There was something about the cat that made her want to get closer. It could be her Symtarian side that felt such an affinity for all animals.

And then again, maybe she should just stay in the petting zoo. The animals there were harmless, and she could cuddle most of them.

"Another time then," Rogar said, breaking into her thoughts.

She didn't want to tell him by the time their relationship got to that point, it would probably be time for him to leave, and it wouldn't matter anymore. But she didn't want to think about that. It hurt too much.

So, she squared her shoulders and faced him. "How do I find my guide? You said there were ceremonies?"

He reached in his pocket and brought out his database. "Let me see what I can find out about them."

She sat down again, watching as he typed in letters. She'd come to the realization his database was just like a mini-computer, and stored just about as much information, except she was positive Rogar would tell her that his system was better.

"Here it is."

She watched the different expressions on his face. When he finally looked up, she was almost certain she didn't want to go through any changing ceremony.

Chapter 21

"I'm telling you the truth. That is what the database says to do," Rogar told Callie, then handed the device to her so she could read for herself.

Callie didn't believe him for a second. She jerked the database from him, and quickly read what was on the screen. Okay, so maybe he had been telling the truth, but was the information accurate? "Is this on the level?"

"I promise. The database wouldn't have false information."

Her eyes narrowed. His expression was bland. Were his eyes twinkling? She couldn't be sure. But if it really did work, wouldn't it be worth trying? It might just save her life. "And you're sure this will work?"

"No."

"I'm supposed to get naked during a full moon, outside, and chant these words while you smear a concoction of questionable ingredients over my body, and you're not even sure it will work?"

"The old leaders must have participated in the rituals or it wouldn't be in the database."

"Were the leaders men?"

"It's a very solemn occasion."

"Unless I get arrested, and believe me, these people here would like nothing better than to see me carted off to jail." Now she knew his eyes were twinkling. "It's not funny."

He quickly sobered. "Of course not."

She marched over to the desk that was inset next to the cabinets, and opened a drawer. Callie couldn't believe she was even considering this. She rifled through the loose papers until she found a calendar, then flipped the pages, looking for the next full moon.

She put the calendar back, and shut the drawer. "The full moon isn't until next week. I'll just have to try to connect before then."

Aww, she had so wanted to go through with the ceremony—not! Tropical scented lotion rubbed on her skin, sure. But what the hell was a mangus root? Did she even want to know? It sounded nasty. If she didn't make the connection, she still might have to go through the ceremony, though. Eww . . .

She squared her shoulders. "What do I need to do, other than a ceremony, to connect with my animal guide?"

"There is something else we can try." He stood, took her hands, and led her to the middle of the living room. "Sit." He motioned to the floor.

She did as he said, crossing her legs in front of her. He did the same, only a few inches separating them.

"Now, close your eyes."

She closed them.

"Empty your mind."

She rolled her shoulders, then let her mind empty. She wouldn't think of anything. Not one thing. She wouldn't even think about not thinking about anything. She would just let her mind empty.

She inhaled, then exhaled.

The cabin was kind of musty smelling. She should open some windows and let it air out. Maybe light some candles. DeeDee's mom always had candles on hand. She was afraid there would be a power outage, and she'd be caught in the dark.

Mrs. Jackson always bought those soy candles. Callie loved

them because the scent seemed to last longer, as well as the candle. She would have to ask DeeDee where her mother had bought the ones she used.

If they didn't cost too much, that is. Mrs. Jackson had really expensive tastes. And why not, she and her husband made oodles of money. If Callie had that much money, she would splurge on expensive candles, and clothes, lots of bling-bling, and nice vacations.

Ahh, vacations. It would be nice to take one.

DeeDee's parents were probably excited their daughter was joining them. Colorado must be nice in the fall. DeeDee once told her the water was clear and unpolluted, and you could see sparkles of gold.

"I don't think you've emptied your mind," Rogar said.

She jumped and opened her eyes. Guilty as charged. It wasn't as easy as he'd made it sound. "How can I empty my mind if you keep talking?

"You have to concentrate on breathing, and let everything else go. When you are able to do that, you'll find your animal guide."

"Okay. Okay." She closed her eyes. She really wanted to find her guide. She vaguely remembered the voice from so long ago. When she had felt lonely and unloved, the voice would soothe away her fears.

What would her guide be? Not a bunny or rhino. No, more like an exotic horse. Yes. She liked that idea. A horse. She'd always wanted a pony. She'd gone on a field trip once and they let her pet a pony. The pony had been gray, with faded white spots on her butt. There had been lots of other horses there, too. She remembered it as though it was yesterday.

A familiar feeling began to wash over her. She moaned, stretching her arms out and reaching toward something . . . something . . .

"Callie!"

She curled into a ball as fog filled the room. The pain wasn't as bad. Not so much like the burning sensation of the last two times. Her arms no longer felt like her arms, nor did her legs feel like her legs.

Her limbs began to stretch, the changes happening inside her, as well as outside. Sweat dotted her forehead, and it was hard to breathe.

Then nothing again. Rogar was right when he said it was like Balam was a shadow. Only she was the shadow. She opened her eyes and blinked, then looked around. Rogar stood in front of her, and she was almost even with his chest.

"You were supposed to empty your mind, not think of an animal."

Had she become the sleek horse she'd been thinking about? She wasn't sure. She had a feeling this wasn't her animal guide, though. The connection that Rogar had talked about wasn't there. It was more like she'd borrowed the animal's body.

Well, she wanted to see. She turned and walked toward the bedroom, where there was a full-length mirror. It sounded like hooves walking across the hardwood floor. Did Rogar find her exotic?

She had a little trouble turning the corner but made it inside, and by then, she wasn't sure she really wanted to look. At least, she knew she wasn't a rhino or she would've taken down half the wall. Try explaining that to DeeDee's parents.

Okay, might as well do this. And then she was looking at herself. Oh, great, this was just great! What, did someone not like her? She'd been thinking about a horse, not a donkey.

She moved a little to the right. Could she at least shift into an animal with a smaller ass—no pun intended? Her ears had to be at least a foot and a half long.

Rogar stepped into her line of vision. Great. She opened her mouth to tell him what she thought about shapeshifting, "Hee-hawwwww." She quickly closed her mouth.

He laughed.

How could he laugh at her? It was so demeaning. He came closer, patting her on the neck.

"I told you that you might experience many animals before you connect with your guide."

She turned her head, nipping at his hand, but he was too fast and moved out of the way, which was probably a good thing since she was a little long in the tooth. She might have done some serious damage.

Oh, God, she had buck teeth.

"Just think about your human side," he told her.

He didn't have to tell her twice. She closed her eyes and concentrated on what it would be like to walk in the woods behind the cabin, or swim in the manmade lake. When she had come the last time with DeeDee, Callie had really enjoyed those activities.

The country club was another story. That had been pure torture. The people there had made her feel like a lower class citizen. The longer the night had progressed, the more depressed she'd gotten.

"Are you concentrating?"

She took a deep breath and closed her eyes. Rogar was right, she needed to learn how to concentrate. She thought of herself standing in front of a mirror, rather than the donkey.

In her mind's eye, she saw herself pulling on a pair of size six jeans—easily pulling them on over her small, tight butt.

The fog rolled across the room and the change began. She took a deep breath, then exhaled as the familiar ache began inside her. She stretched out, then curled inside herself. The burning sensation came, and with it darkness. It almost seemed as though she floated through space while the change took place.

"Callie?"

She blinked, then opened her eyes. When she looked at her hands, she saw she was back in her own body. "Please tell me that wasn't my animal guide."

"When you connect with your animal guide, it will feel totally different from anything else, as though you're sharing each other's bodies and minds. There will be a separation, but a connection as well."

"I'm not sure I like the idea of someone living inside of me—besides me."

"That is why you have not made the connection. Your guide is frightened."

"Of me?"

He nodded. "When your guide first began to speak to you, and you told others, they sent you to a doctor. You made the decision to stop listening, and pushed your guide away."

"But now I'm not."

"The guide was smart and stayed dormant most of the time. When you had a strong feeling about something, your guide gently led you in the right direction.

"The power is in you to reject the guide. You are old enough to consciously make that decision. That is why she's afraid to join completely. If you get scared, you can choose to live without her."

"What happens to her? I mean, if say I don't want to share my body?"

"She will die."

Oh, that was nice. She would be a murderer. "Has anyone ever done that?"

"A few."

A cold chill swept over her. Damn, she'd forgotten she was naked. As if he sensed her discomfiture, he walked to the window, keeping his back toward her. She started to retrieve the clothes she had on earlier, but changed her mind at the last minute, and grabbed sweats and clean underclothes out of her bag, and quickly dressed.

"You can turn around."

Rogar looked disappointed when he faced her. Too bad. She was not going to make this a love nest when she was on a mission.

"I liked the other clothes."

"I'm sure you did, but this is me. I like comfort." And these clothes made her feel less sexy, less horny. No wonder DeeDee had sex on the brain.

"You look cute in those, too," he said after taking a full minute to study her.

"Yeah, right."

He nodded. "Because I know what lies beneath the clothes."

Only Rogar could make her feel sexy wearing baggy sweats. "Okay, how do I make my animal guide trust me?"

"Talk to her."

"Talk to her?" Yeah, right. Did he really expect her to go around talking to her invisible friend? That's pretty much what she would be doing.

"We could always try the ritual."

He sounded too eager. "Okay, I'll talk to myself, but not in front of you." She didn't want to look any more like a fool than she had to.

"I'll leave then."

"That would be great." Then she thought about him wandering around the camp. Not a good idea. "On second thought, I'll leave. You stay inside."

"It might help if you were nearer the goddess who created the animals. I saw woods behind the house. That would be a good place to connect with your guide."

"Do you have a lot of deities on New Symtaria?"

"We have many. We pay homage to them at different festivals. Everyone in the nearby dwellings share food, and there are games. The people enjoy it very much."

"It sounds like fun."

"You could find out for yourself. Come back with me. We are good together."

She shook her head. "This is my home. I worked hard to get through college. It took me longer than some because I didn't have a lot of money, but I made it. I can't throw that all away."

"I understand wanting something very badly."

She had a feeling he was talking about her, but he only needed her so he could complete his mission. Yeah, the sex was great, but it wasn't as though he would want her all the time once he returned home.

"I won't be gone long," she said. She walked through the house, and out the back door.

As she left, she wondered what it would be like to have someone want her all the time. She used to imagine having loving parents, and maybe a couple of sisters or brothers. They could've played together, and even had a few fights, but there would've been a bond that held true.

But then, not all families were fairy tales. She'd come to the conclusion that most were dysfunctional. DeeDee had once told her that her aunt and mother had stopped talking years ago. So maybe families weren't that great.

She stepped out of the clearing and past the trees. She and DeeDee had actually explored these woods. The golf course was on the other side.

Callie walked about halfway between the golf course and the house, saw a tree that had fallen, and made herself comfortable on it. Meditating didn't really work for her so she decided to just talk, as Rogar had suggested. But what should she say?

It had been a long time since she'd actually heard the voice. Her imaginary friend, as the doctor had called her guide. If he'd only known. But the voice had seemed like a friend. Her only real one, besides Alma. Alma had been adopted so that hadn't lasted long.

Callie thought back, trying to remember what it had felt like. Rogar was right when he said she would know when her animal guide connected. The voice inside her had been different.

"I remember you," she finally said, closing her eyes so she could concentrate better. "You came to me when I was all alone, and had no one else. We were friends."

Nothing. But then, Rogar had said the guide was afraid to come out.

"You talked to me mostly at night." She would lie on her bed, one in a row of eight, and there were eight more across from her. Anyone would think with that many girls she wouldn't have been lonely, but it was hard to make friends, especially when they would get adopted, and she knew she'd never see them again.

But she'd had her guide.

"Please don't be afraid. I promise I won't hurt you."

"Hello, Callie."

She let out a sigh of relief. "I've missed you." And she knew she had. It was as though an old friend had returned.

"It has been a long time."

"I know. I'm sorry."

"Don't be, because I really haven't thought about you at all. I mean, you certainly aren't the type to run with my crowd."

Huh? Her eyes flew open. Oh, damn, Constance Gentry. "I was . . . meditating. Getting in touch with my inner self."

Constance let her gaze drift over Callie. "I didn't know people still wore those . . . things."

"They're called sweats."

"Whatever." She flipped her hair behind her with one hand.

Constance still looked the same as she had the last time Callie had the misfortune to run into her. Tall, tanned, and blond. Callie wanted to vomit.

"What are you doing in the woods, anyway?" Callie asked.

She bent and picked up a golf ball. "I shanked it."

"I bet that's not all you've shanked in your lifetime," she muttered.

"I'd heard you were mooching off DeeDee again and staying in her parents' cabin." She laughed. "Mrs. Crane must've been hitting the bottle again. She said you were engaged to a prince." Her laughter was high-pitched enough that it could've broken a champagne glass. "You've got to remember those frogs you've probably been kissing are not going to turn into princes."

They both turned their heads when there was a rustling of underbrush. Rogar stepped out, and Constance sucked air. And for once in her life, Callie felt as though she had the upper hand.

"There you are, darling," Rogar said. "I know you said you wanted to take a walk by yourself, but I got lonely. Oh, I see I've interrupted."

"Not at all, sweetheart." She pasted a smile on her face that was so sweet it probably dripped sugar. "Constance, I'd like to introduce you to Prince Rogar Valkyir."

They might not be engaged, but he was a prince. So what if she was flaunting his royal status—she'd feel guilty tomorrow.

Or not.

Chapter 22

Another blueblood. Rogar briefly studied the young woman. She wore a white band of sorts across her forehead. The other blueblood, Ms. Crane, had worn a white band also.

Maybe it's a sacred symbol, Balam's thoughts blended with Rogar's.

It looks stupid.

Not nearly as fine as your medallion, Balam agreed.

Rogar found her lacking in other areas as well. Other than her white top and white shorts, she also wore her haughty demeanor out in the open. He didn't think he liked her any-more than he had the other two.

And he'd heard everything she'd said, and how she'd acted toward Callie, and Rogar didn't like it. It made him wonder why Callie would want to stay on this planet. She longed for a job she'd apparently trained many years to get, but still didn't have. The Earthlings he'd met wore masks. They smiled and said one thing, while meaning something entirely different.

DeeDee has a good spirit, Balam reminded him.

One out of many.

True.

"Are you really a prince?" Constance asked.

"Yes."

Rogar walked over to Callie and held out his hand toward

her. She took it. Her hand felt small in his. He helped her to her feet, but didn't let go. Instead, he pulled her close to him, protective, but he also enjoyed the warmth of her body.

Constance's eyes narrowed. "I guess you forgot to wear your engagement ring." She looked pointedly at Callie's hand.

"It is being designed especially for her," he smoothly replied. He would need to look up their customs on his database. He didn't know about the ring. The woman looked skeptical.

"Hey, Constance, did you get lost?"

"Over here, Freddie," Constance called without looking in the direction the voice had come from.

It sounded as though many large animals were clomping toward them, but then a man appeared. He looked rather odd. Short, with red hair, and funny dots all over his face. Rogar had never seen anyone with dots.

"Callie Jordon, I heard you were staying at DeeDee's parents' cabin," the man called Freddie said. "How the hell have you been?"

Callie relaxed so Rogar knew this person was not a typical blueblood. That, and he didn't wear the white band across his forehead.

"Hi, Freddie," Callie said, and Rogar heard the smile in her voice.

"Really, Freddie, do you have to make so much noise when you walk? You sounded like a herd of elephants."

He only grinned. Then he met Rogar's gaze, and Rogar saw something besides the odd way the man looked. There was intelligence. This man was no fool.

"I'm Freddie Danbury."

Rogar bowed slightly at the waist. "Prince Rogar Valkyir, Callie's fiancé."

Freddie looked at Callie as though she had done something very good, then nodded.

"Come on, Freddie, let's get back to our game." Constance turned on her heel.

"There's a get together tonight. A benefit auction for some

cause that Matilda Crane dug up. Fancy dress and bidding wars," Freddie said, ignoring Constance. "Why don't you two join us at the club?"

Callie stiffened. "I don't think . . ."

Constance turned. Rogar could see the fury flare in her eyes, but just as quickly it changed to a calculating gleam. "Oh, do, come. And bring your . . . prince."

"We are honored by your invitation," Rogar quickly told her, and could almost feel the dread coming from Callie. She'd changed since they'd arrived at the cabin. Since the Cranes had dropped by. She'd been more on edge, just like when this Constance woman had begun to talk down to her.

"Great, we'll see you then," Freddie said. "And congratulations. You deserve all the happiness you find, Callie."

"Freddie!"

He grinned again, then left.

As soon as they were out of sight, Callie jerked away from Rogar. Planting her hands on her hips, she faced him, and she didn't look a bit happy.

"Why do you keep telling people we're engaged?" she demanded.

"Because they act superior toward you. I don't like it."

"But we're not engaged."

"You will never see these people again so it doesn't matter."

She loudly exhaled. "And I'm not going to their damn auction!"

"Are you afraid?"

"No, I don't like these people. Why would I want to be around them?"

"To show them you are better. They only gauge a person by their wealth. Tonight, you will be like Cinderella."

She frowned. "How the hell do you know about Cinderella?"

"When DeeDee told me women liked fairy tales, I looked it up on my database. Cinderella was listed, so I read the story. I enjoyed it very much."

"Well, you're wrong about all women liking fairy tales. I don't want the fairy tale. I don't even believe in them."

"For one night, wouldn't you like to give them a taste of how they treat others they consider below their level?" She didn't look convinced. "Face your enemies, Callie, then conquer them."

She didn't say anything, so he knew she was thinking it over.

"Okay, maybe I would, but what you're suggesting would only be make-believe."

"Everyone needs a little fantasy in their life from time to time. It makes things more exciting."

She shrugged. "But I don't have anything to wear, so it doesn't matter."

"We will duplicate."

"Duplicate?"

"Like the money."

She sighed deeply. "I have a feeling this is not going to be good."

"It will be very good." He reached out and stroked his hand down the side of her face, and felt the shiver that ran through her. "You always make me want you."

"I didn't do anything." She visibly swallowed.

By the Goddess Aricepta, Callie didn't have to do a thing but be near him. Had she cast a spell upon him? Some women he knew practiced the art of spell casting, his mother and sisters did. Rogar's father had once laughingly said that was how she had captured his heart. But his brothers and sisters knew better. Their mother was a dark-haired beauty. Many men had wanted her, but Rogar's father was the one she chose.

"Fore!"

He looked up as a white ball landed nearby. "Why do they yell fore, then toss their ball into the woods?"

"It's just a game."

"Your games are silly."

She smiled. He liked the way she smiled.

"Let's go back to the cabin," he said. He didn't like the constant interruptions.

She nodded.

As they walked, he thought of something he'd wanted to ask. "Why did Freddie have dots? Is he an alien?" He was thoughtful for a moment. "Although I haven't seen anyone until this day that had dots."

She chuckled. He liked that, too. When DeeDee had stopped by to leave Callie her birthday present, she had told him Callie didn't laugh much, and if Rogar hurt her, she would personally see him castrated. He'd promised he wouldn't. After she left, he typed in castrated. He'd decided he would make certain that he wouldn't hurt Callie.

"Those are called freckles. Most redheads have them," she said. She looked up at him and smiled.

Her lips were too tempting. No one could blame him for what he was about to do. He lowered his head until his lips were touching hers. His tongue caressed hers, the heat of the kiss shooting downward, leaving him shaking. He wanted this woman more than breathing.

He pulled away, each breath strained. "What spell have you cast upon me?" he murmured as he buried his face in her hair, breathing in her scent.

"I could ask you the same thing."

He pulled back, looking into her eyes. "Leave with me right now. Zerod cannot harm you on New Symtaria." He waved his arm. "These people are fools. They think wealth is the most important thing in life, and if you aren't one of them, you're not accepted into their ranks."

She shook her head, tears filling her eyes. "I can't. It's more than that. These people mean nothing to me. What I have might not seem like much to you, but it's a part of who I am. I've lived—breathed—every thought has been that I would someday work with the big cats at the zoo. I'm next in line for the animal keeper job. You're asking me to give it all up. To leave Sheba, to leave DeeDee, I can't." She ducked out of his arms and ran the rest of the way to the cabin.

Rogar had seen the single tear run down her cheek before she turned away and fled. A sharp pain stabbed him in the heart at the mere thought that he would hurt her. His gaze dropped to the ground, and he noticed the flowers growing in patches. He would make her feel better by bringing flowers to her.

Then he would ask her not to tell DeeDee that he'd hurt her. He wasn't sure how DeeDee would manage to castrate him, since he was obviously the stronger one, but he didn't know what an Earthling was capable of doing, and he chose not to find out.

Callie felt like a fool. Why had she run away? Crying, no less. She rarely cried. A long time ago, she realized tears never solved anything. The only time she cried was when she watched *Steel Magnolias* or *Beaches*. But other than a sappy movie, she didn't cry.

She frowned.

Maybe when a new baby was born at the zoo, or when an animal died, then she would cry, too. But those were the only times.

She shook her head. It didn't matter why she cried. She just didn't like it when someone saw her. Damn it, she couldn't leave the only thing that had given her stability in her life. She belonged right where she was, except maybe living in a new house where she could have pets. She bet she couldn't have a pet on New Symtaria. And if she did, it would probably shift into a person and scare the crap out of her.

No, her life was what she knew, what was familiar, for better or worse. Yes, she liked Rogar a lot, but she wouldn't leave with him.

The door opened behind her. She stiffened.

"I brought you flowers to make you feel better," he said as

he came around in front of her and thrust them under her nose.

She took one look at the red petals and sniffed. *I will not cry! I won't!*

"I've made you cry again. I'm sorry."

"It's okay," she finally managed to say, hugging the flowers close to her chest.

"Then you won't tell DeeDee?"

She shook her head. It dawned what he'd just asked. "What has DeeDee got to do with this?"

"DeeDee said she would castrate me if I hurt you. I looked it up on my database. I don't think it would be a pleasant experience."

She opened her mouth, then closed it. DeeDee told Rogar she would castrate him? She started laughing. He frowned, and she laughed harder.

He squared his shoulders, looking quite affronted. "I tell you that I don't think I want to be castrated, and you laugh? If you had that threat hanging over your head, you wouldn't laugh."

He was priceless. One second, she thought Rogar knew everything there was to know about Earth, then in the next, he comes up with something like this.

"DeeDee would never do that. She couldn't. It was just a figure of speech to let you know she would be furious with you if you ever hurt me."

He seemed to think that over, then nodded. "I see." He exhaled deeply. "Good. I was afraid she might have special powers, and would cast a spell to make my testicles fall off."

"Cast a spell? You have people who can do that?"

"My mother and sisters can, and there are others." He shrugged.

Interesting. "Tell me more." She took her flowers to the kitchen and put them in a glass of water. DeeDee was the only person who had ever gotten her flowers. Odd that she would feel warm all over because Rogar had brought her some, too.

He sat on the sofa. She joined him, careful not to sit too close. She wanted to know more about New Symtaria, and arm's length from Rogar was still a temptation.

"We have many tribes. The same as you have many races on Earth."

"But some can cast spells?"

He nodded. "Each tribe brings something of use. My mother's tribe prays to Hadda, who makes everything on land grow and bear fruit."

"Are there many gods and goddesses that you worship?"

"There are many, yes. Once they walked the land, and were one with us. They were part animal, part human. They were very good, and had special powers that helped the people. There are many tales of how, when they passed from this life, they were carried to the next realm by a golden ark."

"They sound like the saints who used to be on Earth. Well, except they weren't part animal." It seemed strange talking to Rogar about the planet where he lived. He made it sound like a wonderful place. She looked down at her hands, then met his eyes again. "Someday, I would like to see New Symtaria. Would that be possible? I mean, to see it, but then come back here?"

His smile was slow. "Yes, that would be possible."

She smiled, just because he was. But then, something changed in the look he was giving her. It became more intense, and she saw his need. Tingles of awareness wrapped around her. She straightened, and cleared her throat. "You said you could duplicate a dress for me to wear tonight?"

Disappointment flashed across his features, but just as quickly, it was gone. He reached into his back pocket and pulled out the database.

"What kind of dress do you want?"

Oh, wow, this might be fun. "A designer dress?"

He typed in the letters, then handed it to her. "Just touch which one you would like to have most."

She recognized a lot of the names. It wasn't that she was materialistic or anything, but ohmygod, if Rogar could duplicate a dress, this would be a really cool device to have around. She felt like a kid in a candy store. She clicked on a designer. Pictures of dresses appeared on the screen—six in all.

"If you want to see more, then slide your finger down."

She jumped when he spoke, not realizing he'd moved next to her. Maybe she was more materialistic than she'd thought if she didn't notice him moving nearer.

When he looked at her, she quickly slid her finger down the screen. She really needed to pay attention. A bevy of dresses appeared at the touch of a finger.

"That one would look good on you," he said.

He had good taste. It was a black strapless that clung to the body, then flared in soft folds at the knees, before flowing softly to the floor.

"Would you like to try it on?"

She looked at him through narrowed eyes. He couldn't really make a dress appear out of thin air—could he? "Yeah, make it happen." She handed him the database.

He grinned. "You don't think I can."

"Not really. Cool fantasy, though."

She used to wait excitedly for the Christmas catalogs to arrive at the orphanage. By the time she'd scrounged one, the pages were dog eared and smudged from the many hands that had already poured over them. She hadn't cared. Her head had been too full of dreams that one day she would have a family, and they would sit around a gaily decorated tree on Christmas morning and open presents. It sure beat the hell out of reality, and the one present she would get at Christmas, which was usually clothes. Not that she hadn't appreciated them, but toys would've been more fun.

So now Rogar was giving her anything her heart could desire. Yeah, it sounded too good to be true.

"Thumb," he said.

"Huh?"

"I need your thumb so the database can read your measurements."

She laughed. Now she knew he was pulling a fast one. But he only quirked an eyebrow. Okay, she'd play along. She stuck her thumb out. When he took it, she tried not to think about the warmth of his touch, or the tingles that traveled down her arm.

"That should do it," he said as he let go of her hand.

It took her a second to realize he'd spoken. She curled her hands in her lap. "Now what?"

"We wait."

"And how long before it . . . appears?"

He glanced down at the screen. "Right about . . ."

Lights swirled in the middle of the room like a psychedelic tornado. When it cleared, the dress was there in front of her, as though someone wore it, except no one was.

"You did it," she said, unable to take her eyes off the beautiful creation.

"Of course, I told you I could. Now do you feel better about going to the party?"

Oh, yeah, she was more than ready. So what if she was being petty, and knew that in the long run she wouldn't gain a thing.

But damn, it was going to feel really good. Sort of like Cinderella—only kick ass.

Chapter 23

"We need to keep a low profile," Callie told Rogar as he pulled in front of the country club.

"I understand."

"Maybe this wasn't such a good idea."

"Too late."

The valet opened their doors. She tried to smile, but knew she didn't quite pull it off.

He squeezed her hand as they walked down the sidewalk. "Have courage, Callie."

Callie could've told him all her bravado had left about an hour and a half ago, but she bit her tongue. He was right. She held her head high as they walked inside the club. A man in uniform silently appeared and took her wrap, then handed each of them a paddle with a number boldly printed on it and a sheet of paper so they could sign their name next to their number.

Rogar looked as though he didn't know quite what to do with the paddle.

"It's so you can bid during the auction." Not that they would be bidding or anything. She figured once around the dance floor, and they could sneak away.

As soon as she signed her name, she handed the paper to Rogar and he did the same. While he signed, she turned, catching her reflection in the full-length mirror. She hadn't dared to look while they were at the cabin. At least, not at every-thing altogether. She'd been afraid she would see a flaw, then lose her nerve.

"You're beautiful," Rogar whispered close to her ear.

"Is that really me?" The woman in the mirror looked nothing like the woman who usually dressed for comfort, throwing on a pair of sweats or shorts, depending on the sea-son.

No, the woman staring back at her looked as though she belonged. The black dress molded to her body, the strappy heels hurt like hell, but they were sexy, and they made her feel so feminine. She could stand a little pain for one night.

But the diamonds at her throat, and on her wrist, sparkled with the colors of the rainbow, pure and clear. They were the icing on the cake. This is what Cinderella would have felt like. If only she could have this all the time.

You can.

She jerked her head around, looking at Rogar.

"Did you say something?"

He shook his head. At that moment, Constance glided into the foyer. She took one look at Callie and her mouth dropped open.

Callie had read stuff like this happening in her romance books. The heroine would get her revenge, but it never felt quite as sweet as she had thought.

The books were wrong.

This felt oh so sweet. "Constance." Callie's gaze skimmed over the other woman. From her creamy-white dress, to the tiny string of pears at her throat, and the white heels. She met the other woman's gaze. "Did we overdress," she asked inno-cently.

"No, you look . . . is that a Versaci?'

"Yes, it is."

"I've always wanted . . ."

"Wow, Callie, nice ice. You know, you clean up really well," Freddie said as he joined them in the foyer.

Constance glared at him. "Don't be crude."

"Rogar, are you sure you want to go inside?" Freddie grinned. "It's kind of like sending you into the lions' den. They've all heard there'll be royalty here tonight."

Callie inconspicuously squeezed his hand when she saw his puzzled look. Instinctively, she knew he was about to ask if they could shapeshift. "I'm sure they're not lions, nor will they eat us."

"No, but watch out. There are some catty women who show their claws occasionally."

Constance's laugh was so cold it almost cracked when it hit the warm air. She sauntered over to Rogar and took his arm. "Nonsense. Freddie is exaggerating."

Before she could protest Constance's easy way with Rogar, Freddie hurried over and took Callie's arm, and they all went inside.

The dining area was packed. Tables that sat four to six couples were draped with white cloths and set with white dishes. Sparkling chandeliers sprouted from the ceiling like upside-down mushrooms, bathing the room in bright light.

A band played an unobtrusive melody on a raised stage. In front of them a dance floor was polished to a high shine. It looked as magical as the time she'd joined DeeDee and her parents. She'd been sadly underdressed. Tonight, she was Cinderella, and this time she'd brought her prince.

Except Constance had draped herself on him. Callie didn't care for the way she pressed her body against Rogar, either. In fact, Callie didn't like it one bit.

"And that's the biggest cat of them all," Freddie leaned over and whispered in Callie's ear.

His voice startled her, she'd been so intent watching Constance flirt with Rogar that she'd zoned out on everything around her. Freddie's words sank in, and she laughed. Rogar glanced over his shoulder and frowned. Callie thought he might have been about to say something, but Constance tugged on his arm, effectively drawing his attention back to her.

"Methinks someone might be jealous." Freddie whispered close to her ear again. "Not only do you have a prince, but one who is totally taken with your charms. Smart man. Unlike the fool that I was."

Startled again, she looked at him.

"Oh yes, fair lady, I had a huge crush on you when DeeDee brought you with her that summer. You didn't even look in my direction."

"You had a crush on me?" No, surely he was only joking.

"Remember the flowers in front of the cabin door every morning?"

"They were for DeeDee. That boy she liked so much . . ."

He shook his head. "Nope, completely my idea, and he got the credit. Then we left, and I never saw my true love again."

She was more than a little shocked. Then she remembered something. "Didn't DeeDee tell me you got engaged a few months later?"

"Rebound." He sighed deeply. "I was settling for less. And now it seems as though I've missed the boat again."

"I'm sorry."

But she had a feeling he wouldn't take to the bottle and drink himself into oblivion since his gaze was already straying. Even while speaking to her, he checked out a petite blonde sitting at a nearby table.

"I really hate to see you suffer so much," sarcasm dripped from her words.

"What? Oh." He grinned, and didn't look a bit embarrassed that he'd been caught checking out the other women.

"You can sit at our table, Rogar," Constance announced.

Callie looked around and saw there wasn't room for her.

"Freddie, why don't you take Callie to the table over there. I'm sure you two have a lot of catching up to do." She waved her hand toward the only table that was still empty. Probably because it was in the far corner.

"This table seems a little too crowded," Rogar said. "I think

I'll join them at the other one." He bowed, then tucked Callie's arm in his, and they walked away.

Freddie grabbed his drink. "Outsmarted again, old girl."

"Shut up, Freddie," Constance hissed.

Callie couldn't resist looking over her shoulder. Definitely a Kodak moment. Constance looked as though she was about to blow a gasket. Callie hoped she did.

"She's a bitch," Freddie said nonchalantly.

"So why do you hang out with her?" Callie asked as Rogar pulled her chair out. As soon as she was seated, they followed suit.

"I love watching just how much of a snob she can be. It's kind of like a train wreck as it's happening." He turned to Rogar. "Get ready for a lot of train wrecks tonight. I want to apologize ahead of time because they're too stupid, and too full of themselves, to know how cruel they can be."

Rogar leaned back in his chair. "But not you."

"Touché. But you see, I only live on the fringes of this group. I do have my moments, though. It comes from the people I keep company with."

She'd always thought of Freddie as one of the nice ones. There were a few at the *Camp in the Pines* that she could stomach being around.

Freddie leaned back in his chair. "My mother was my father's secretary, so I'm not a pure blueblood. He divorced his socialite wife, and married my mother. It was true love until a few years later, when my father found someone younger, and divorced my mother. She had thought it would last forever. One day, she hung herself. Checked out without even saying good-bye. No note, nothing." He twirled the olive on a toothpick around in his glass.

"I'm so sorry, Freddie," Callie said. "I didn't know."

"Depressed people are not always aware of what they do," Rogar said.

Freddie suddenly smiled. "It would seem that *I've* depressed everyone." He frowned. "Not sure why I opened up like that. Don't normally. I guess I wanted you to know I've felt their barbs, too." He downed his drink, then motioned for a nearby waiter.

"Then walk away from them," Rogar said.

"When my father kicked the bucket, he left me a considerable fortune, since he was between wives at the moment. The only thing he didn't bother to teach me was how exactly to live." He waved his arm. "This is all I know."

The waiter took their drink orders. Callie had a feeling she knew why Freddie had opened up—he was drinking double martinis, and she doubted that had been his first. She and Rogar ordered wine.

Ms. Crane walked to the center of the dance floor. She wore a poofy-pink dress that sparkled almost as much as the chandeliers, and like deer that had been caught in headlights, everyone shifted their attention to her.

Her hair was almost as poofy as her dress. All that might not have been so bad, but her bony shoulders were bare, her rouge too dark, and it looked as though she wore false eyelashes. She reminded Callie of a scarecrow coming off a week of hard drugs.

"That's enough to give everyone nightmares for a few weeks," Freddie murmured.

Callie snorted, then quickly covered it with a cough.

"Is she ill?" Rogar asked.

Freddie shook his head. "No, that's how she usually dresses for these things. She just has more money than everyone else, so no one has the nerve to say anything to her face."

One of the waiters handed Ms. Crane a microphone. She tapped it once, the sound bouncing off the walls, followed by a loud screech. The waiter hurried to turn it down, then handed it back.

"It works," she said, stating the obvious. "Before we get started tonight, I want to let everyone know that we have royalty with us tonight." She beamed like a lighthouse on a foggy night. "Prince Rogar Valkyir. Please give him a warm welcome. We're so happy to have him join us." She waved her arm toward him.

Callie felt as if she might as well have faded into the wallpaper. Why was she even here? She didn't even like these people. Sure, she was wearing fancy clothes and expensive jewels, but she was still the same Callie.

Rogar stood, bowed slightly, then held his hand out for Callie. She really wished he hadn't done that, but she smiled and stood.

"Oh, yes, forgive me. And his fiancée is also with him," Ms. Crane said nervously.

They sat back down as their drinks arrived. Freddie took a long swallow of his. "Notice how they accidentally leave us unimportant hangers on out of the mix? Ah, yes, they are taught from birth how to let the undesirables stand on the fringes of their circle." He grinned and winked at her. "While we just sit back and enjoy their antics. Great sport, really."

Callie laughed. She couldn't help it. Freddie had a good sense of humor.

"I'm sorry," Freddie spoke to Rogar. "You obviously have wealth, and prestige, and here I am putting down the bluebloods. I apologize."

"We don't have class distinction where I'm from," Rogar said.

"But you're a prince. I find that hard to believe."

He shrugged. "Everyone works toward the common good of all the people. We're a simple . . . country."

"It sounds like paradise."

Rogar's gaze fell on Callie. "It is."

As warmth crawled up her cheeks, she quickly took a drink of her wine.

"Enjoy your meal, because as soon as it's over," Ms. Crane spoke into the microphone, "—we'll start the auction. I expect to raise a lot of money for the local zoo."

Zoo? Callie perked up. Okay, maybe this wouldn't be a

total loss. She liked the idea the money raised tonight would actually go for something good. Not that they would stick around long.

Their food was brought out. Since it was catered, they didn't have a choice, but it tasted a lot better than the food they'd been eating. She wasn't much of a cook, and Rogar had already shown his talents in the kitchen, which she'd just as soon he not repeat.

Rogar and Freddie talked during the three courses, and she mostly listened.

"So, you have a lot of brothers and sisters?" Freddie asked.

Rogar grimaced as though it pained him to talk about them. "More than I like to think about."

She cocked an eyebrow.

"I have two brothers and three sisters. They're all very stubborn," Rogar said.

"Oh, much like you then," she said with wide-eyed innocence.

"I think you're making a joke at my expense," Rogar said.

Had she offended him? Nope, there was that twinkle in his eye again. "And I did it very well, too," she said. She started laughing. Rogar and Freddie joined in.

Callie reached for her wineglass, glancing around the room as she did. Constance was looking straight at her, venom spitting from her eyes, but she quickly glanced away when their gazes locked. After tonight, Callie had better watch her back. Not that she planned on associating with these people again.

As the waiters cleared the tables, Ms. Crane made her way back to the center of the dance floor. One of the staff wheeled out a cart that was covered with a pretty blue silk scarf.

Callie leaned closer to Rogar. "We can sneak away any time," she whispered.

"I'd like to see what happens."

"All they'll do is bid on stuff that is brought out, the highest bidder wins the item, then the money will be donated to the local zoo."

"It sounds interesting."

Did it really matter if they stayed a bit longer? "Okay, then we'll hang around for a while."

Ms. Crane removed the scarf to reveal a vase. "First up we have a lovely china vase donated by the Burberrys."

As Ms. Crane continued to extol the quality of such a fine vase, Freddie leaned over. "Everyone cleans out their attic for this event. It's a good way to get rid of junk they don't want anymore," he whispered, then shrugged. "But it is for a good cause." He raised his paddle. "One thousand."

Ms. Crane beamed. "Going once, twice, sold to Freddie Danbury!"

"Well, I've done my duty for the night."

Several more pieces were sold. Then another item was brought out. Ms. Crane whisked off the scarf. Callie sat straighter in her chair, drawing in a breath. It was a beautiful tawny statue of a jaguar, and it looked just like Sheba.

The bidding started. How much did she have in her savings?

"We have one thousand, one thousand five, are there any more bids? Going once." Ms. Crane looked around the room. "Going twice."

It was a shame. She would've really liked to have the jaguar. Her savings account was practically nil. Besides, she'd promised herself that she would never touch it for any reason, even if it meant eating tuna every day until she got her next paycheck.

But it was a really beautiful piece. She sighed, wishing for once in her life that the fairy tale was real.

Rogar raised his paddle. "One million dollars."

Chapter 24

There was a collective gasp from the crowd. Callie's head whipped around, her mouth dropped open.

"Good show." Freddie began to clap.

"Did I understand you correctly, Prince Valkyir?" Ms. Crane squeaked. She quickly cleared her throat without moving the microphone away. It sounded like a roll of thunder barreled across the room. "You bid one million dollars?"

"One million, yes. Is that acceptable? Callie seemed particularly fond of the little statue."

"Oh, that's . . . yes . . . wonderful. Well done!" She laid down her microphone, and clapped her hands. Everyone in the room joined in.

"This isn't keeping a low profile," Callie frantically whispered as she leaned over, keeping a smiled pasted on her face.

Ms. Crane marched over, and personally handed the jaguar to Callie.

"I will have someone deliver the money tomorrow, if that is acceptable?" Rogar told her.

Ms. Crane still seemed to be in a daze. "Yes, that will be fine."

"I think I'll just go and freshen up a bit," Callie said as the people in the room settled back into their seats. She needed a moment to collect her thoughts. Sheesh, Rogar was going to give Ms. Crane a million in counterfeit money. If she ever discovered the ruse, Callie was sure to go to jail. This was definitely not good.

She went inside one of the stalls and closed the door, plopping down on the toilet seat. They shouldn't have come. So what if they would've been snubbing the cream of society. It wasn't as though they hadn't snubbed her a zillion times or more.

She dropped her head down to her hands. She knew exactly why she'd wanted to come tonight—to get a little back. She wanted to be the one who came out on top for a change.

It had felt good, too. It probably shouldn't have, but it did. Did that make her a bad person? Probably.

But she hadn't known Rogar was going to bid a million dollars on the jaguar. She sighed deeply. It was a beautiful piece. A smile curved her lips. And he'd gotten it for her. He must've sensed how much she wanted it.

There was the little matter of buying it with fake money, but it really was the thought that counted.

She was as bad as him.

Maybe she could give it back and say they had changed their minds. That might work. She would probably have to grovel. Bleh, that left a sour taste in her mouth.

She stilled when some women came into the bathroom talking about the auction.

"Can you believe how much was bid on the little tiger figurine?"

It was a jaguar you idiot, Callie thought to herself.

"Don't you think he's just the hottest guy in the room?" One of the women asked. Callie didn't recognize her voice, but her words made her preen just a bit. Rogar was hot. And even better, he was all hers—for a little while.

"Soooo hot! He must love Callie a lot to spend that much on her."

Pffft. Of course he didn't love her. Liked maybe, but certainly not love. Still, warm tingles swirled inside her stomach.

"I doubt it's love. More like infatuation."

Callie grimaced. She recognized that voice—Constance.

"I mean, really, he's scraping the bottom of the barrel to claim her as his fiancée," Constance continued. "He's a prince from a foreign country. What the hell does she know about polite society?"

"True," one of the women chimed in. "Remember when she showed up the first time with DeeDee? I really doubt she'd ever had a manicure in her life."

"And her bathing suit had to have come from Wal-Mart," another giggled.

Callie knew they were right. Her suit had come from a discount store, and she had never had a manicure. She always did them herself because it was all she could afford.

"He'll dump her," Constance continued. "Just wait and see. She's a little slut pretending to be something she's not."

They left the bathroom.

Callie sat there. They were right. Except about the slut part. And even if she went back to New Symtaria with Rogar, they wouldn't be a couple or anything. He was a prince, and she wasn't anything, except a pauper.

Just plain Callie Jordon. Even her name had been given to her by the woman who ran the orphanage. Maybe she had known red tape would keep Callie from being adopted, so it was better to go ahead and give her at least that.

But damn it, Constance had no right to put her down. She was a mean bitch who thought every one was beneath her. Poor Freddie had been taking her crap for years. Someone should put a stop to her behavior. Make her see what it's like to feel embarrassed and out of place.

She gritted her teeth and curled her hands into fists, imagining what it would feel like to punch her lights out. If she could she'd . . .

Callie gasped, doubling over and grabbing her middle. Oh, God, what was happening? She was dying. The food had been tainted. Maybe Constance had added poison to Callie's. She wouldn't put it past her.

Through a haze of pain, she felt something familiar. Oh, no, this wasn't happening. It couldn't be happening. Not here, not now. She hadn't been thinking about an animal. Why was she shifting? Fog filled the stall. She drew in her arms and legs close to her body as the room began to go dark.

Slowly the deep ache inside her began to subside, and everything returned to normal. Well, except everything was dark. She blinked, then looked down at her feet. Only, she didn't have any. Had something gone wrong? Maybe she'd lost her legs during the transition, and she'd have to drag herself out to Rogar . . . eww . . . with stumps where her legs used to be.

No, wait, there they were, except she was apparently standing on the toilet. Her legs were actually long . . . and skinny. She raised her arm.

Wings?

She was a bird. Bird wasn't bad. It sure beat rhino, although the thought of squashing Constance had merit.

She experimented and flapped her wings, almost losing her balance. That was a close call. Okay, she needed to see what had happened. She wobbled, but made it to the top of the stall door, and bumped her head on the ceiling. What the hell? She perched there for a few moments while she regained her balance.

Better.

Now to get to the counter. She took a deep breath, then took off. It turned out to be more of a long jump, rather than bird in flight.

She stared at the mirror.

Oh, this was just freakin' great. She couldn't have shifted into a pretty little dove, or a cute parakeet? No, she was a pink flamingo with long spindly legs. She turned to the right and got a full side view. Her plumage was a soft pink and, in some places, deep red. She looked like a Vegas showgirl. Minus the sexy part.

Callie pranced down the counter, then turned, tail feathers ruffling. Not bad, for a novice.

The bathroom door opened and a very matronly woman ploughed inside. She took one look at Callie, and screamed as she fled. The door swung violently back and forth. Callie caught glimpses of the people at the tables watching the woman, their expressions a mixture of shock and surprise.

Not good! Everyone would be in the bathroom in just a few seconds. How the hell would she explain she'd shifted into a bird? No, not good! As the door swung out, she went the same direction.

Maybe this wasn't good, either. Everyone stared at her. She was so not the life of the party. She looked at Rogar, who hurried to the French doors and opened them wide. Bless him.

She flapped her wings and took flight. Probably not as graceful as a real flamingo, but not too bad if she said so herself.

This was cool. The screams from the women, and some of the men, were rather annoying, but flying was cool. She flew over Constance and her bitches, then turned back. When she flew over the next time, Constance looked up.

Bombs away!

Constance screamed.

Making a poo deposit probably wasn't the nicest thing to do, but that's what birds did. She looked back once. Bull's eye! Revenge was damned sweet.

The French doors were right in front of her. She swooped down and out. Flying was great! The wind rushed past her as she glided through the air. Maybe this was her guide. It felt good, right.

Hey, guide, are you there?

Silence.

Maybe not, but she could get used to this. She flapped her wings, closed her eyes, and became one with the night.

Splat!

Her eyes flew open.

Splat again!

Ugh, a swarm of bugs zipped past, but she could barely see them. She had bug guts splattered on her face. Oh, yuck!

She aimed in the general direction of the cabin. So much for flying. At least her beak hadn't been open. She landed on the front porch, then began to meditate about her human side. It didn't take nearly as long to change back, or to realize how chilly it was outside. The fog that always accompanied the change hadn't made things any warmer. Shivering, she hurried to the backdoor, found the key under the flowerpot, and flung it open.

Callie went straight to the bathroom and washed her face, nausea welling inside her. This was really, really gross. As soon as she felt clean, she ran to her bedroom and pulled on a pair of sweats. Her body was one big goose bump. Before she finished dressing, she heard the Hummer pull up. She quickly jerked on a pair of thick socks before hurrying to the front door. She opened it as Rogar came up the steps, taking them two at a time.

"You made it home," he said. The worried creases on his forehead faded. "Why did you shift?" He closed the door behind him as he came inside. "Were you in danger?"

"I didn't mean to shift. It . . . just happened." Oh, God, what if she shifted at work or when her landlady came over for the rent?

"You look ill," he said, and led her toward the sofa.

"I feel ill. Rogar, I didn't try to shift."

"What happened?"

She grimaced when she began to think about it. "Constance showed up. She was being her usual bitchy self and began telling her friends how low class I am. I got angry."

He relaxed. "Ah, that explains it. When a Symtarian becomes very emotional, they will often shift to an animal form. Their guide, if they've connected. With men, it's usually after very passionate sex."

Like Rogar did after they made love. She didn't know why that should please her, but it did. Well, except she had to dive for the nearest door before he finished the change.

She was still a little confused, though. "Why now? This never happened before."

"Because you're becoming more in sync with your animal guide. The more you shift, the closer you'll get to her."

"I haven't found her, but I thought I heard her talking to me tonight."

"That's good. You only have to trust that she will lead you in the right direction."

"But what if she's wrong? Does that ever happen?"

He shrugged. "Sometimes. But they're better able to observe our actions. They're not directly connected, so they can see with a better perspective than we can. Sometimes we want to listen with our heart, rather than our heads."

That made sense. Sort of.

"But wouldn't that work both ways?"

"I often tell Balam if I think he's wrong."

"Does he listen?"

Rogar laughed. A deep resonating sound that sent shivers of pleasure over her. She realized again just how hard it was going to be to let him go.

"I don't think Balam ever listens to me, but he is a good friend."

"And you're not afraid he'll . . . uh . . . hurt one of your friends?"

"He wouldn't."

"You're sure he wouldn't harm anyone?"

"Yes. Very sure. Would you like to meet him?"

For a brief second, excitement flittered through her. Of course she wanted to meet him. Her dream was to work around the big cats. They were magnificent animals. But to be up close and personal?

"Balam wants to meet you," he urged.

She narrowed her eyes. "If he eats me, I swear I'm coming back to haunt you."

"Everything will be fine. Remember, Balam is also a part of me, just as your guide is a part of you."

She nodded, then took a deep breath as he closed his eyes. Her nerves stretched taut when he began to change. As always, a thick fog rolled in. What the hell was she thinking? She couldn't stay in the same room as a jaguar. She started to get up.

Trust Rogar. Balam won't harm you.

Callie stilled, tears filling her eyes, because she finally recognized the voice from her childhood. "You're my guide." She felt as though she had found an old friend.

The fog cleared. There was a deep, guttural purr beside her. She flinched. Then swallowed hard as she stared into the dark eyes of the black jaguar.

"Hello . . . uh . . . Balam." Her voice squeaked. She only hoped he didn't think she was a mouse.

When Balam came to his feet on the seat beside her, she shifted away. As though that would make any difference. If he wanted, he could be on her in a heartbeat, mighty jaws clamping down on her head. She closed her eyes, taking a deep breath, and trying to dispel that image from her mind.

The big cat moved closer. Callie stayed perfectly still. Balam smelled her hair, her shoulder. Was he deciding if she would make a good meal? This was not good. Why had she let Rogar talk her into meeting his guide? Why had . . .

A big tongue licked up the side of her face. Oh, great, he was tasting her.

But then he laid down, his head across her lap, and turned on his back. Before she could wonder what he was going to do next, one humongous paw reached up and caressed her face.

She hadn't expected that. She looked into the jag's eyes and saw something there she hadn't previously seen: kindness, gentleness.

Tentatively, she stroked his fur. He closed his eyes and purred. Then it dawned on her. She was petting a jaguar. Hell, a jaguar was lying in her lap. Sure, he was really heavy, but this was cool.

They probably sat there for hours, with her gently stroking his fur. Sometimes it seemed they were silently communicating. Not only was she getting to know Rogar's guide, but maybe in an odd sort of way, her own.

She must have dozed as the hour grew late, because the next thing she knew, Balam was moving. She yawned and opened her eyes, then glanced down. But it was no longer Balam, Rogar had returned.

She smiled down at him. "Thank you."

"I told you he wouldn't hurt you. He's too much a part of me to ever harm you. Besides, he said he liked you, and that you give good back rubs."

"I never thought I'd ever get that close to a jaguar. In the classes I took, they taught on the side of caution."

"But that's not the Symtarian way when it comes to animals. We are taught to be one with them."

"I think Balam was right."

Still half asleep, she smiled. "Right about what?"

"You do give great back rubs."

Her hand stilled as his words sank in. She was lightly caressing his back, running her fingers through his hair. Her gaze drifted over him.

And he was quite naked.

Chapter 25

Rogar sat up. "I want you." Which was obvious, but Callie couldn't blame him. Not when she was touching him like this. Innocent? Yes. Sensuous? Painfully so. And by the gods, he hoped she didn't stop.

It wasn't as though he could turn off his emotions when she was around. On the contrary, it was more as though each of his senses were heightened when she was near.

He studied her. She nibbled her bottom lip, not commenting. Why did she fight the attraction? He knew she felt the same. Was Callie afraid he would seduce her into going back to New Symtaria with him? That he wouldn't fight fair?

She'd be correct in her assumption.

The thought of leaving her behind shook him to the core. He'd come to care for her so much in such a short time. He didn't want to go home without her. Was seducing her the answer?

It would be underhanded and dirty.

He only hoped it worked.

Rogar leaned in, brushing strands of hair from her face. "Spend this time with me—while we still can be together."

She sniffed. Not the response he'd hoped for. He nuzzled her neck, then swirled his tongue inside her ear. She gasped, clutching his shoulders.

That was more like it.

He brought his lips to hers. She caressed his tongue with hers. Flames of desire flared inside him. No woman had ever ignited his passion as quickly as Callie. Maybe she had bewitched him. But what a sweet bewitching it was.

He slid his hand under her top. Sweet torture! She wore nothing beneath it. His erection throbbed with the need to bury himself deep inside her, but he didn't want to rush. No, it was much better to draw out their mating.

He cupped her breast, his thumb scraping across the taut nipple. Still he needed more. He ended the kiss, pulled her top over her head, and tossed it to the side, then drew in a deep breath as he stared at her. She was perfection.

"I . . . I . . ." she stuttered, bringing her hands up to cover what he so desperately wanted to look at.

"No, my sweet. You're beautiful." He brushed her hands away. "Your breasts are perfect." He cupped one, running his thumb over the tight nipple.

She sucked in a breath, her eyes drifting closed.

It wasn't easy to pull away, but he stopped touching her.

She opened her eyes and looked at him. He saw the question forming on her face, and knew she wondered why he'd stopped.

"Look," he said. "Your nipples are a dusky rose . . . perfect. Your breasts just full enough for me to cup in my hands. No, look," he told her when she would have turned her eyes away. "Watch as I caress them, take each one into my mouth."

He lowered his head and sucked one delicious nipple into his mouth rolling the nub around with his tongue. She gasped and pulled his head tighter to her.

He moved to the other side, running his tongue over her nipple, teasing, before sucking it inside his mouth. His hand slid beneath the waistband of her sweats, running over her flat stomach, reaching down, touching her, feeling her dampness, knowing she wanted him as much as he wanted her.

He jerked when her hand snaked between their bodies,

and she in turn began to touch him, to stroke her finger lightly over his erection.

"Yes, just like that," he told her. His breathing became labored as her grip tightened just a little. She massaged him, then slid his foreskin down, then up with oh-so aching slowness. Exquisite torture! He wouldn't be able to stand much more.

He knew the routine, and grabbed his pants that were on the sofa where he had shifted form, and pulled out a package that contained a sheath. He'd decided since Callie apparently wanted this protection, that he wouldn't argue with her. He wasn't about to take the chance that she might refuse him. That would drive him insane. He quickly rolled the sheath down his erection.

The pressure built inside him until he thought he might explode. He tugged her sweats off, then pulled her onto his lap. She straddled his legs, rubbing herself against him. He watched her face, saw the passion, and it fired his desire even more. He cupped her butt, pulling her in tighter against him. Then in one swift movement, he raised her, lowering her body onto him.

She gasped. "Oh, yes, that's what I want. That feels . . . yes . . ."

She gripped his shoulders, sliding her body sensuously up and down him, her slick wet heat embracing him in ecstasy. He tightened, trying to hold back, but it seemed like forever since they'd made love.

Her body jerked. She gasped. Her eyes closed.

He let go, giving way to his own orgasm. Felt the waves of passion quiver through him. This was good. Very good.

With a deep sigh, Callie laid her head against his chest. Her body was soft against him. He knew deep in his heart that she was meant to be with him.

But something else was happening. He felt Balam growing stronger inside him. He groaned, unable to stop the tide that rocked him to the core.

Callie jumped up. "Not again!"

He couldn't stop the change. Too much passion flowed through his body.

The ache grew inside him, the burning began to build as fog enveloped him, just before he shifted. It would have been nice lying in her arms, feeling her naked body pressed against his.

It was much later that his heart slowed to a normal pace. He opened his eyes and looked through Balam's.

Where is she, old friend?

In the bedroom. She shut the door. I think she's still a bit leery around me.

That will change with time.

I have no doubt. Go to her.

Rogar shifted. He walked down the hallway, then eased open the door of the bedroom. She'd left a light on. It bathed her in a soft glow. He watched the even rise and fall of her chest.

Rather than join her, he went into the bathroom. Shower first, then he would crawl beneath the cover, and pull her naked body against his. He could get used to having Callie around.

As in forever?

Rogar smiled as he continued on without even a stumble. *Yes, Balam, I could get used to her forever.*

She would make a good lifemate.

I only need to convince her of that. Rogar wasn't sure it would be that easy, but he kept those thoughts hidden.

She doesn't like change. It might be harder than you imagine.

Rogar turned the water on in the shower and stepped beneath the spray. *You doubt I can?*

No, but it will take a bit of finesse.

He laughed. *Are you going to give me lessons?*

Silence.

Had he offended Balam? His animal guide could get quite touchy at times.

No, I think you should be able to manage quite well, Balam told him.

Thank you. Rogar grabbed the soap and began to lather his body. A pleasant smell reached his nostrils. Maybe he would take some things back with him to introduce to their world. His mother and sisters would like the scented soaps. They were always anxious to try new aromas.

Our genes have mixed so we share some of the same traits, Balam continued. *You get your strength and agility from me. Also, your prowess with the women.*

Rogar snorted. Balam was full of himself. *And what do you get from me?*

Silence.

It is rather one-sided, isn't it? Balam stated matter-of-factly.

Now you're a comedian.

Thank you.

Rogar shook his head as he finished rinsing the soap from his body, then turned off the water, and stepped out of the shower. After drying, he slung a towel around his hips, and knotted it at his waist.

When he walked out of the bathroom, her eyes were open, but she had that sleepy, seductive look about her, and it made him want her all over again.

"Good. I liked Balam, but I'd rather snuggle with you," she said with a yawn.

He chuckled. "I would rather snuggle with you, too."

Her cheeks tinged a rosy red. How could she still be embarrassed, after they had been so intimate with each other?

He strolled to his side of the bed, then unknotted the towel, letting it fall to the floor. He watched her face, saw her pupils widen, and more—he saw the hunger in her eyes. Maybe it wouldn't be so hard to convince her to return with him.

"Next time we'll shower together. I would like soaping your body," he told her.

She visibly swallowed, her gaze finally moving to his face. "I don't think we would have gotten very much showering done."

"True." He pulled the cover back and saw she had on a thick nightgown. He shook his head.

"What?"

"You are wearing clothes to bed again."

She frowned. "It gets cold at night."

"Not when you're sleeping with me." He reached down and tried to tug the gown up, but it was stuck under her. Her face turned a darker shade of red.

"Fine." She pulled it off and tossed it on the floor, before jerking the cover up to her chin.

"I enjoy looking at your body as much as you enjoy looking at mine."

Her eyes widened. "I don't!"

He raised his eyebrows.

"I mean . . . you have a great body and all. . . ." Her forehead wrinkled. "Okay, I do enjoy looking at you." To give credence to her words, her gaze drifted over him. She sighed. "You have a magnificent body."

He grinned.

Her frowned deepened. "And a big . . . ego."

He switched off the light and crawled beneath the cover, pulling her body close to his. "Go to sleep." He kissed the top of her head. Having Callie next to him felt so right. He wouldn't like it if she wasn't there. Balam was right. Now Rogar had to convince her that leaving with him would be the correct thing to do.

Callie snuggled closer to Rogar, and tried not to think about someday. Not having him lying close like this was too painful. She'd always taken things one day at a time, and if something good happened, then that was great, but if it didn't, then she wouldn't feel the deep disappointment that was sure to come.

It had taken her a long time to stop looking forward to things that never happened. Like when the children were paraded in front of perspective parents. She always hoped that someone would adopt her, but they never did.

Unresolved legal issues and red tape had been the case in the beginning. By the time that was settled, she'd known she was different. She supposed the prospective parents had sensed it as well.

Once, when she was eight, she thought she might have a good chance of being adopted. A nice older couple took her home for a trial period. Callie fell in love with them. So much that she told them about the voice who spoke to her.

They brought her back quick enough. Shortly after that, she was taken to see the doctor. By the time she learned to stop listening, to make the voice go away, no one wanted an older child who had been seen by a psychiatrist.

It was hard to be positive when she was surrounded by negativity.

She suddenly smiled. But getting a little back felt pretty good. Tonight had been . . . kind of fun. For once, she had come out on top.

She nibbled her bottom lip. Pooping on Constance hadn't been very nice. Not that she hadn't deserved it. She should've been pooped on years ago. Callie wondered how hard it would be to change into a bird again. The bird wasn't her animal guide, so it might prove difficult. Besides, it would be just her luck there'd be a hunter close by and pop a shot off. Kersplat. That would be the end of her.

She snuggled closer to Rogar, heard his even breathing, and knew he slept. She inhaled, then smiled when she caught the floral smell of the bath soap DeeDee's mom always used. It was a nice scent. Not very manly, but nice all the same. Not that Rogar had to prove he was a man. No, he certainly didn't need to prove anything in that area.

She yawned, just before drifting off to sleep. Her dreams

were filled with her and Rogar living on New Symtaria. The two of them roaming the valleys and walking on the beaches. Peace and tranquility.

Callie came awake slowly, her eyes fluttering open. She glanced at the clock. After nine. She never slept this late. She yawned and stretched, her arm reaching across the bed, but the other side was empty.

She listened, but didn't hear sounds from any other part of the cabin. Where was Rogar? She sniffed. He wasn't burning anything. There was plenty of junk food in the kitchen, though, so maybe he'd gotten hungry. She'd probably find him eating the rest of the cream-filled cookies.

Tossing the cover off, she got out of bed, and strolled to the bathroom naked. She caught her reflection in the mirror, and realized she was becoming more comfortable in her own skin. She shook her head. There had been a lot of changes in her life since Rogar had come into it.

Hmm, she wasn't sure they had all been for the better. He had turned her world upside down. Plus, Zerod had found her, and now wanted to kill her. If Rogar hadn't shown up, Callie might have lived her life in complete obscurity.

And boredom.

Her thought?

Callie's hand stilled as she was about to turn on the faucet. She didn't think so.

"You're here, aren't you?" she asked.

Silence.

"I remember you. We were friends once."

But you wanted me to go away.

Callie inhaled a sharp breath. "I was young and afraid. I didn't know what was happening to me. I want to get to know you."

Only to send me away again. You are not ready to accept that part of yourself.

Callie opened her mouth, but no words came out. What

could she say? That they could live in harmony for the rest of their lives?

"I'm so confused."

Silence. Callie knew her guide had buried herself again.

She washed her face, then turned off the water, and reached for a towel. When she looked into the mirror, she thought for a brief moment she saw different eyes staring back at her. Dark eyes flecked with gold. She blinked, and the image was gone, and she once more stared back at her own face.

Had it been a trick of the light? Suddenly, she felt drained. She needed to talk to Rogar about what was happening. She grabbed the white terry cloth robe off the hook on the door, and slipped her arms inside. After tying the belt, she hurried from the room.

He wasn't in the kitchen, or the living area. She walked to the front porch. The Hummer was still parked in the driveway. She started to go back inside when she heard a golf cart coming down the trail. Constance was driving, but Rogar was on the seat beside her.

Fury burned through her. She clamped her lips together, and narrowed her eyes.

It wasn't enough that Rogar was with a woman Callie loathed, no, Candice looked bright-eyed and beautiful, while Callie was only wearing the robe. She was also barefoot, and her hair still tousled. She ran her fingers through it as they pulled close to the porch.

What the hell was Rogar doing with Constance anyway? Damn it, Callie really didn't want to have to deal with the other woman this early in the morning.

Constance smiled up at Callie, but there wasn't an ounce of warmth in it.

"I see you're finally up." Her gaze scanned Callie. When she met Callie's eyes once more, Constance gloated. "Not a morning person, are you?"

Rogar climbed out of the cart, impervious to the underlying sarcasm passing between the two women.

"You've been up for a while," Callie said. "You should have woken me."

Constance's eyes narrowed. "Remember what I said, Rogar." She smirked. "The offer is on the table." She turned the cart, and left without saying another word.

Callie met his gaze. "What offer?" There was no way they could have discussed business since, as far as she knew, Constance's family wasn't involved in interplanetary import and export.

Rogar turned and watched the cart disappear around the corner. "She wanted us to become lovers."

"She wanted . . . lovers! That bitch!" She started down the steps, but before she could even step off the first one, Rogar scooped her into his arms and carried her inside.

"I told her no, I was very satisfied with the lover I already have."

She felt somewhat better. Then she eyed him with more than a little suspicion. "Are you telling me the truth?"

"I would never lie to you."

"Why were you even with her?"

"I took a check to Ms. Crane. It was a nice, early morning walk."

Now he was writing hot checks? Oh, God, she was definitely going to prison. "But you don't have a bank account."

"I created one with my database. The money has been transferred to the account. Everything is taken care of. It was relatively simple."

"That still doesn't explain why you were with Constance." Was that really her questioning him like a jealous girlfriend? Yes, it was, and yes, she was jealous of Constance. Jealous might not be the right word.

Territorial?

Not that Rogar was her exclusive property. He would leave soon, and probably find someone new. Ouch, that hurt.

"I was with Constance because she drove by and offered me a ride. I was anxious to get back to you, so I accepted."

She smiled as a warm, tingly feeling tickled her tummy. "You were?"

He dropped a kiss on her lips before he set her on her feet. "Yes, I was. I don't know how to cook and I'm starved."

She cocked an eyebrow. "That is so not funny."

There was a knock on the door. They both turned. If Constance was on the other side, she'd belt her one. Rogar might not be hers forever, but he was hers for right now.

"I'll get it," she said, then marched to the door, ready for battle.

Chapter 26

Callie opened the door, surprised to see Freddie. "Good morning."

"God, you're even beautiful when you first wake up. You have that look about you."

She frowned. "What look?"

"The look that says you've been well-loved." He sighed. "Too bad I wasn't the guy you were with."

"Did you want something?" Rogar asked as he came up behind Callie. "Besides Callie that is."

She glanced over her shoulder. Was that a note of jealousy she heard in his voice? His stern expression said it just might very well be. She kind of liked the idea that someone would be jealous over her.

Freddie seemed to weigh his options, then sighed deeply. "Since I apparently can't have her, how about a cup of coffee?" He pushed the door open wider, and strolled inside. "Computers are a marvelous invention, you know. You can find out about anyone with the touch of a finger. Like the fact there is no prince of New Symtaria, nor is there even a country." He went around the kitchen bar to the cabinets, opening them until he found the coffee.

She realized her mouth was hanging open, and snapped it closed. Crap, what were they going to do now? She cast a worried glance at Rogar, before shutting the front door. "Uh . . .

what are you getting at?" she asked as she walked over to the bar.

He took the glass carafe to the sink and filled it, looking up only after pouring water into the machine. "Nothing much, except there isn't a prince called Rogar Valkyir anywhere in the world."

She gave a short, unconvincing laugh. "It's a very small country. I doubt it's even listed."

Freddie looked at Rogar. "The guy is leading you down the wrong path Callie. He's a con man. Believe me, I've met my share of them. I can't believe you've fallen for his lines."

"I haven't lied to anyone," Rogar said.

Freddie's eyes narrowed, and for the first time in her life, Callie realized looks can be deceiving. There was a lot more to Freddie than anyone suspected.

"Then what is the name of your country?" he asked, voice as cold as ice.

"New Symtaria."

Freddie shook his head. "Symtaria would have popped up on the search engine. Symtaria, new or old, doesn't exist."

Callie felt as though the room was quickly closing in on her. Please, please, please just drop it Freddie, she silently prayed.

"I'll give you one hour to clear out. Alone. Then I'm calling the police, whether you've left or not." He shook his head. "Why would you lie to Callie like that? She's never done anything to anyone. She's the only real and decent person I've ever met."

"I didn't intend to hurt Callie," Rogar told him.

"But you have. She'll be lucky if she doesn't get in trouble. Did you just assume she would clean up the mess you're leaving behind? The million dollar bid last night?" His lip curled into a sneer. "I doubt someone like you has ever seen that much money."

"It's not like that," Callie broke in.

"Callie, don't buy into his game. The jewels you wore last

night were probably fake, or worse, stolen. I have lawyers who can help you if you need them. Don't worry."

She looked at Rogar, silently begging for help.

"I am not from your planet," Rogar said.

Callie groaned. That was not the kind of help she had been praying for.

Freddie began to slowly inch around the bar, moving closer to her. "Another planet. That's a little hard to buy, buddy."

This was not going at all well.

Rogar looked calm, not at all disturbed that Freddie now knew he was an alien. Not that Callie thought for one minute Freddie believed Rogar. No, from the expression on Freddie's face, she was pretty sure he thought Rogar was a nutcase. She wasn't too sure this had been the right way to go.

"Tell me more about this planet you say you're from," Freddie urged.

Callie knew the drill, keep the crazy guy talking so they could make an escape. Been there, done that.

"We're alien shapeshifters. I've come to take Callie home."

"She is home." Freddie was closer to her now.

"He's telling the truth, Freddie," she ventured. She might as well back up Rogar's story.

Freddie stepped in front of her. She thought it was sweet that he would try to protect her. Not that she needed protecting.

"He's only brainwashed you, Callie. I also have a psychiatrist on call who's really pretty good. He's helped me a lot."

"Would you like me to prove it to you?" Rogar asked.

"Not Balam." Freddie might have a coronary if Rogar suddenly shifted into Balam. She certainly didn't want his death on her conscience.

"Not Balam," he assured her.

"Who's this Balam?"

"It doesn't matter," she said. "How are you going to prove it?"

"Yeah, how?" Freddie leaned an elbow on the bar, practically daring Rogar to prove himself, but she could see his body was still tense, as though he waited for the perfect opportunity to grab her so they could make their escape.

"I've come to the conclusion there are certain things Symtarians can do that people from Earth can't."

Freddie snorted.

Rogar pointed his finger toward the lamp on the table beside the sofa. When he wiggled his finger, the lamp moved a few inches.

"Wow, you never mentioned you could do that," she said.

"A magician's trick." Freddie scoffed, and opened both hands, then waved them back and forth. With the snap of a finger, he produced a rose, which he gave to Callie.

"I forgot you did magic tricks, Freddie. That was good." She automatically brought it to her nose. Silk. Oh, well.

Rogar frowned. "Your gravity is slightly different from ours." He closed his eyes, and slowly began to raise his hands, as he did, his body gravitated upward.

"Wow, he's good." Freddie was transfixed as he watched Rogar.

Apparently, he'd forgotten that he'd pegged Rogar as crazy. Callie's lips turned down. Freddie didn't seem as upset as he had. From the rapt expression on Freddie's face, he certainly wasn't as worried about her safety as he once was. Men!

"How'd you do that?" she asked.

Rogar's feet settled on the floor once again. "I've noticed little things since coming to Earth. There must be something in the gravitational force."

"I can't do that." Callie crossed her arms in front of her. She was lucky if she didn't trip over her own two feet.

"Probably because you're part Earthling. It might be something to explore. I have a theory about the gravitational force being somewhat different, which could have some effect on a Symtarian's molecular structure."

She took one look at Freddie. Rogar had talked his nerdy language, but Freddie still didn't look as though he believed Rogar could be from another planet.

"I saw someone in Vegas who could do that," Freddie said.

"Balam?" Rogar looked at Callie.

Callie really hadn't wanted to take it this far, but it seemed they had no choice. She nodded.

A light fog began to fill the room.

"What's happening?" Freddie straightened, looking around.

"It's the only way we can make you believe," Callie told him. "The Symtarians are a race of shapeshifters. They have animal guides that share their body."

"Where are the cameras?" He looked around.

"There aren't any."

Rogar groaned, drawing their attention. The fog wasn't so thick that they couldn't see Rogar drop to the floor on his hands, then groan as he curled into a ball. Not so dense they couldn't see flesh change to fur, hands become claws.

"I . . . I . . ."

She took Freddie's hand in hers. The color had drained from his face. "It'll be okay. Balam is a black jaguar. He's also Rogar's animal guide."

"He really is from another planet." Freddie sat down hard on the stool.

"Yes."

The mist cleared. Balam opened his mouth and roared. Freddie tilted sideways on the stool. Callie grabbed him before he could fall off.

"That's a jaguar. They eat people," Freddie pointed out.

"He won't eat you."

"Are you sure?"

"Not positive."

Freddie's eyes were wide when he turned them on her. "What do you mean, you're 'not positive'?"

"He won't," she quickly told him. Then, to prove her words, she walked over and knelt in front of Balam. "Hello, again." She smiled, then rubbed the cat behind his ear. Balam purred, rubbing his head against her cheek. Callie would never get over the fact she could get this close to a jaguar.

Balam raised his head, looking over her shoulder, then trotted into the other room.

Freddie watched the cat leave, then looked her way, as if he only now remembered she was still in the room. His infatuation was really short lived. She would give him credit for trying to protect her, though. Meeting an alien apparently took precedent over his concern for her safety. The story of her life.

Freddie seemed to come out of his daze. He snapped his fingers. "You shapeshifted into that flamingo last night." He looked at Callie. "That was you, wasn't it?"

She could feel the heat rise up her face. "Yes."

He laughed. "You certainly hit your target. I've never seen Constance that pissed before."

"But we're keeping a low profile," she quickly told Freddie, and only hoped he would keep this to himself.

"Low profile?" he repeated.

"Yes."

He reached over the bar and grabbed the paper he'd brought with him, then spread it out. She groaned when she caught a glimpse of Rogar's picture splattered across the front page.

Visiting Prince Bids One Million
For Porcelain Statue at Benefit Auction

This wasn't good.

"It went over the AP's so I'm sure the bigger papers picked it up as well," Freddie said. "I mean, who wouldn't. It's a good story."

Rogar emerged from the bedroom completely dressed.

"Look at this." She held the picture up for him to see.

Rogar moved closer, his frown deepening. "I didn't know anyone was taking pictures."

"Nearly everyone has a camera phone these days. It wouldn't have been hard for them to take this," Freddie said, staring at Rogar as though he was some kind of god.

"Zerod will know our location." Rogar walked to the window, as if he expected their enemy to show up any second.

Cold chills of foreboding ran up and down her arms.

Freddie looked from Rogar to Callie. "Who's Zerod?"

"A particularly evil man who wants to destroy mixed bloods."

"You're part alien," Freddie said.

She nodded.

"That means you're on this Zerod's hit list."

"I won't let harm come to her," Rogar promised.

Freddie studied Callie. "That's wild that you're part alien. All this time, and you never told anyone?"

"I didn't know," she said.

"We have to leave." Rogar turned and met Callie's gaze. "We're no longer safe."

"I have a place . . ." Freddie began.

"No, we can't run forever," Callie said.

Freddie grimaced. "Go to the police . . ."

"And tell them what? That an alien wants to kill me? I'd just as soon not be the one locked up."

He straightened. "Then Rogar and I will protect you."

She shook her head. "It's not your fight."

"I'll make it my fight."

"No, Callie is right. Besides, Zerod is powerful. You would be no match for him. But I am eternally grateful for your courageous offer."

"Where will you go?' Freddie asked.

"Home," Callie said. "If we're going to stand our ground, then I want it to be on my turf." She took Freddie's hands in hers. "After we leave, don't come back to the cabin. It might not be safe."

He nodded, then surprised her by grabbing her close to

him in a hug. The angry cry of a jaguar filled the small space. Freddie jumped back, his face ashen.

"What the hell was that?"

She quickly shifted her attention to Rogar who didn't look at all pleased. "You better leave," she told Freddie.

"Sure." He hurried past Rogar, gave him a sideways glance, then left.

"Did you have to do that?" she asked.

"I didn't like him touching you."

"It didn't mean anything."

"It meant more to him than you realize." He marched past her and walked toward the bedroom.

"Just don't start marking your territory," she mumbled, but had to admit it felt nice that he was jealous.

She hurried after him. It took them only a few minutes to gather their things and leave in the Hummer. She wasn't sad to leave the camp. Especially Constance.

"We'll need a plan of action," she said. "A trap. He needs to be destroyed."

"It is against our law to kill another Symtarian," he said.

"But it's okay for him to kill me?"

"Our laws need to be changed. When that was written, we were all of pure blood."

"Well, excuse me for living."

He reached across the seat and took her hand. "We're not a cruel race, Callie. The laws were created to protect everyone."

"Except there are people like Zerod out there who want all the non–pure bloods destroyed."

"He's a rogue. There will always be his kind in every society."

"You're right." She sighed. "Then what can we do?"

"Cage him. Then I will transport him back to New Symtaria, where he will be locked away forever."

"The only place I know with a cage that can hold him is the zoo." That wasn't a bad idea when she thought about it.

He shook his head. "No, how could I keep you safe, if you're at work?"

She suddenly smiled. "Don't you see, it's perfect. We'll tell Mr. Campbell that you've decided it would be interesting to work with the cats at the zoo. He thinks the reason I'm taking off is so I can convince you to come to work for him. You can tell him you need me as your assistant."

"I'm still not sure. Too many people."

"We'll work something out."

"There's still one other solution."

She shook her head. "I won't let Zerod run me off."

He finally nodded. "You would make a fine warrior."

She tried not to smile at his words, but lost the battle. "You think I'd make a good fighter?"

"No, a warrior. There's a difference. A warrior plans his battles. A fighter just fights because he enjoys battles."

"You have female warriors on New Symtaria?"

He nodded. "One of my sisters is a warrior." He suddenly frowned. "She's too aggressive sometimes. You would like her, though. Maybe you can meet her someday."

Someday. She was starting to hate that word. As in, someday Rogar would leave. He didn't know it, but the thought of his returning to New Symtaria was getting harder for her to imagine.

Would her memories be enough to sustain her on cold winter nights? Would her soft blanket and her flannel pj's be enough to keep her warm?

She had a feeling they wouldn't be.

Chapter 27

Mr. Campbell leaned back in his chair, puffing out his chest like a rooster about to let loose and crow. "Of course Callie can work with you. Can't break up a winning team. The media will love this. I wouldn't doubt if the mayor took an interest." He beamed. "I've always thought I could run for office if the opportunity presented itself. This might just be the chance I've been waiting for."

It was all she could do to keep from gagging. She'd always thought her boss was pretty much of an ass. Now he was proving he was. Maybe Mr. Campbell should be reminded that he was supposed to be thinking about the zoo and not his supposed political career.

She squared her shoulders. "And it should bring in revenue for improvements at the zoo."

"What? Oh, yes, we have to keep everyone happy—including the animals. They're why we're here."

His smile didn't even come close to sincere.

"We'll need privacy so I can get to know the cats." Rogar looked comfortable sitting in the chair. As if he was the one in charge, and truth be known, he was.

"Anything you want."

"Then we'll be working at night," Rogar said.

"But, how will we get all the publicity I want? You can't . . ." Mr. Campbell sputtered.

"Just until I'm comfortable with the big cats. I really don't think you want the media filming one of us being attacked and ripped to shreds. That might have the opposite effect."

Mr. Campbell nodded, leaning back in his chair. "You're right. I hadn't thought about that."

Great, he was more concerned with his reputation than the thought they might be killed by one of the animals.

He sat forward again. Elbows resting on his desk. "I'll give you a week."

"Two."

"Done." He shuffled some papers on his desk. "When Callie told me that you had agreed to work with the cats, I called a couple of guys down at the newspaper. Surely it won't hurt to at least have your picture taken, to sort of whet everyone's appetite."

"I think that's a good idea," Rogar said.

Mr. Campbell came to his feet, grinning widely. "Great! I'll just tell them to set everything up outside in front of the office. Come out whenever you're ready." He hurried out his office door.

Callie could tell Rogar saw through the other man's act, but this would be their chance to draw Zerod out. They would be ready for him this time. Once they got him inside a cage, Rogar would transport him back to New Symtaria where he would face charges for his criminal activity.

She would be safe.

And she would probably never see Rogar again. She closed her eyes, swallowing back the tears that threatened.

"Callie?" Rogar said her name like a whisper drifting on a warm breeze.

She rapidly blinked away the tears. "I'm ready." She came to her feet.

"Don't worry, it will soon be over. Zerod will not be able to hurt you. I'll make sure of that."

She was more worried about the fact Rogar would probably be leaving soon. Not that she wanted to die or anything.

They walked out the door to where the media was waiting. She would make sure she cut the picture out of the paper so she would at least have that to cling to. She was so pathetic.

You could go with him.

Callie stumbled. Rogar put a firm hand on her elbow.

You're back.

I never left. I've always been here.

I don't want you to leave . . . ever.

I won't.

When will I meet you?

Soon.

What do I call you?

Katun.

"Katun," she tested the name on her tongue.

"What?" Rogar looked at her.

She smiled as a reporter snapped another picture. "Katun is her name. The name of my guide."

He smiled and hugged her close. Did he know how she felt right now? As though she had found an old friend whom she'd thought had been lost forever. Yes, she suspected he did. Rogar was good about knowing how she felt.

As the reporters asked questions, Callie basked in the feeling that she had somehow become whole again. Deep down, she knew there would be more. It was as though her senses were coming alive. The very air around her seemed to crackle with energy.

"Tell us what it felt like when you jumped into the pit with the ferocious jaguar?" one of the reporters asked.

Her brow knit. Sheba wasn't ferocious. Sure, she was a wild animal, but Callie wouldn't exactly call her ferocious. Sheba did only what came naturally to her. No one could blame her for that.

A volley of rapid fire questions were aimed at Rogar, but he easily answered each and every one.

"I'll be back in a bit," she whispered to him, then headed toward the jaguar's cage. She felt a little guilty leaving him with the two reporters, but she would only be gone a few minutes. There was still twenty minutes left before the zoo opened. She could at least say hello to Sheba and make sure the jaguar was okay.

It took her about five minutes to walk to that side of the park. She sighed with relief when she saw Sheba in the pit, lying in the sun, except she looked a little droopy.

"Hey, Sheba," she said as she approached the enclosure.

The cat's head jerked up. Sheba cried out. Callie could've sworn that the jag looked glad to see her. And maybe she was. Callie rested her arms on the cement ledge. Sheba got up and moved closer, making Callie smile.

"So much has happened in my life, Sheba, that sometimes I think I'm being turned inside out. I don't know what to do anymore. I'm part alien, imagine that, and I can shift into another animal form, except I don't know my guide yet. Well, not exactly."

She closed her eyes for a moment. When she opened them, everything looked the same, except she knew she was different.

"And I've fallen in love with Rogar."

She closed her eyes and let that sink in for a few seconds. It was true. She had fallen in love with him.

"He's the first person who has come into my life and made me feel whole, as though I know where I belong. Except he wants me to go with him to New Symtaria, his planet, and I'm scared. Will I feel just as out of place there?"

And what if he didn't love her? She didn't know their customs. What if leaving totally screwed up her life even more? Would he bring her back? Would she still be next in line for the job she wanted? So many questions.

She sighed. "Then there's the problem that if I stay, Zerod could find me. He came to my house, and Rogar saved my life. If we draw him out, if he falls into our trap that we'll set here at the zoo, then maybe it would be safe to stay. I'm just not sure about anything, except that I'll never push my guide away again. I truly feel as though I've found a long lost friend."

*   *   *

Callie was quiet on the drive back to her house. Rogar left her to the silence. But as soon as she walked inside the house, she turned, and hugged him close to her. He held her without saying a word.

"When you said I would know my guide, you were right. It's different from anything I've ever experienced. Her thoughts aren't the same as mine. I feel as though we're two complete individuals, but at the same time, we're also a part of each other. Is it that way for everyone?"

"Yes."

She looked up at him. "When do you think I will get to meet her?"

"When the time is right."

"She said soon."

"Then it will be soon."

She frowned. "You knew I would feel like this."

"I was almost certain."

She stepped away. "This is still my home. I can't leave. It's the only sure thing I've ever had in my life."

"But it isn't your home," he told her. "You belong on New Symtaria."

"My gut tells me to stay. Don't ask me why, I just know this is where I need to be."

"You may never meet Katun, then. You still don't know what animal form she is. It could be dangerous for both of you if you shifted." He raked his fingers through his hair. "I care deeply for you, Callie. Come, if only because you want to be with me."

She saw the need on his face, but deep down inside, she knew something held her here on Earth. She shook her head. "I can't."

"Is it because of the job you want?" he asked with something close to disbelief in his voice.

She turned away from him, unable to look at the longing on his face. "I don't know what it is. I just know this is where I need to stay. I'm sorry."

There was a long pause in which she wondered what he was thinking, but she still couldn't bring herself to look at him.

"As soon as I take care of Zerod, I'll leave. I won't ask you to come with me again. If you should decide to travel with me to New Symtaria, I would be very pleased."

"Thank you." That sounded lame, but what was she supposed to say? God, was she making the right decision?

They slept the afternoon so they would be more alert that night. Rogar in the bed, Callie on the sofa. It was as though she was already putting distance between them. Odd how cold the bed was without her beside him. He ached to pull her close, to feel her body next to his, to . . .

A deep sigh interrupted his thoughts.

You're definitely in love with her.

I know, he told Balam.

You'll be hell to live with until you convince her that she has to return to New Symtaria with you.

And exactly how am I supposed to do that?

Give her what she has here. Make New Symtaria more tempting than Earth.

You would think I'd be enough temptation.

Balam snorted. *Rather full of yourself, aren't you?*

She damned well tempts me. Why shouldn't I tempt her?

Make her want to leave with you, more than she wants to stay.

"Okay, okay, I'll try." How the hell was he going to convince her when they didn't cage animals on New Symtaria? They were free to roam at will. No one harmed the guides, and the guides didn't harm the humans. She wouldn't have the job she so desperately wanted.

Occasionally, there were rogue hunters that had to be caged, but there were specially trained guards who cared for those humans or guides. It wasn't a good job. They weren't a perfect society.

He sat on the side of the bed. His stomach growled and he realized it had been a while since he'd eaten. As he went to the other room, Rogar caught a glimpse of Callie sleeping on the sofa, and walked closer.

Her breathing was even, as though she slept peacefully. And why wouldn't she? It wasn't as though she cared for him as much as he did her. How could he be so stupid as to fall in love with her?

His body trembled. He did love her. He loved her with all his heart.

She stretched.

He went back into the kitchen, not wanting her to see him right now. The last thing he wanted from her was pity. He was such a fool. On New Symtaria he had women practically falling at his feet, but it was Callie that had taken him to his knees.

"I'm starved," she said.

He glanced over his shoulder. She wore that sleepy look that reminded him of when they mated. He quickly faced the cabinet and opened it.

"You have nothing to eat."

"Because I never have much money for food," she grumbled.

"Pizza." He looked up the number, then punched it in.

"You really like pizza, don't you?" she said after he placed the order.

"It's good." He cleared his throat. "About tonight. I want you to get out of there if Zerod shows up."

"Do you think he will?"

"No, not really. He hasn't had time to pick up our scent."

She raised her eyebrows. "Can you do that? I mean, smell someone's scent?"

He shrugged. "Sometimes. It depends. A guide can sometimes detect another Symtarian, but not always."

"Can you detect my scent?"

He wished she would let it go, but he could tell by her expression she was just curious enough to keep asking. So be it, she wanted to know, he would tell her.

"Yes, I know your scent. It's the wildflowers that burst with fragrance after the danger of a freeze has passed. It's sultry, lazy nights. It's the scent of the forest." He stopped in front of her. "It's everything that I love."

She didn't move when he grazed his knuckles over her cheek, or when he lowered his head and brushed his lips across hers. Fool, his mind screamed, but he couldn't seem to stop. If nothing else, he would have his memories.

When he ended the kiss, they were both breathing hard. "I don't like sleeping alone," he finally said.

"The sofa is uncomfortable."

"Good, then you will sleep with me from now on."

"Until it's time for you to leave."

He heard the catch in her voice, and knew this was as hard for her as it was him. "We won't speak of leaving. Not until that time comes."

"Okay."

He forced himself to let her go, and went to the cabinet, bringing down two glasses. The silence was thick with unspoken words.

The doorbell finally rang.

Her smile was sad. "Pizza."

Glad for something to do, he went to get their food. The same young man was on the other side of the door.

"I kept it nice and hot, sir, and I threw in some cinnamon swirls—no extra charge."

"That was thoughtful." Rogar reached in his pocket, and brought out a thick wad of money. He peeled off several bills and handed it to the boy."

The kid swallowed hard, then took the money, shoving it into the pocket of his jeans. "Thank you very much!" He handed Rogar the drinks and the pizza, then jogged back to his vehicle. When Rogar turned, Callie was smiling.

"What?"

She walked forward and took the bottle of soda. "The normal tip is around five dollars, not five hundred."

"You think I gave him too much?"

"I think if you stay here very much longer, you'll pay for his college education."

He nodded. "Education is a good thing."

She suddenly sobered. "You could stay, you know. Think how much you could learn about Earth while you were here. You know, be an explorer or something."

"I can't."

"But why not? It's the perfect solution."

"I cannot." He walked to the kitchen and set the box on the table.

"It could work."

"I'm sorry."

She set the bottle of soda on the table and planted her hands on her hips. "Oh, I see, it's okay for me to give up everything I've ever known and go to another planet far, far away. But when I suggest you stay here with me, you won't even consider it."

He sighed. Things had been going so smoothly. "I'm a prince. I have responsibilities."

"Ohh, now I'm impressed. I guess I'm too low class that you would even consider staying with me."

How had she managed to twist his words? "You know that's not what I meant."

"I'm just beginning to think I might not know you as well as I thought I did," she said quietly. "I'm going to take a shower." She glanced at the clock on the wall. "It won't be long before it's time to leave."

"You need to eat."

"I will. I just want to shower first."

He let her go, watching until she went inside the bedroom and closed the door. He didn't want to leave her. He wanted her to be a part of his life, but he had a feeling she was already gone.

Chapter 28

Callie was antsy. Three nights had passed, and still nothing from Zerod. Not a hint that he was even in the area. Their pictures had been plastered all over the front page of the paper, taunting him to show his face. Telling him they weren't scared of what he might attempt.

She stopped at the fence in front of Sheba's cage. Rogar would probably kill her himself because she'd slipped away, but she had to get out of the building for a while. Rogar was busy with the lion's cub. Somehow, it had cut its foot. She smiled. The cub was a cute little fellow. Always into one thing or another. Besides, she wouldn't be gone that long. Rogar probably wouldn't even miss her.

And if Zerod showed up, she had a can of mace in one pocket of her jacket, and a small gun in the other, and she knew how to use them both. Not that she was a marksman or anything, but DeeDee was a damned good shot. They'd gone to the firing range a few times. DeeDee had shown Callie how to load, aim, and fire a gun. Callie wouldn't think twice about pulling the trigger, either.

The strain of the last few days eased as she neared the jaguar's cage. "What do you say, Sheba? Will Zerod show himself tonight?"

The jaguar growled from deep in her throat as though she understood.

"Yeah, I know. I don't like him, either. Rogar will protect me, though." She had no doubts that he would come running if she needed him. Could she do the same? He wanted her to go with him.

"I can't just pick up and go live on another planet. This is where I belong, right?"

Callie crossed the fence, and knelt in front of the cage. It was dangerous, she knew. Sheba wasn't like Balam. But Callie couldn't stop herself.

Sheba had treated Rogar like a long lost friend. Would Sheba sense Callie's guide? On the other hand, Balam was a jaguar. Callie still didn't know what her guide was. It could be a rabbit. Sheba might have been looking at her all these years as a meal, rather than a friend.

"Someday, we'll really get to know each other," she said. "Of course I can't leave Earth. Never seeing you again would be unthinkable."

Sheba purred as if she agreed, then came to her feet, and ambled across the cage, stopping in front of Callie. Sheba rubbed her head against the bars.

Tentatively, Callie raised her hand, felt Sheba's fur like a warm caress. Strong emotions flooded Callie as her eyes filled with tears. She had no idea why it meant so much for her to touch Sheba, but it did. Maybe because she had longed to so many times, but never had the courage. She had Rogar to thank for that.

"I have to get back. Rogar will worry. I'll try to sneak in another visit before we leave in the morning."

As Sheba went back to her corner of the cage, Callie hurried back to the animal keepers' building, and Rogar. The lioness still made her nervous, but Rogar seemed perfectly comfortable with her, too.

Some people would think she was crazy to want to work with the big cats when she was a little scared of them, but she also felt this incredible pull to be around them.

Before she reached the building, a man stepped from the

shadows. Her heart pounded inside her chest. She opened her mouth to scream, but no sound came out. She fumbled inside her pocket for the gun.

"I was getting worried about you," Rogar said.

She ran the rest of the way to him, throwing her arms around his neck.

"You're trembling."

That was an understatement. "I thought you were Zerod." Oh, yeah, she was real brave.

"I'm sorry. I wasn't that quiet as I walked down the sidewalk, though."

"I guess I was lost in thought."

He frowned. "I don't want you this far away from me again. If I had been Zerod . . ."

He left his sentence unfinished, but Rogar didn't need to go into any detail. She could guess what would have happened.

"What were you doing?" he asked.

Her cheeks grew warm. She was glad the only light in this area came from the full moon. "I was checking on Sheba."

"You were with her that first night, too."

"I couldn't have a pet." She shrugged. "I sort of adopted the jaguar." Excitement began to build inside her. "This time was different, though. She actually walked over to the bars, and I pet her."

"You love her very much, don't you?"

"I do. Over the years that I've been here, I've poured my heart out to her." She chuckled. "Sheba is a good listener."

"I could be a good listener, too." His hand lightly stroked her arm.

Callie closed her eyes, her heart pounding. He wasn't asking her to leave, just telling her what it would be like if she did.

"Make love to me," she whispered. She suddenly needed to feel him inside her, needed that connection with him.

"It would be dangerous."

She placed her fingers over his lips. "I want to make love to you right here, right now, then every time I walk past this spot, I'll think about you." She stepped out of his arms and removed her jacket before she began to unbutton her shirt. He was still watching her when she slipped it off.

"Callie." His voice was ragged with need.

"Don't think. Just make love to me."

She unfastened her bra and let it fall to the ground. He groaned, before grabbing her against him. Her breasts crushed against his chest, her nipples hard from the cool breeze.

Rogar had once told her he wanted to make love to her outside. This was the perfect place. She felt as though she was deep in a jungle. Making love here would give her a memory that would last a lifetime. It would have to last that long.

She raised her head, felt his lips against hers, then his tongue stroking, caressing, loving. His hands slid over her rib cage, then back up to cup her breasts in the palms of his hands. She moaned when he rubbed his thumbs over her nipples. Pleasure shot down, settling between her legs.

He ended the kiss, but she didn't waste any time unfastening his jeans, then sliding the zipper down. She ached to hold him.

Rogar toed off his boots, then shoved his pants off the rest of the way while she did the same with her clothes. He scooped them up, then tugged her deeper into the wooded area. As soon as they were out of view of any guard who might wander by, he dropped their clothes on the ground and pulled her into his arms.

"I want to taste you," he said. "All of you."

He licked across her nipple. She leaned against a tree for support. He licked across the other nipple before sucking it inside his mouth.

She grasped his head, pulling it even closer, as sensations swirled inside her. It felt so good. She couldn't think, she didn't want to think, she only wanted to feel what he was doing to her body.

He licked over her stomach, then between her legs,

She drew in a sharp breath as his tongue slid over her, then sucked the fleshy part of her sex inside his mouth. She felt naughty, she felt embarrassed—oh, God, she felt so freakin' good!

He grabbed her butt, bringing her closer, tighter, keeping her against his mouth as he sucked, running his tongue over her sex. She couldn't move even if she had wanted to, which she didn't. It felt so wonderful.

She grasped the sides of the tree, holding on. There was nothing in the world that could harm either of them. The only thing that mattered was this moment in time.

The fire inside her began to build, taking her higher and higher. Flames licking her. Passion building.

Her legs began to quiver as she came. She cried out, then stifled it. Waves of pleasure washed over her. She didn't think her legs would hold her up, but she didn't have to worry. Rogar picked her up, then laid her down on top of their clothes.

She felt a familiar burning ache begin inside her. She was going to shift.

It's not time, Callie.

Whatever, she thought dreamily.

She began to relax, and the feeling slowly went away.

Then Rogar was entering her. He began to move, slowly at first, then faster. She wrapped her legs around his waist. Heard his groan of pleasure as he sank deeper. Her body ached once again for the release that only Rogar could give her.

He cried out at the same time the world burst into a multitude of colors around her. She gasped. Rogar collapsed on top of her, then rolled to his side.

Silence.

Only the sound of their labored breathing.

Her world slowly came back into focus.

When he moaned, she knew what was about to happen. Okay, she didn't mind Rogar seeing her naked, but she felt a little odd when it was Balam. She grabbed her clothes just as the fog rolled in and jerked them on. She was dressed when the shift occurred.

"It's me, Balam." She warily eyed the cat, hoping he would remember her.

Balam came to his feet with a roar.

Ben clomped through the brush at the same time, raised his gun, then fired. Callie stared at the security guard in disbelief.

Balam! Rogar!

She turned just as Balam went down.

Oh, God, she was going to be sick. She turned on Ben.

"You shot him."

Chapter 29

"Looks like I was just in time, too," Ben said. "I heard rustling around and pulled my tranquilizer gun. You're safe now. Well, until the medication wears off, but we'll have him in a cage long before then."

She looked at the downed jaguar. Balam was panting as he tried to focus, the dart poking out his flank.

Ben pushed the button on his radio. "Ray, bring the Jeep with the trailer hitched to it. Grab that canvas, too. We got a jaguar to get locked up."

"Uh, did you say a jaguar was loose?"

"Don't worry. I knocked him out. There's enough medicine in him to keep him quiet for a while."

Static, then, "Sure thing. Wow, I can't wait to hear about this one."

While they were talking, Callie removed the dart. "I'm so sorry. I'll get you out, I promise." She shoved his clothes behind a log, and pushed some leaves on top of them, glad there were so many on the ground.

"How'd he get out?" Ben asked.

"I guess the door wasn't secure." She held her breath, hoping he would believe her.

Ben squinted. "Don't remember a black jaguar."

"He's new."

Ben nodded. "Better be more careful."

"I will." She exhaled a deep sigh of relief.

In less than ten minutes, Ray came lumbering up in the Jeep, the trailer bouncing behind him. Ben motioned for him to back it up, bringing it as close as they could without hitting a tree. Callie hurried to help roll Balam onto the canvas Ray had laid out.

"Careful, don't hurt him."

"I'm the one who's going to have a hernia. What's he weigh? Two hundred?"

"One ninety, maybe," Ray said.

They put him on the cart. Callie chose to ride with Balam to the cages. "It'll wear off in about an hour or so, I promise," she whispered. Why had she thought making love in the zoo was a good idea? It had been stupid. She only hoped the tranquilizer wouldn't have any lasting effects.

They stopped in front of the cage next to Sheba. She paced inside hers as if the other jaguar made her nervous. This wasn't good at all. Sheba might have accepted Rogar, but she apparently did not like Balam.

"I don't think she cares for the new jaguar," Ben voiced her thoughts.

"I'm sure everything will be okay," she said.

Ben's radio crackled again. Ben pulled it out of the holster on his hip and pushed the button.

"What's the matter now?" he asked.

"The gorilla is going ape shit." Apparently, he realized what he'd said and began to laugh while still holding the button down.

Ben frowned. "Smart ass," he mumbled, then pushed the button again when the other guy let off. "I'll be right there." He turned to Callie. "You'll be okay?"

She nodded.

Ben looked up. "Full moon. All the animals go crazy. Never fails." He started toward the Jeep. "If you have any more problems, just give me a holler."

"I'm sure I'll be fine now. Thanks, Ben."

As soon as he drove off, she quickly opened the cage and hurried to Balam. He was still sleeping. She ran her hand over his dark coat. "You are so going to have a headache when you wake up." And as long as he woke up before morning, they would be fine. She really doubted the zoo's visitors would appreciate viewing a naked alien in a cage.

On second thought, maybe they would. Rogar was a hottie, no two ways about it. She certainly enjoyed looking at him. She shook her head. Sheesh, crazy thoughts. Sometimes she wondered about her mental state.

Sheba was still creating a ruckus so Callie went to her, leaving Balam's cage open just a bit in case the drug wore off early.

"What's the matter, girl? Balam wouldn't hurt you. There's nothing to be afraid of."

"Isn't there?" Zerod asked as he stepped from the shadows.

Callie felt the color drain from her face as cold dread filled her. "Ben!" She turned, but already knew he was long gone.

"I really doubt he'll be able to help you. In fact, I'm certain he'll be with the gorilla the rest of his shift. It was so easy to create a diversion. I'll have to thank the guard for knocking Balam out for me, though. An error in judgment on my part, I'm afraid. I planned to attack sooner, but I got rather caught up watching the two of you mate."

"You bastard," she snarled.

"I can see why Symtarians have enjoyed mating with women from Earth." He reached out and caressed her face. When she jerked away, he only laughed. "There's a wildness about you that almost matches that of our women. Maybe I'll mate with you before I kill you."

"I'd rather die than have you touch me."

He bowed slightly. "As you wish."

His hands were around her throat before she could run. She stumbled back against Balam's cage. He made an angry noise from deep in his throat as he tried to protect her, but she knew he wouldn't have the strength.

She attempted to get to her pocket where the gun was, but couldn't quite reach it. *How could I have thought I'd be a match for Zerod?*

Her world began to go dark.

Zerod applied just enough pressure that she was able to get a little oxygen into her starving lungs. Just enough that she could hear his words. Not enough that she had the strength to defend herself.

"You look a lot like your mother," Zerod said. "She was a very beautiful woman. But I see some of your father as well. He was such an easy kill. No sport at all."

"I hope you die a painful death," she managed to gasp.

He chuckled, then turned serious. "Not until I wipe everyone not of pure blood off every planet. Our blood should never be mixed." He lowered his head, his lips pressing against hers in a quick kiss. She almost gagged.

Their gazes locked. She saw the hatred in his, and knew she was going to die tonight. There was so much she still wanted to do. So much she still wanted to see.

"Good-bye, Callie Jordon." He squeezed harder.

Lights danced in front of her eyes as the sounds around her diminished. She vaguely heard his voice.

"They'll think Balam killed you when I'm done. They'll think he ripped your body to shreds. I won't have to harm Rogar, they'll put Balam down for me, and Rogar with him."

She tried to tell Zerod what she thought of him, but no words formed as her oxygen was completely cut off. This was it. The end. What did she have to show for her life here on Earth? She hadn't even gotten the job she'd worked so hard for.

Or to tell Rogar she loved him.

She loved him. She did. With all her heart.

Callie tried to raise her hand, to hit at Zerod, but she didn't have the strength.

Suddenly, she felt a great weight push her against the bars of the cage. She fell to the ground, oxygen filled her lungs. She took great gulps as the fog cleared from her brain.

Zerod screamed. She opened her eyes. Sheba, not Balam, had attacked him. How had she gotten out? Callie shook her head to clear it, but when she looked again, she saw that Zerod was changing into his animal guide with a swiftness that could only come with age. He would kill Sheba. The jaguar wouldn't be able to fight his experience.

Anger swelled inside her fast and furious. Fire burned deep in her belly as a familiar ache grew and fog moved over her. She stretched, welcoming whatever help she could give.

This time the shapeshifting felt different. She felt different. She groaned. Then blinked.

Together we will conquer him, the voice inside her spoke.

Katun?

We meet at last my friend.

Callie blinked, and knew she was seeing through the eyes of her jaguar guide. And yes, she knew she was jaguar. Callie didn't need a mirror this time.

She could feel Katun's power, her strength, as she joined forces with Sheba.

Zerod's animal guide was no match for the two of them. They continued pressing forward, attacking from both sides, until they had him backed into Sheba's cage. Sheba rammed her head against it and the door clicked shut.

Zerod's injuries were many. He growled one last time, then dropped to the straw bed, waiting for his injuries to heal. But for now, he was out of commission, and they were safe.

Thank you, Katun.

You are welcome, my sister.

Callie smiled, liking the idea that they were sisters. Then just as suddenly, she collapsed to the ground. What was happening? Had she been injured? She closed her eyes as she began to shift back to her human side.

So much had happened.

I'm not ready to say good-bye, Katun.

You have other things to attend to that I cannot help you do.

What other things?

But Katun was already gone and fog was rolling in. Rogar hadn't mentioned other things that Callie needed to do when she changed into her animal guide for the first time. Maybe there was a procedure that she was supposed to follow, or a ceremony.

She blinked several times until her vision cleared. Callie knew she had shifted back to her human form. She looked around. There was a woman kneeling beside her. A very beautiful woman, with long dark hair. And she wore a gentle smile.

"Hello, Callie." Her voice was like soft music.

There was something familiar about her, but Callie couldn't put her finger on what it was. "Who are you?"

"I am Recina."

"Do I know you?" She looked at the other woman, and noticed Recina wore her shirt. Nothing else, just her shirt, but it reached the top of her thighs.

"You know me as Sheba."

She quickly sat up and glanced around. Sheba was gone. Her gaze went back to Recina. "You're Symtarian?"

Recina nodded. "Yes."

"Did someone send you to watch over me all these years?" It didn't make sense. Sheba had been at the zoo almost as long as Callie. Too long for someone to live in a cage just to watch over her.

"Once I found you, and it took many years, I knew I had to stay close although it meant I would lose some of my freedom. I also knew that Zerod would detect my Symtarian scent, but not so much my animal guide's scent, especially when I was surrounded by other animals."

Callie could feel her heart begin to pound as tears pooled in her eyes. "But why would you do that?"

"That's what mothers do, Callie. They love their children more than anything else." And just so Callie would truly understand. "I'm your mother."

Chapter 30

"You're my mother?" Callie said, but she knew Recina spoke the truth. Now Callie knew why she felt such a connection here; it was Sheba. She'd felt that bond between them.

"I am," Recina told her.

Callie threw her arms around Recina and hugged her tight. "I've missed having you in my life. Please don't ever leave me again. I've felt so lost and alone without you."

"I won't, my child." She held Callie just as tight. "I've wanted to hold you close so many times, but I was afraid to take the chance of shifting."

There was a groan behind them. She looked over her shoulder and saw the fog.

"Rogar is shifting." Then Callie realized there was going to be a lot of naked people in the zoo. Not good if a guard happened by. Poor old Ben would have a heart attack. "I'll get his clothes." She jumped up, but at the last minute, turned back. "Don't leave."

"I won't."

Callie hurried back to where she and Rogar had made love, and grabbed his shirt off the ground. "Great way to meet your mom, buck naked." She shook her head as she slipped Rogar's shirt on, which fit her more like a short dress.

This is what I needed to finish, wasn't it, Katun?

Yes, my sister.

Have you always known about Sheba?

Only recently did I begin to suspect.

You're a jaguar. She smiled, liking that her guide was an animal she dearly loved.

Yes.

I'm glad.

She hurried to finish buttoning her shirt, then grabbed up Rogar's other clothes, and hurried back.

Balam had shifted back to Rogar while she was gone. He was sitting up, but he still looked groggy. He glanced up when he heard her approach.

"Tell Ben that if he shoots Balam again, the jaguar will eat him."

She smiled. His gaze swept over her.

"You're okay?" he asked.

She nodded. "And you?"

He shrugged. "Groggy."

"This is my mother."

"I know. We've been talking."

"And I met my animal guide."

"Katun?"

She nodded, unable to speak her happiness because she was afraid she would sound like an idiot if it all bubbled out, and she was more likely to do that in her excitement.

"You hadn't met your guide?" Recina asked with astonishment.

She shook her head. "It's a long story."

Recina smiled. "We have all the time in the world." She looked at Rogar, her smile still firmly in place. "And you two have mated?"

"Yes," Rogar told her.

"Uh . . ." Callie looked between the two.

Recina seemed to realize what she had just asked. "I'm

sorry. My mother raised me with all the traditions of a Symtarian. I'm afraid I've always been of that culture. I knew someday I would see my home again."

But Recina had just said she would never leave her? Had it been only words?

"We'd better get Zerod locked away where he can do no harm," Rogar said.

He was right. They would all have time for questions and answers later.

But she was starting to feel very confused.

"I never thought I would have the chance to wear clothes again," Recina said after they were back at Callie's house. They had just changed into some of Callie's clothes.

"Thank you for watching over me." Callie couldn't stop herself from giving her mother another hug. This was her mother! All these years and she'd been watching over Callie the whole time.

Recina held her close for a moment, then with a sniff, stepped back. She cleared her throat as she glanced around. "This is where you have lived?"

"It was all I could afford." Callie saw the shabbiness even more now that her mother was here. She would've hoped for her approval, but she could understand her disappointment.

Recina put her arm around Callie and pulled her close once again. "It's not your fault. You survived, we both did, and that's all that matters. Surviving has made you strong, I can see that. I guess I felt bad because I couldn't give you everything that I would have liked to give you."

"You gave me more than I ever dreamed."

Rogar walked in the front door. "I have Zerod safely locked away on my craft. He won't be able to get free. Once we're back on New Symtaria, he'll pay for his crimes." Rogar looked between the two of them. "It's time for me to return."

Callie's heart skipped a beat.

Go with him. It's where you belong, Callie. It's where I belong, too.

"Callie?" Rogar asked.

"I . . ." She looked at her mother.

"I can't tell you what to do."

"But I spent all that time going to college, and then there's DeeDee, and . . ."

"Follow your heart," Recina said. "But know that I will stay if that is what you choose."

Callie wasn't sure what she should do.

"I love you, Callie," Rogar told her. "I love you with all my heart. If you decide not to leave, I'll give up everything to come back and be with you."

She saw by his expression that he was serious. He would give up the planet that he loved, his people, just to be with her. But could she ask him to do that?

Or could she travel far, far away to New Symtaria?

It wasn't hard to figure out when she really thought about it.

She ran to Rogar and threw her arms around his neck. "I love you, too, and yes, I'll go back with you."

He swung her around, laughing before lowering his lips to hers in a searing kiss that left her breathless.

You made the right choice, Katun said.

I know.

And she did know. She'd always felt there was something missing in her life, but she'd never known what it was, until now.

Facing the unknown would take a lot of courage, but it was better than living the life she'd been living. Actually, when she thought about it, she hadn't really been living, only watching as life passed her by.

Don't miss INSTANT TEMPTATION, the third in
Jill Shalvis's Wilder brothers series, out now . . .

"I didn't invite you in, TJ."

He just smiled.

He was built as solid as the mountains that had shaped his life, and frankly had the attitude to go with them—the one that said he could take on whoever and whatever and you could kiss his perfect ass while he did so. She'd seen him do it, back in his hell-raising, misspent youth.

Not that she was going there, to the time when he could have given her a single look and she'd have melted into a puddle at his feet.

Had melted into a puddle at his feet. Not going there.

Unfortunately for her senses, he smelled like the wild Sierras; pine and fresh air, and something even better, something so innately male that her nose twitched for more, seeking out the heat and raw male energy that surrounded him. Since it made her want to lean into him, she shoved in another bite of ice cream instead.

"I saw on Oprah once that women use ice cream as a substitute for sex," he said.

She choked again, and he resumed gliding his big, warm hand up and down her back. "*You* watch Oprah?"

"No. Annie does, and once I overheard her yelling at the TV that women should have plenty of both sex *and* ice cream."

That sounded exactly like his Aunt Annie. "Well, I don't need the substitute."

"No?" he murmured, looking amused at her again.

"No!"

He hadn't taken his hands off her. He still had one rubbing up and down her back, the other low on her belly, holding her upright, which was ridiculous so she smacked it away. She did her best to ignore the fluttering he'd caused, and the odd need she had to grab him by the shirt, haul him close and have her merry way with him.

That was what happened to a woman whose last orgasm had come from a battery operated device instead of a man, a fact she'd admit, oh, *never*. "I was expecting your brother."

"Stone's working on Emma's 'honey do' list at the new medical clinic, so he sent me instead. Said to give you these." He pulled some maps from his back pocket, maps she needed for a field expedition for her research. When she took them out of his hands, he hooked his thumbs in the front pockets of his Levi's. He wore a T-shirt layered with an opened button-down that said WILDER ADVENTURES on the pec. His jeans were faded nearly white in the stress spots, of which there were many, nicely encasing his long, powerful legs and lovingly cupping a rather impressive package that was emphasized by the way his fingers dangled on his thighs.

Not that she was looking.

Okay, she was looking, but she couldn't help it. The man oozed sexuality. Apparently some men were issued a handbook at birth on how to make a woman stupid with lust. And he'd had a lot of practice over the years.

She'd watched him do it.

Each of the three Wilder brothers had barely survived their youth, thanks in part to no mom and a mean, son-of-a-bitch father. But by some miracle, the three of them had come out of it alive, and now channeled their energy into Wilder Adventures, where they guided clients on just about any outdoor adventure that could be imagined; heli-skiing, extreme mountain biking, kayaking, climbing, *anything*.

Though TJ had matured and found success, he still gave off a don't-mess-with-me vibe. Even now, at four in the afternoon, he looked big and bad and tousled enough that he might have just gotten out of bed and wouldn't be averse to going back.

It irritated her. It confused her. And it turned her on, a fact that drove her bat-shit crazy because she was no longer interested in TJ Wilder.

Nope.

It'd be suicide to still be interested. No one could sustain a crush for fifteen years.

No one.

Except, apparently, her. Because deep down, the unsettling truth was that if he so much as directed one of his sleepy, sexy looks her way, her clothes would fall right off.

Again.

Wasn't that just her problem. The fact that once upon a time, a very long time ago, at the tail end of TJ's out-of-control youth, the two of them had spent a single night together being just about as intimate as a man and a woman could get. Her first time, but definitely not his first. Neither of them had been exactly legal, and only she'd been sober.

Which meant only she remembered.

"Merilee said I could bring a date to the wedding, then got in this dig about whether I was seeing anyone, or between losers. I'd really hate to show up alone."

He'd learned not to trust that gleam in her eyes, but couldn't figure out where she was heading. "You only just broke up with NASCAR Guy." Usually it took her two or three months before she fell for a new man. In the in-between time she hung out more with him, as she'd been doing recently.

Her lips curved. "I love how you say 'NASCAR Guy' in that posh Brit accent. Yeah, we split two weeks ago. But I think I may have found a great guy to take to the wedding."

Damn. His heart sank. "You've already met someone new? And you're going to take him as your date?"

"If he'll go." The gleam was downright wicked now. "What do you think?"

He figured a man would be crazy not to take any opportunity to spend time with her. But . . . "If you've only started dating, taking him to a wedding could seem like pressure. And what if you caught the bouquet?" If Nav was with her and she caught the damned thing, he'd tackle the minister before he could get away and tie the knot then and there.

Not that Kat would let him. She'd say he'd gone out of his freaking mind.

"Oh, I don't think this guy would get the wrong idea." There was a laugh in her voice.

"No?"

She sprang off the washer, stepped toward him, and gripped the front of his rugby jersey with both hands, the brush of her knuckles through the worn blue-and-white-striped cotton making his heart race and his groin tighten. "What do you say, Nav?"

"Uh, to what?"

"To being my date for the wedding."

Hot blood surged through his veins. She was asking him to travel across the country and escort her to her sister's wedding?

Had she finally opened her eyes, opened her heart, and really seen him? Seen that he, Naveen Bharani, was the perfect man for her? The one who knew her perhaps better than she knew herself. Who loved her as much for her vulnerabilities and flaws as for her competence and strength, her generosity and sense of fun, those sparkling eyes, and the way her sexy curves filled out her Saturday-morning sweats.

"Me?" He lifted his hands and covered hers. "You want me to go?"

She nodded vigorously. "You're an up-and-coming photographer. Smart, creative." Face close to his, she added, eyes twinkling, "Hot, too. Your taste in clothes sucks, but if you'd let me work on you, you'd look good. And you're nice. Kind, generous, sweet."

Yes, he was all of those things, except sweet—another wimp word, like doll. But he was confused. She thought he was hot, which was definitely good. But something was missing. She wasn't gushing about how *amazing* he was and how *crazy* she was about him, the way she always did when she fell for a man. Her beautiful eyes were sharp and focused, not dreamy. Not filled with passion or new love. So . . . what was she saying?

He tightened his hands on hers. "Kat, I—"

"Will you do it? My family might even *approve* of you."

Suspicion tightened his throat. He forced words out. "So I'd be your token good guy, to prove you don't always date assholes."

"Ouch. But yes, that's the idea. I know it's a lot to ask, but please? Will you do it?"

He lifted his hands from hers and dropped them to his sides, bitter disappointment tightening them into fists.

Oblivious, she clenched his jersey tighter, eyes pleading with him. "It's only one weekend, and I'll pay your airfare and—"

"Oh, no, you won't." He twisted away abruptly, and her hands lost their grip on his shirt. Damn, there was only so much battering a guy's ego could take. "If I go, I'll pay my own way." The words grated out. He turned away and bus-ied himself heaving laundry from his washer to a dryer, try-ing to calm down and think. What should he do?

Practicalities first. If he agreed, would it affect the exhibit? No, all she was asking for was a day or two. He could escort her, make nice with her family, play the role she'd assigned him. He'd get brownie points with Kat.

"Nav, I couldn't let you pay for the ticket. Not when you'd be doing me such a huge favor. So, will you? You're at least thinking about it?"

Of course he'd already accumulated a thousand brownie points, and where had that got him? Talking about *roles*, she'd cast him as the good bud two years ago and didn't show any signs of ever promoting him to leading man.

He was caught in freaking limbo.

The thing was, he was tired of being single. He wanted to share his life—to get married and start a family. Though he and his parents loved each other, his relationship with them had always been uneasy. As a kid, he'd wondered if he was adopted, he and his parents seemed such a mismatch.

He knew "family" should mean something different: a sense of warmth, belonging, acceptance, support. That's what he wanted to create with his wife and children.

His mum was on his case about an arranged marriage,

sending him a photo and bio at least once a month, hoping to hook him. But Nav wanted a love match. He'd had an active dating life for more than ten years but, no matter how great the women were, none had ever made him feel the way he did for Kat. Damn her.

He bent to drag more clothes from the washer and, as he straightened, glanced at her. Had she been checking out his ass?

Cheeks coloring, she shifted her gaze to his face. "Please, Nav? Pretty please?" Her brows pulled together. "You can't imagine how much I *hate* the teasing." Her voice dropped. "The *poor Kat can't find a man* pity."

He understood how tough this wedding would be for her. Kat had tried so hard to find love, wanted it so badly, and always failed. Now she had to help her little sister plan her wedding and be happy for her, even though Kat's heart ached with envy. Having a good friend by her side, pretending to her family that she'd found a nice guy, would make things easier for her.

Yes, he was pissed that she wanted only friendship from him, but that was his problem. He shouldn't take his frustration and hurt out on her.

He clicked the dryer on and turned to face her. "When do you need to know?"

"No great rush, I guess. It's two weeks off. Like I said, I'll probably leave Monday. I'll take the train to Toronto, then on to Vancouver."

"It's a long trip."

"Yeah." Her face brightened. "It really is fun. I've done it every year or so since I moved here when I was eighteen. It's like being on holiday with fascinating people. A train's a special world. Normal rules don't apply."

He always traveled by air, but he'd watched old movies with Kat. *North by Northwest. Silver Streak.* Trains were sexy.

Damn. He could see it now. Kat would meet some guy, fall

for him, have hot sex, end up taking him rather than Nav to the wedding.

Unless . . .

An idea—brilliant? insane?—struck him. What if he was the guy on the train?

What if he showed up out of the blue, took her by surprise? An initial shock, then days together in that special, sexy world where normal rules didn't apply. Might she see him differently?

If he analyzed his idea, he'd decide it was crazy and never do it. So, forget about being rational. He'd hustle upstairs and go online to arrange getting money transferred out of the trust fund he hadn't touched since coming to Canada.

It had been a matter of principle: proving to himself that he wasn't a spoiled rich kid and could make his own way in the world. But now, principles be damned. Train travel wasn't cheap, and this was a chance to win the woman he loved.

Unrequited love was unhealthy. He'd break the good buddy limbo, stop being so fucking pathetic, and go after her.

But first, he had to set things up with Kat so she'd be totally surprised when he showed up on the train. "Yeah, okay." He tried to sound casual. "I'll be your token good guy. I'll fly out for the wedding."

"Oooeeee!!" She flung herself into his arms, a full-body tackle that caught him off guard and almost toppled them both. "Thank you, thank you, thank you." She pressed quick little kisses all over his cheeks.

When what he longed for were soul-rocking, deep and dirty kisses, mouth to mouth, tongue to tongue. Groin to groin.

Enough. He was fed up with her treating him this way. Fed up with himself for taking it. Things between them were damned well going to change.

He grabbed her head between both hands and held her steady, her mouth inches from his.

Her lips opened and he heard a soft gasp as she caught her breath. "Nav?" Was that a quiver in her voice?

Deliberately, he pressed his lips against hers. Soft, so soft her lips were, and warm. Though it took all his willpower, he drew away before she could decide how to respond. "You're welcome," he said casually, as if the kiss had been merely a "between friends" one.

All the same, he knew it had reminded her of the attraction between them.

She would be a tiny bit unsettled.

He had, in a subtle way, served notice.

Token good guy? Screw that.

He was going to be the sexy guy on the train.

And here's a sneak peek at UNDONE, the historical romance anthology featuring Susan Johnson, Terri Brisbin, and Mary Wine. Turn the page for a preview of Susan's story, "As You Wish."

Fortunately for the earl's pressing schedule, the night was overcast. Not a hint of moonlight broke through to expose his athletic form as he scaled the old, fist-thick wisteria vines wrapped around the pillars of the terrace pergola. The house to which the pergola was attached was quiet, the ground floor dark save for the porter's light in the entrance hall. Either the Belvoirs were out or already in bed. More likely the latter, with only a single flambeau outside the door.

He'd best take care.

Kit had described the position of Miss Belvoir's bed-chamber—hence Albion's ascent of wisteria. Once he gained the roof joists of the Chinoiserie pergola, he would have access to the windows of the main floor corridor. From there he could make his way to the second-floor bedchambers, the easternmost that of Miss Belvoir. Where, according to Kit, she'd been cloistered for the last month, being polished by her stepmother into a state of refined elegance for her bow into society a few weeks hence.

Which refinements, in his estimation, only served to make every young lady into the same boring martinet without an original thought in her head or a jot of conversation worth listening to.

Hopefully, there wouldn't be much conversation tonight.

If he had his way there wouldn't be any. He hoped as well that she wouldn't prove stubborn, but should she, he'd stuff his handkerchief in her mouth to muffle her screams, tie her up if necessary, and carry her down the back stairs and out the servants' entrance. It was more likely, though—with all due modesty—that his much-practiced charm would win the day.

Pulling himself over the fretwork balustrade embellishing the pergola, he stood for a moment balanced on a joist contemplating which window would best offer him ingress. His mind made up, he brushed himself off, navigated the vine-draped timbers, and reached the window. Taking a knife from his coat pocket, he snapped open the blade, slipped it under the lower sash, and pried it up enough to gain a finger hold.

Moments later, he stood motionless in the dark corridor. The stairs were to the right, if Kit's description was correct. After listening for a few moments and hearing nothing, he quietly made his way down the plush carpet and up the stairs. A single candle on a console table dimly illuminated the hallway onto which the bedrooms opened. Pausing to listen once again and distinguishing no undue sounds, he silently traversed the carpeted passageway to the last door on his right.

It shouldn't be locked. Servants required access if the bell pull by the bed was rung. For a brief moment he stood utterly still, wondering what in blazes he was doing here, about to abduct some untried maid in order to seduce her. As if there weren't women enough in London who would welcome him to their beds with open arms. Considerable brandy was to blame, he supposed, along with the rackety company of his friends who had too much idle time on their hands in which to conjure up wild wagers like this.

Bloody hell. He felt the complete absence of any desire to be where he was.

On the other hand, he decided with a short exhalation, he had bet twenty thousand on this foolishness.

Now it was play or pay.

He reached for the latch, pressed down and quietly opened the door.

As he stepped over the threshold he was greeted by a ripple of scent and a cheerful female voice. "I thought you'd changed your mind."

The hairs on the back of his neck rose.

His first thought was that he was unarmed.

His second was that it was a trap.

But when the same genial voice said, "Don't worry no one's at home but me. Do come in and shut the door," his pulse rate lessened and he scanned the candlelit interior for the source of the invitation.

"Miss Belvoir, I presume," he murmured, taking note of a young woman with hair more gold than red standing across the room near the foot of the bed. She was quite beautiful. How nice. And if no one was home, nicer still. Shutting the door behind him, he offered her a graceful bow.

"A pleasant, good evening, Albion. Gossip preceded you." He was breathtakingly handsome at close range. Now to convince him to take her away. "I have a proposition for you."

He smiled. "A coincidence. I have one for you." This was going to be easier than he thought. Then he saw her luggage. "You first," he said guardedly.

I understand you have twenty thousand to lose."

"Or not."

"Such arrogance, Albion. You forget the decision is mine.

"Not entirely," he replied softly.

"Because you've done this before."

"Not this. But something enough like it to know."

"I see," she murmured. "But then *I'm* not inclined to be instantly infatuated with your handsome self or your prodigal repute. I have more important matters on my mind."

"More than twenty thousand?" he asked with a small smile.

"I like to think so."

He recognized the seriousness of her tone. "Then we must come to some agreement. What do you want?"

"To strike a bargain."

"Consider me agreeable to most anything," he smoothly replied.

"My luggage caused you certain apprehension, I noticed," she said, amusement in her gaze. "Let me allay your fears. I have no plans to elope with you. Did you think I did?"

"The thought crossed my mind." He wasn't entirely sure yet that some trap wasn't about to be sprung. She was the picture of innocence in white muslin—all the rage thanks to Marie Antoinette's penchant for the faux rustic life.

"I understand that women stand in line for your amorous skills, but rest assured—you're not my type. Licentiousness is your raison d'être I hear: a very superficial existence, I should think."

His brows rose. He'd wondered if she'd heard about Sally's when she mentioned women standing in line. She also had the distinction of being the first woman to find him lacking. "You mistake my raison d'être. Perhaps if you knew me better you'd change your mind," he suggested pleasantly.

"I very much doubt it," she replied with equal amiability. "You're quite beautiful, I'll give you that, and I understand you're unrivaled in the boudoir. But my interests, unlike yours, aren't focused on sex. What I do need from you, however, is an escort to my aunt's house in Edinburgh."

"And for that my twenty thousand is won?" His voice was velvet soft.

"Such tact, my lord."

"I can be blunt if you prefer."

"Please do. I've heard so much about your ready charm. I'm wondering how you're going to ask."

"I hadn't planned on asking."

"Because you never have to."

He smiled. "To date at least."

"So I may be the exception."

"If you didn't need an escort to Edinburgh," he observed mildly. "Your move."

"You see this as a game?"

"In a manner of speaking."

"And I'm the trophy or reward or how do young bucks describe a sportive venture like this?"

"How do young ladies describe the snaring of a husband?"

She laughed. "Touché. I have no need of a husband, though. Does that calm your fears?"

"I have none in that regard. Nothing could induce me to marry."

"Then we are in complete agreement. Now tell me, how precisely does a libertine persuade a young lady to succumb to his blandishments?"

"Not like this," he said dryly. "Come with me and I'll show you."

"We strike our bargain first. Like you, I have much at stake."

"Then, Miss Belvoir," he said with well-bred grace, "if you would be willing to relinquish your virginity tonight, I'd be delighted to escort you to Edinburgh."

"In the morning. Or later tonight if we can deal with this denouement expeditiously."

"At week's end," he countered. "After the Spring Meet in Newmarket."

"I'm sorry. That's not acceptable."

He didn't answer for so long she thought he might be willing to lose twenty thousand. He was rich enough.

"We can talk about it at my place."

"No."

Another protracted silence ensued; only the crackle of the fire on the hearth was audible.

"Would you be willing to accompany me to Newmarket?" he finally said. "I can assure you anonymity at my race box. Once the Spring Meet is over, I'll take you to Edinburgh." He blew out a small breath. "I've a fortune wagered on my horses. I don't suppose you'd understand."

This time she was the one who didn't respond immediately, and when she did, her voice held a hint of melancholy. "I do understand. My mother owned the Langley stud."

"That was your mother's? By God—the Langley stud was legendary. Tattersalls was mobbed when it was sold. You *do* know how I feel about my racers, then." He grinned. "They're all going to win at Newmarket. I'll give you a share if you like—to help set you up in Edinburgh."

Her expression brightened, and her voice took on a teasing intonation. "Are you trying to buy my acquiescence?"

"Why not? You only need give me a few days of your time. Come with me. You'll enjoy the races."

"I mustn't be seen."

Ah—capitulation. "Then we'll see that you aren't. Good Lord—the Langley stud. I'm bloody impressed. Let me get your luggage."